'We all thoug[ht] [my]
lord Nerra d[ead...]

'And a different na[me to match your]
face, sweetbriar?'

He laughed and Rosalind joined in. Things might not
be so very bad, after all. 'Oh, we thought we were all
dead, my lord, for certain...'

'Then this Nerra has a fearsome reputation, my lady?'

Rosalind nodded. 'Oh yes, my lord. They call him the
fifth horseman——'

'As in the Apocalypse?'

'Yes, my lord. They say he cuts a swathe of death and
destruction wherever he goes. No one is safe—especially
not the women——'

De Bourne reached down and cupped her chin firmly
with one brown hand. Raising her head, he looked deep
into Rosalind's eyes. 'I should have introduced myself
properly. I am your new lord, Mahel de Bourne.
Commonly known as Nerra——'

Born in Somerset, Polly Forrester has been writing for as
long as she can remember.

Her working career began with twelve years as a
humble office clerk. Escaping to combine her love of
history and the countryside in a new career as a writer,
her work is used by several national publications.

She now lives in the depths of rural Gloucestershire
with a cat, a dog and a flock of very eccentric poultry.

Previous Titles

KNIGHT'S PAWN
JEWEL UNDER SIEGE

WINTER OF THE WOLF

Polly Forrester

First published in Great Britain 1991
by Mills & Boon Limited

© Polly Forrester 1991

Australian copyright 1991
Philippine copyright 1991
This edition 1991

ISBN 0 263 77199 7

Masquerade is a trademark published by
Mills & Boon Limited, Eton House,
18–24 Paradise Road, Richmond, Surrey, TW9 1SR.

Set in Times Roman 10 on 11 pt.
04-9103-78034 C

Made and printed in Great Britain

CHAPTER ONE

AUTUMN had been defiled. Ripe blackberry scents from the woodland edge had been stifled by rank animal smells and the smoulder of burning wood. The low slant of early morning sunshine lit not wisps of mist in the valley but smoke from camp-fires. Cawing rooks in nearby elms laughed to see the sweat of men and horses dappling the bracken like dew.

Rosalind knew that this was the end. Three weeks ago the anarchy had reached the Tirolds' own castle. She had been on her own with the staff, left to hold out under a cruel siege.

Every day they had expected Ascelin to return from Gloucester to help them. Now it was too late. Rosalind had managed to keep hope alive in her staff for three weeks, but now the stories would have to change. Instead of assuring them that their master was sure to be on his way, she must start thinking of plausible excuses for him. Again.

She would have to claim that the messenger could not have got through. Or that Ascelin and his men must have stopped to thrash the Empress's men at some point along the way. Any story would do, Rosalind thought sadly. It was bound to be less painful than the truth.

Wild rumours had been whispered through the countryside for months. King Stephen was becoming increasingly unpopular. His rival to the throne of England, the Empress Matilda, had seized her chance to create mischief. Now chaos and anarchy stalked the land.

Rosalind knew that her husband Ascelin was not the sort to be seen running from a fight. He would rather buy his way out of trouble a long time before things came to blows.

She looked down from the roof-top refuge where she had herded the indoor staff for safety.

Seated on a horse a little way distant from the besiegers was the real reason why Ascelin hadn't come to save his own castle.

Nerra de Bourne. The Black Wolf, they called him. A ruthless mercenary whose services were priced far beyond the means of a lowly tenant in chief. Ascelin Tirold had abandoned his wife and staff to their fate.

From this distance it was difficult to make out more of de Bourne than his shape. He sat hunched in his saddle, overseeing preparations for a final storming of the castle. Stories of his brutality were legendary, and Rosalind held the little silver cross about her neck with nervous fingers.

The plain black of Nerra de Bourne's banner and shield told an unforgiving story.

'Oh, my lady...'

'Sh.'

Rosalind clasped the hand of Crispin, her young musician. The autumn sun made him seem even more frail and fair, his robin-bright eyes dulled with fear.

'Just because you're afraid, Crispin, it doesn't mean that you have to frighten all the others. They've got enough of their own worries without yours.'

That was what her mother had told her, so long ago. The morning of her first marriage.

Rosalind gave herself the luxury of thinking back. William had been kind, knowing how nervous she was at leaving home for the first time.

When William had died, Ascelin Tirold had not been slow to stake his claim. Land, land and more land was Ascelin's aim. He kept close to King Stephen and his favourites, ever ready to put himself forward for any vacant territory.

Rosalind was brought back to the present with a jolt. As she gazed at the mercenary leader far below, he had nodded sharply in signal to his men. A great racketing roar tore through the early dawn as the Empress's men doused red-hot fires at each corner of the castle walls with cold water.

Steam billowed up with a hiss of splitting stone. The Empress's men sprang forward with picks and crowbars to prise open the castle wall at its seams. Then the battering-ram began its work on the great double gates securing the castle yard. The end was in sight for Rosalind and her staff.

Three weeks of holding out, and all for nothing. Rosalind would have carried on resisting, but the arrival of de Bourne himself the day before to supervise his soldiers had drained away all her will.

Left to their own devices, his men had at least been prepared to sit and wait.

De Bourne was different. He wasn't content to play cat at the mousehole. All Rosalind could hope was that he would be merciful to her staff.

A splintering crash sent rooks scattering from their trees in an explosion of cawing. Three more hefty blows from the battering-ram were urged on with yells of delight by the Empress's men. With each smash the leather hinges of the gate gave a little more. Wood buckled, iron bent.

Suddenly a torrent of men was pouring over, through and under the hanging and battered gates. The watchers on the roof made the sign of the cross. Many threw themselves on their knees, begging the cold empty sky for mercy.

Soldiers swarmed through the castle courtyard, heading for stable, smithy and stores. With a rattle and slither of hoofs a horse screamed. Men still outside the gate yelled and surged forward in anticipation of rich pickings.

Within the castle yard, half a dozen men scaled the steps up to the castle door itself. A roar from de Bourne stopped them.

His horse was wild-eyed at having to squeeze through the gaping gate socket, but the mercenary leader forced it on regardless. Dismounting at the foot of the castle mound, he leapt up the steps three at a time. Lesser mortals were bundled aside in his haste.

'He won't get in, my lady. We're quite safe. I locked the door...' Crispin said nervously.

Rosalind did not reply. There came the sound of two splintering blows, a kick, then an almighty thunder as the door bounced back on its hinges.

The sound of mailed feet rushed up from below as the soldiers followed de Bourne's lead. Rosalind nearly gave in to fear and sank to her knees with the others, but de Bourne was among them before she had time.

'Priest!'

His strong, wolfish features and mane of shaggy black hair struck terror into them all. The castle staff shrank back in silence as de Bourne strode through them.

'We—we have no priest, sir. He died——'

'What? Who said that?'

He swung around, an expression of black hatred on his face. Rosalind was the only one left standing. Trembling from head to foot, she stepped forward.

'I—I am Rosalind Tirold, sir...'

The sound of her precious belongings being looted and spoiled below was the only thing that kept Rosalind from fainting away altogether. She had to stay calm. The staff were depending on her.

'This castle belongs to my husband, the lord Ascelin Tirold——'

'Wrong.' De Bourne glared, one gloved hand to the side of his face. 'This castle belongs to me, held for the Empress Matilda, rightful heiress to the throne of

England!' This was announced in a mighty roar as he glared at his captive audience.

'We—are all loyal to…King Stephen here…' Rosalind said in the ensuing hush.

De Bourne advanced towards her, his voice thick with venom. 'Madam, yesterday forenoon I split a tooth on a beef bone. Pain I can endure, but fools and women never. As you are plainly both, get me salve or surgery— either—but hold your tongue!'

'Our priest used to manage such things, my lord. Since he died last week——'

'I don't want history. I want rid of this toothache. See to it.'

He stalked off to the stairway and went back down towards the hall.

'I'm not having him speak to you as though you were a common servant, my lady!' Crispin saved his indignity for when de Bourne was out of earshot. Relieved at having survived their first meeting with the dreaded Black Wolf, the rest of the villagers murmured their approval.

'Dear Crispin—everyone—there are to be no heroics!' Rosalind looked at them all in turn. 'He's built like a champion fighter. And he's well practised, too, by all accounts. There's no one here would be a match for him.'

She wondered if she was addressing her staff for the last time. There was no knowing who would live or die now. De Bourne's reputation had swept all before him. His name was a byword for brutality.

Leading the way down into the castle, Rosalind knew that she had to remain calm. If he had any Christian feeling whatsoever, Nerra de Bourne would not attack without provocation.

Rosalind stopped short. What if he wasn't a Christian? Tales were told about his Levantine mother—perhaps she had been an infidel. That would make de Bourne an unknown quantity. There was no telling how he might choose to act.

De Bourne was sitting at the trestle table, broad shoulders hunched. About him his men emptied trunks and trampled the disarray in their search for loot. Hens were startled into flapping riot, which set all the dogs barking. De Bourne paid no attention. He had split open a cask of wine, rinsing each mouthful around his teeth with a grimace before swallowing it. Wine leaked from the broken cask like blood over the rushes covering the floor.

Rosalind turned and looked about her people, who were edging along behind her.

'Marty, you're the strongest. See if you can help my lord de Bourne.'

She pushed the blacksmith's apprentice forward. Marty was solid as a barn door, but gentle by nature. As the boy worked himself up to confronting the mercenary, de Bourne swung round to face him with an evil grin.

'Come on, then, boy—the young lions are starting without me!'

A thin scream came from out in the yard. Rosalind could bear the noise and destruction no longer.

'My lord—make them stop! All this ruination! It isn't necessary, surely?'

De Bourne raised his eyebrows. Coal-black eyes laughed at her as he took another drink. 'It's only natural, sweet. The old order changing. When young lions move in to oust an old king they start by destroying the cubs. To make way for a strong young generation of conquerors. That's why I call my boys the young lions. You wouldn't have any Tirold cubs hidden about the place, would you, sweet?'

Rosalind's stomach twisted in anticipation of all the old taunts. 'No, my lord—and if I did, you can be sure that I wouldn't let them fall into the hands of brigands like you.'

'Oho! My little sweet turning out to be more of a sweetbriar, is she? I can see I'll have to watch out for thorns.'

His dark eyes had narrowed before he turned away to face Marty. Rosalind was torn between revulsion and fear. The realisation was growing that Ascelin would try and use de Bourne's presence in the castle to rid himself of her with the least inconvenience to himself. When King Stephen quashed the rebels Ascelin would cite the Black Wolf's presence in his castle as proof of her infidelity.

Rosalind would be thrown out of the home that she had once shared so happily with William, while Ascelin got everything.

Marty stood before his new master, a pair of pincers in his hand. He clicked them continually in his nervousness, which didn't do de Bourne's temper any good at all.

'Good God, boy!' he burst out. 'I could have pulled a dozen teeth in the time you're taking!'

The mercenary leader took a grip on the edge of the trestle table and opened his mouth. While Marty fiddled about, hardly daring to look at what he was doing, Rosalind's eyes were riveted upon de Bourne.

His powerful fingers gripped the table-top until the swarthy knuckles showed white. Pain dewed his dark features, but de Bourne made no sound despite Marty's worst efforts.

The fourth bone-crunching jerk drew the tooth and sent Crispin sliding to the floor. De Bourne wiped his folded glove across his face and roared with laughter.

'Weak men for a weak king! Tend your milksop, sweetbriar—we'll have some fun with him, later!'

Rosalind knelt beside Crispin, who was green and groaning. She looked up at de Bourne in helpless appeal.

'He's only a musician, my lord . . . He isn't strong . . .'

'Don't worry. The lads'll soon rough a bit of strength into him, sweetbriar. He'll learn what it means to show weakness.'

De Bourne took a mouthful of wine, then went to the curtained garderobe beneath the stairs. At least he didn't spit it out on the floor, Rosalind thought. She wondered how is was possible for such a brute to have better manners than her own husband.

When the mercenary strolled back out into the hall he was beaming with self-satisfaction. The drawn tooth had been towards the back, and no gap in his smile was apparent. Rosalind was reminded of the bright white teeth of the wolves that Ascelin hunted down, and shuddered. De Bourne seemed just as dangerous.

'Well, sweetbriar, there's not much use in standing about looking at each other, is there?' he said almost light-heartedly, then turned a terrifying rage on the servants. 'Haven't you lot got work to go to?'

De Bourne's soldiers and most of the staff scuttled away like coneys released from a trap. Only Crispin remained. He quailed in Rosalind's arms, and clung to her.

'What's to happen to the staff, my lord?' Rosalind asked in a small voice.

De Bourne bent down until his face was within a hand's span of hers. 'I'm going to eat them all for dinner!'

Straightening up, he withdrew, and went to sit on the edge of the table. Dipping out another cup of wine, he drank, but never once took his eyes from Rosalind. When the cup left his lips he was laughing. 'Don't look so serious, sweetbriar! I'm not hungry—yet.'

'No, my lord.'

De Bourne laughed again, pulling off his second glove and pushing them both into his belt. 'Are you always so biddable, sweetbriar?'

It was surprising the change that six months could bring.

'Yes, my lord.'

'Then I can see that you and I are going to get along very well. Get rid of that...' He waved a hand airily in Crispin's direction. 'Then you and I can get down to business.'

Crispin and Rosalind exchanged a nervous glance. Neither moved until de Bourne stepped forward. Then they shrank back.

The mercenary leader caught hold of a handful of Crispin's jacket and lifted him bodily out of Rosalind's arms. Setting the young musician on his feet, de Bourne gave him a none too gentle shove in the direction of the door.

'Go!'

Rosalind started to tremble. She put her hands on to the floor to steady herself, but it was no use. The fear built up within her until she could stand it no longer. She gave in to it, and lay down in the autumn-crisp rushes that covered the floor.

Crispin turned back. 'Oh, my lady——!'

'Get out!'

Rosalind heard de Bourne draw his sword and take two hurried paces. In that same instant the door opened and then slammed. Crispin had escaped.

She was all alone.

There was silence for a moment, then a deep sigh from de Bourne. 'Oh, get up, woman. For heaven's sake— you're making the place look untidy.'

When he made no move to drag her up as he had done to Crispin, Rosalind raised her head slowly.

He was sitting on the edge of the table once more. While his right hand balanced the sword lightly against the bench, his left hand was to his mouth.

'Bad luck to draw a sword without drawing blood.' He met her terrified stare with a curious gaze. 'I suppose you're wondering, as they all do?'

Standing up, he strolled to her side and crouched down. When he pushed his left hand towards her Rosalind saw red blood beading the grazed, cyprus-shaded skin.

'Yes, I bleed, and yes, it's red, like pure Frankish blood. Now, can we please get on to the business in hand?'

His voice was deep, but soft. Its country burr was quite different from the cultured tones of Ascelin's friends at court, but Rosalind knew that her husband would never dare ridicule Nerra de Bourne. Always supposing that Ascelin ever dared to show his face at the castle again, which she doubted.

Shame was a bitter medicine that Rosalind had learned to swallow meekly. When she spoke, her whisper was dull with foreboding. 'What do you wish me to do, my lord?'

She heard de Bourne pacing about slowly, considering his next move. When he stopped there came a rasping of fingers over roughened chin, then a muffled rustle as he folded his arms.

'The first thing you can do is order me hot water, towels and soap, if you get such things out here in the wilds. While that's being sorted, you can show me around.'

Rosalind managed to look up into his face at that.

'Around? Here?' She was mystified.

'Of course! What sort of man goes to the trouble of getting himself a place to live in without wanting to go over every inch?' De Bourne looked about proudly. 'I've got great plans for this place. As soon as I heard about it I said to myself, ''Mahel, that's the one for you!'' I've never had a house of my own before...' he finished, a little self-consciously.

Rosalind was amazed. She sat up, still nervous but surprised out of her sheer terror.

'Mahel?'

'That's my name.' He grinned, clearly expecting some question of hers to take the heat from his discomfort.

'Oh,' Rosalind breathed in relief. 'We all thought that you were the lord Nerra de Bourne——'

'And a different name brings a smile to your poor pale face, sweetbriar?'

He laughed, and Rosalind joined in. Things might not be so very bad, after all.

'Oh, we thought we were all dead, my lord, for certain...'

She accepted the hand he offered to help her to her feet. He did not seem half so frightening now. Indeed, his dark eyes seemed almost merry as he looked her up and down.

'Then this Nerra has a fearsome reputation, my lady?'

Rosalind nodded. 'Oh, yes, my lord. They call him the fifth horseman——'

'As in the Apocalypse?'

'Yes, my lord. They say he cuts a swathe of death and destruction wherever he goes. No one is safe—especially not the women——'

She stopped. Although he was looking almost jolly as he listened to her, there was something about this Mahel de Bourne that made her wary. The quick movements of his eyes, the gypsy darkness of his skin and hair...

'Oh, my lord...forgive me if I have spoken out of turn...the lord Nerra—is he a relation of yours?'

'You could say that.'

De Bourne turned his back upon her. Taking this as a sign of his great displeasure, Rosalind sank in a low curtsy. Head bowed, she waited for him to compose himself.

'My lady—Rosalind, wasn't it?'

'Yes, my lord,' she murmured as he turned and walked towards her.

De Bourne reached down and cupped her chin firmly with one brown hand. Raising her head, he looked deep into her eyes. 'I should have introduced myself properly. I am your new lord, Mahel de Bourne. Commonly known as Nerra——'

Terrified, Rosalind tried to spring away but de Bourne gripped her firmly.

'But I won't hurt you, if you do as I say.'

Rosalind could force herself to be brave, in front of the staff. Now she was quite alone. Heroism was not in her nature, and her legs finally gave way.

De Bourne caught Rosalind up, one strong hand supporting her as he sheathed his sword.

'I'm not in the habit of repeating myself, sweetbriar,' he said in a low voice, very close to her ear. 'Listen, and learn. Apart from tales of my wicked, black-hearted pastimes, the gossips will have told you that I'm a *poulain*—half Frank and half Levantine. Yes?'

His fingers were digging into her arm cruelly. Rosalind could not speak for fear, but managed to nod.

'Your fellow countrymen treat *poulain* worse than curs. The only way to get any respect at all is to be better than they are. Well, I'm the best. Hear that unholy racket outside?'

Rosalind nodded again, weak with fear.

'That's my men. Animals, every one. My young lions! The only way I can keep order is to be totally ruthless. If any one of them goes too far, he'll suffer for it at my hand. They know it, and it controls them.' His grip on her arm slackened a little. 'And I'm as fell with the people we meet up with, too. That's why the gossips talk. If a man turns truculent, he's got rid of. The same goes for women, too. Those that are good and biddable survive.'

He might have intended his words to reassure Rosalind, but they had quite the opposite effect. When he let go of her arm she slid to her knees again.

'Oh, for heaven's sake, girl! Get up! Don't you understand simple words? You're quite safe, as long as you do exactly as I say. Right now I'm asking you to show me around. That's all. No dark, satanic rites or evil practices. Not yet, anyway!'

He laughed, and put out one hand to tousle her hair. Rosalind flinched away. Amusement disappeared from de Bourne's eyes, the merry light in them flickering and dying.

'It doesn't come off, sweetbriar. There'd be no sooty Levantine handmarks on your pretty, pale hair.'

'I know,' Rosalind said quickly. Despite his hardened reputation she had recognised the fleeting look that had haunted his eyes. Shame had looked back at her often enough from her own looking-glass.

'Are people cruel to you about it, then, my lord?' she said quietly.

'I thought I was the only one with a licence to be cruel.' At once the look of casual amusement had returned to his face. 'Now, move. I want to see every nook and cranny that this place has to offer. I'm a man of property now, and I want to make the best of it.'

He went towards the wooden steps leading to the upper floor. At their foot he turned and clapped his hands, summoning her. 'What did I say, sweetbriar? Obedience at all times. Shout for some hot water, then up those steps, and be quick about it.'

He was actually waiting to let her go up first. Rosalind could hardly believe it. Almost immediately, however, she began to suspect his intentions.

'After you, my lord...'

'I want obedience, not cringing. Go on.'

Rosalind went to the main door and opened it. The riot outside had moved to the kitchen block, and crowds of staff, soldiers and villagers tussled and shoved about the low building. Rosalind caught sight of Crispin cowering in the forge with Marty and called them over.

'Oh, my lady... We thought he must be doing something awful—we're all too scared to confront him...'

'It's all right, Crispin. There's a good chance he's not as black as he's painted. Tales always grow in the telling.'

'His men are bad enough, my lady. They're working through the stores like rooks through a seedbed...'

Rosalind remembered de Bourne's words, and wondered if he could be persuaded to restrain his men. Determined to try, she gave the two boys the mercenary's list of requirements then went back into the hall.

De Bourne was still waiting beside the stairs. He was looking about the dimly lit hall with a hint of pride. Every inch the confident new landowner, Rosalind thought, realising how she might manipulate him.

'My lord...' she began hesitantly, 'your winter supplies are suffering. These are cold and hungry hills—if your stocks are plundered this early in the season, there may be famine later...'

'My stocks?' he murmured in an undertone, then strode past her to the door. Flinging open the door, he gave a piercing whistle, then shouted some orders to the rabble.

'That's fixed them,' he said, closing the door firmly. 'Rioting through my property? I'll show them.'

If Rosalind hadn't been so nervous she would have laughed at his disgruntled tone.

'Go on, then, sweetbriar. Up you go.'

She looked at the tall mercenary who made such a commanding figure. Everything about him, from the fierce set of his jaw to the heavy cut of his boots, spoke of relentless efficiency. Rosalind was afraid.

'What is it, sweetbriar?' He winked mischievously, fingering his sheathed sword. 'Is this what's worrying you?'

In one movement he had released the sword belt from about his waist. Holding the sword out to Rosalind, he urged her to take hold of it. 'It must always be close at hand, sweetbriar. You take care of it for a minute, if it makes you feel safer.'

The sword was remarkably light for its size. A little reassured, Rosalind ran up the steps. She stood a respectable distance away as de Bourne arrived at the upper floor.

'I think I'll take another look out from the roof, sweetbriar.'

Rosalind nodded towards a ladder in one corner. As de Bourne went towards it he called back to her, 'I'm afraid you're going to have to come, too! You'll have to show me how far my new lands stretch.'

Meekly Rosalind did as she was told. A boarded walkway ran around the roof, where lookouts could keep watch over the countryside. The high morning air here was bright and cold, very different from the smoky gloom of the hall.

De Bourne stepped out on to the walkway and stood, hands on hips, surveying his new domain. Autumn was still only flirting with the scenery as yet. It was content for the moment with ruffling gold through the bracken, and speckling a tree here and there with touches of yellow or red.

'Quite a view, eh, sweetbriar? Hills and dales, trees and downland... I bet you're out here on the roof all the time.'

'No, my lord. Ascelin—my husband—does not permit it.'

The mercenary looked at her sharply. 'You should have told me before. I've got no wish to come between husband and wife in that way.'

'You ordered me here, my lord...'

'Good grief! You've got a tongue in your head, girl, haven't you?'

At that Rosalind felt a little aggrieved. 'You told me to obey, my lord. What else was I to do? I was afraid to speak out.'

He moved to stand in front of her, taking her face in both his hands and raising it. 'Then if you won't speak, sweetbriar, I can see I shall have to read your eyes.'

His work-hardened thumbs were almost touching her lashes, and Rosalind blinked automatically.

'All I can see at the moment is fear. Don't be frightened, little one. If you behave yourself, there will be no trouble from me.'

Rosalind looked up into his eyes. There was none of Ascelin's scorn for her there, only a curious light adding lustre beneath his dark lashes.

'You have beautiful eyes, sweetbriar. Blue as that patch of clear sky. They should smile more. Come on! We don't want your dear lord and master coming home to find I've frightened all the fun out of you! That isn't the intention.'

There was a soft edge to his voice that made Rosalind as nervous as his earlier warnings had done. She tried to back away, and in doing so nearly dropped de Bourne's sword.

'Ah! Careful—that's a very precious thing, sweetbriar. Are you finding it heavy?'

'A little, my lord. It's an awkward thing to carry.'

'You get used to it,' he said simply. 'Let me relieve you of it.'

Taking the sword and its belt from her, de Bourne fitted it back around his waist.

'As we're up here, sweetbriar, you might as well show me the sights. How much of this beautiful view is mine?'

'All of it, as near as makes no difference, my lord.' Rosalind moved away from him with some relief. 'See that line of cleared trees in the distance? That's the beginning of my parents' land. Their boundary used to come nearly as far as the walls of this castle, but they gave William a lot of land when I came to him in marriage.'

'William? I thought you said his name was Ascelin?'

'My first husband. He was already an old gentleman when we married. To my eternal sadness we only had ten years together...'

Rosalind had become frightened again, scared of what Ascelin might do if he got to hear of the bitterness in her voice.

'Then you will have cubs hidden somewhere.' De Bourne leaned on the parapet with folded arms. 'It would have been as well to have told me straight off. If the lads were to come across them they might not have my understanding of the matter——'

'I have no children, my lord,' Rosalind burst out. That was the hateful truth—let him make of it what he would. She was used to the ridicule.

De Bourne continued to look out over his new lands. After a long time he cleared his throat, and spoke without turning around. 'Try putting some weight on. You're nothing but skin and grief, child.'

Rosalind was puzzled at this sudden change of subject.

'Is that an order, my lord?'

He sighed with exasperation. 'Put on a little more condition, my lady, and...' standing upright, he crossed quickly to the other end of the roof, speaking as he went '...other things should follow.'

'I was never so thin before William died...' A blush tempered Rosalind's anger. 'Everything seemed— seems... in order. Yet still I've remained—like this. The fault is mine...'

Of course it was. Ascelin had told her often enough.

De Bourne finished his tour of the roof and returned to the trapdoor leading back downstairs. Despite the chill autumn breeze he looked uncomfortably hot. When Rosalind was halfway down the ladder he spoke again. 'They say young Tirold's barely out of napkins.'

'He's eighteen, my lord. Quite a few years younger than I am.'

'There's your answer, then,' De Bourne said briskly as he strode past her along the upper hallway. 'A bit more meat on your bones and a good young husband—you'll fall in no time, sweetbriar.'

The words were kindly meant, even if they were roughly spoken.

That made the pain even harder to bear.

'Oh, don't cry, for pity's sake, girl! I've just given you some good advice. There's plenty would charge for that.'

Tears flowed, and would not be stopped. Rosalind stood at the foot of the stairs and cried. All the grief pent up through so many anxious months flooded out unchecked.

Her senses deadened by distress, Rosalind did not notice his approach until one strong arm was about her shoulders.

'There, sweetbriar. It'll happen. One day...' he said with difficulty.

'It won't. It won't—and—and it's all my fault...'

'What does your mother have to say about it?'

Rosalind shook her head. 'I—I don't see her... Ascelin...doesn't like me going out...'

'Can't she come here? If your parents only live along the track——'

'No. We don't have visitors.'

'Ascelin doesn't like it?'

Rosalind nodded.

'The more I hear about your husband, the more I like him.' De Bourne laughed bitterly. 'Cheer up, sweetbriar. Nothing's ever as black as it's painted—not even me!'

The comforting arm slipped away from her shoulders as the sound of movements came from the hall below.

'There's lots of things you can try, if you haven't already. I'll get your mother over here.'

'She won't come, my lord,' Rosalind gulped, trying to hide her tears from Marty and Crispin as they arrived with hot water and towels for de Bourne. 'My parents are for King Stephen, not your Empress. They won't have any dealings with rebels.'

'Everybody has dealings with me,' de Bourne's voice rumbled a warning as he glared at the two lads. 'Now, take me to your chamber, sweetbriar. I might as well stake my claim to the best room in the house.'

Rosalind led him to the room she shared with Ascelin when he chose to stay at home. Impressed at the cleanliness and large, netted window, de Bourne threw himself down on the bed and bounced a few times.

'It's a shame Count Geoffrey can't spend a bit less on hunting and a bit more on home comforts like these,' he said, putting his hands behind his head to watch Crispin and Marty arrange bowls, water, soap and towels on the scrubbed wooden table in the corner. 'We live like paupers in the court of Anjou, sweetbriar. No wonder the Empress wants to take up her rightful place in England. It's quite civilised here. She'll leave Geoffrey back in Anjou with his hawks and hounds, and then they'll both be happy. Theirs is one marriage that was definitely *not* crafted in heaven!'

The lads withdrew, leaving Rosalind and de Bourne alone. Unwilling to put her darkest fears into words, Rosalind could only press herself back against the wall and watch him with large, frightened eyes.

De Bourne looked straight back at her. His gaze pinned her to the wall, and would not let her go.

At last he rose from the bed. Unpinning the brooch at his neck, he let his cloak fall away, then pulled his padded overtunic off over his head. He made no allowance for Rosalind's shame but stood there in only his shirt and breeches.

'I should run along, sweetbriar. Nice girls don't hang about where a man's trying to have a wash and brush-up.'

Without waiting for her to go, de Bourne stripped off his shirt and went to the basin. After a moment's surprise, Rosalind seized her chance and bolted out of the door.

De Bourne's laughter chased her down the stairs and to the safety of her staff.

It was some time before the mercenary came downstairs to find Rosalind again. Crispin and Marty had carried his trunk of belongings upstairs between them, so de Bourne was dressed in some style when he entered the hall.

A dark grey tunic belted with golden links reached down to his knees, showing expensive woollen leggings beneath. Neat new shoes crafted in soft leather made less sound than his heavy riding boots. Out of his working clothes, Mahel de Bourne looked less threatening and far more approachable. He sounded more cheerful, too.

'That's better. Getting rid of that troublesome tooth is a job well done. Thanks...' He looked from Marty, hunched over the fire, to Rosalind.

'Marty,' she whispered.

'Thanks, Marty.'

He slapped the young man on the arm and Marty ducked instinctively.

'What *have* you been telling them, sweetbriar? I may have been like a bear with a sore head before—or even a wolf with a sore mouth...' nobody laughed except de Bourne '...but that's better now. I can get down to enjoying my new acquisition. Lead on, sweetbriar—I want to get to know this place like the back of my hand.'

De Bourne extended one of those hands to Rosalind. It was a dark paw, shaded with fine sable hair at the wrist. When she hung back, the mercenary stretched out and took her hand by force. 'Remember what I said, my lady.' He put his head down close to hers to whisper. 'Behave, and no harm will come to you.'

Marty and Crispin were of no use. They hung about at the fire, unwilling to offer any resistance.

'Bye, boys! We'll see you later. If my lady Rosalind is a good girl.' He grinned down at her.

Hustling her out into the castle yard, de Bourne pulled Rosalind to a halt beside the knot of soldiers still loitering at the kitchen door. The men were alert immediately, casting lascivious eyes over Rosalind until de Bourne growled at them ferociously, 'See this?' He thrust her forward. 'A spoil of war. It's got my mark on it. Any man found handling the goods knows what to expect.'

At once the leers died away. De Bourne raked them all with a glare that showed he meant what he said, then pulled Rosalind aside.

'They won't touch you now, sweetbriar.' De Bourne laughed softly as he took her away. 'All you'll have to contend with is my attentions.'

He laughed, and squeezed her arm.

'And we should start as we mean to go on. The stables first, I think.'

Rosalind felt his hand tighten, and knew there was no escape. She was the Black Wolf's prisoner, and his unwilling prey.

CHAPTER TWO

ROSALIND was half frantic with fear. She could not risk making a scene in front of the poor staff, who had more than enough to worry about. Instead she tried to pull away from de Bourne, but he held her fast.

'What's up, sweetbriar? Anybody would think that you didn't like my company!'

'When my husband gets here he'll——'

'He'll what, sweetbriar? He doesn't take very good care of you, leaving you here on your own for any rascal to catch.'

De Bourne was nudging her in the direction of the stable block.

'No my lord!' The entreaty came out louder than Rosalind had expected, and she shrank again. If he wouldn't be reasoned with, what then? 'I'm a good woman, sir—a good wife——'

'I don't doubt a word of it. Although you seem a mite too retiring to my mind, lady. No matter. I'll curb you of that fault before long. I don't mind mettlesome women, but dullards I won't harbour.'

He bundled her through the stable door to the hay-scented gloom within. With his fearsome reputation, Rosalind knew very well what to expect. That made what actually happened all the more bewildering.

'Which one's yours, sweetbriar?'

De Bourne was studying the horses now, not her. He moved down the line of rounded, chestnut-glossed rumps.

'I—I don't ride any more, my lord. Not since I married Ascelin...'

'You should. It would put some roses back in your cheeks. You're not an invalid, girl.'

He brushed the nearest horse with an expert hand.

'Fine animals, these. Your husband know a bit about them, does he? I might consider letting him stay on here, in that case.'

He wandered to the end of the line, engrossed in watching the horses.

'Ascelin has many good qualities, my lord...' Rosalind said uncertainly.

'And a loyal wife. That's worth something to even the biggest scoundrel.'

De Bourne strolled back to stand between Rosalind and the stable door. She was cornered. He put one hand to the wall beside her head. Blocking any escape, he leaned forwards and brushed a stray strand of blonde hair back from her face. In the half-light his eyes glittered wickedly. Rosalind found that the steady, knowing gaze held her captive.

'There's no one here, sweetbriar. The stable door's standing open—no one but a too suspicious mind could suspect that you're doing anything but showing me around. One kiss. That's all——'

'No!' Rosalind twisted away, trying to escape, but de Bourne put his hand lightly on her shoulder. He was laughing.

'Well done, sweet! The worst men can sometimes attract the best women, then.' He did not move away, but stayed grinning down at her. Black Wolf, Rosalind thought as she pressed herself away from him and into the limewashed walls. The name is well earned. He preys on lesser mortals.

'I won't touch you now, sweet,' he murmured, but still did not move. 'You surely can't blame a man for trying? Especially not one with my reputation.'

Rosalind stood still. There was something about his voice now that reassured her, in a strange way.

'I was wondering...' De Bourne gave her a sly look. 'Something has been puzzling me for quite a time. I need advice. From a good woman—although in my line of work I meet so few.' He was smiling again, daring Rosalind to try and escape past him.

'Sweetbriar, when a woman finds herself in your position—desperate, yearning for a child that is denied her—how far would you go to find a cure?'

Rosalind had thought of it so many times, and her fear was forgotten for a moment in remembering.

'Oh, to the ends of the earth, my lord...'

The answer seemed to annoy him, for he pushed away from the support of the wall and stood upright. His expression was hard and unyielding.

'Would that include...' he seemed to search for words deep within himself '...committing a sin?'

Rosalind was so horrified that it drove away the last of her fear. 'Certainly not, my lord! How dare you suggest——?'

'I wasn't suggesting anything.' De Bourne seemed openly irritated now, fiddling with the hilt of his sword.

Rosalind didn't care. She wasn't going to have her reputation put in doubt.

'I am married to Ascelin for good or ill, my lord. I won't ever do anything to break my vows——'

'Not even if he flaunts his infidelities in front of you, blames you for everything, makes your life a misery?'

'I shan't stay here and listen to this! What right have you got to say such things? I don't care who you are or what your reputation, my lord, I won't listen to your wicked talk!' She tried to rush past him, rage lending her courage. 'What do you know about it, anyway?'

De Bourne caught her tightly by the arm.

'More than you might imagine.'

Rosalind swung around and found that his sable eyes were tormented.

'You are truly driven to distraction by your childlessness?'

'Yes, lord—yes! Do you want it written in blood? What more torment can you put me through?' Rosalind was sobbing now, but with hopelessness, not fear.

'Yet you still wouldn't consider——'

'Never! Take your hands off me!'

He did not, but the grip slackened. There were no more questions. Rosalind's sobs gradually faded away. When she looked up at him again his eyes were veiled, as though thinking of things long ago and far away.

Feeling her gaze, he looked down and smiled. 'Thank you, sweetbriar.'

'For what? I haven't done anything,' Rosalind said crossly, taking the chance to pull her arm away from his loosening grip.

'You've answered a question that has dogged me for a long time. And it looks as though I've managed to spark a bit of spirit into you, sweetbriar!'

'You are an evil-minded rascal, my lord. If you take revenge on me for speaking the truth, then that will prove the point.'

De Bourne withdrew his sword half an inch from its sheath. 'Ah—I see. When I slice your pretty head from those delicate little shoulders, you'll have won the point, will you?'

Rosalind stood stock-still. Through the open stable door she could see life going about outside. The gentle stamp and rustle of the horses about her would go on; de Bourne would go on, regardless of what might happen next. Rosalind screwed up her courage and stood her ground.

De Bourne watched her carefully, a hint of animal cunning in his eyes. After an age he reached forward and tousled her hair. Rosalind flinched, but he had already turned and walked towards the door.

'Come on, then, sweetbriar! There looks to be a lot
more of this place for me to see yet. We can't waste time
in idle gossip here!'

She watched him stroll out into the early morning
sunlight. De Bourne didn't look to have a care in the
world. He certainly didn't look like a man who had
turned from seducer to tyrant to sightseer in a matter of
minutes.

Rosalind pulled her skirts around her and followed
him. She had been made even more suspicious of de
Bourne. Her first nervousness had now taken on a different form. It had become a fear of the changeable, not
the dark terror brought on by brute force.

For the rest of the morning Rosalind escorted de Bourne
around his new property. She was wary, and careful to
keep him at arm's length at all times. For his part, the
Black Wolf treated her with a cold respect.

The soldiers, villagers and castle staff were even more
nervous than Rosalind. Wherever she took the new lord
and master, crowds melted away with frightening docility.
There was none of the cheerful good humour that was
usual when Ascelin was away from home.

Dinner was served early. As the whole morning had
passed without de Bourne holding a full massacre or
selling the villagers into slavery, the tension began to ease
a little. Although there was a respectful silence in the
hall, the staff no longer cowered quite so fearfully.

'This is the life,' de Bourne said as he washed his hands
in the bowl of hot water that Crispin offered him. 'I'm
going to like it here. You say this boy's a musician,
sweetbriar. Is he good enough to play a tune or two over
my dinner?'

Rosalind took one look at Crispin's white face and
knew all his talents would be frozen by fear.

'We are only simple country people, my lord.' Rosalind dried her hands carefully. 'I'm sure our pleasures would not please someone of your standing.'

'Rubbish! Back in Anjou we made our own entertainment. Had to. No wandering minstrels would call in to risk an evening with Geoffrey when he was on form.' De Bourne gave a rough laugh.

The Count of Anjou was well known for playing hard and fighting even harder. Rosalind had heard the most shocking stories, passed secretly about. A morning spent with de Bourne had made her wonder for the first time how many were actually true.

'Perhaps you might like to entertain us yourself, then, my lord?' She concentrated on the meal that was being dropped on to the trencher before her. 'I've heard that Count Geoffrey's court is very good at farmyard impressions.'

When he neither struck her down nor shouted, Rosalind risked a smile. Time spent with the Black Wolf was showing her that she was as likely to surprise him as the other way about.

To Rosalind's shame, de Bourne reached out and pinched her cheek. What made matters worse was that she could not help but blush. Colouring up was her only reaction, however. Beginning her meal as though nothing had happened, Rosalind studiously ignored her neighbour.

De Bourne was not to be silenced by that alone. As they settled to beef stew and dumplings, he said in a low voice, 'I can see I'm going to have to watch you, my lady! Encouraging a bit of spirit is one thing—turning you into a sparky little rascal is quite another.'

He paid little attention to his meal, preferring to wait for Rosalind's reply. When none came he took a mouthful of wine then said carelessly, 'All right, I'll entertain one and all after dinner's finished. It's a good job you're a woman of the world, sweetbriar, that's all

I can say. Some of our Angevin songs can be pretty earthy, even to my experienced ears——'

'Crispin!' Rosalind was so tense that the word came out as a squeak. The young musician rose from his seat by the fire and came forward. De Bourne laughed silently, much to Rosalind's fury.

'I like teasing you, sweetbriar. It has such pretty results.' He held one hand a few inches from her cheek. 'Phew! You could toast bread near that!'

'Crispin,' Rosalind said evenly, trying to ignore de Bourne's laughter. 'My lord wishes entertainment. Some music, please.'

The boy looked from Rosalind to de Bourne, then back again.

'What's the matter with him, sweetbriar? Cat got his tongue?'

Rosalind cleared her throat and said slowly, 'If the penalty for not pleasing the lord Ascelin is a sound beating, then Crispin can be forgiven for being nervous before *you*, my lord.'

'True.' De Bourne ate a little more of his meal while Crispin and Rosalind waited.

When the Black Wolf had taken a further drink and dabbed at his mouth, he leaned forward. Crispin took a step back.

'Come here, boy, for heaven's sake. Play us a good tune or two, and you'll be well rewarded. If it's not to my liking, though...' de Bourne sucked his teeth and frowned, dark brows knitting together '...retribution will be swift. Now, get playing.'

That warning finished any hope there might have been of Crispin playing well. He sat beside the fire, nervously plucking all the wrong notes, and wavering through a succession of fear-forgotten songs.

As the meal ended, so Crispin's frayed nerves finally gave way. He stopped and awaited his fate like a little bird dazed by a weasel.

'Well done, Crispin!' Rosalind said aloud, then added in a whisper to de Bourne, 'Don't punish him, my lord. He was doing his best in very trying circumstances. It was quite good, after all.'

'It was rubbish.' De Bourne leaned back against the wall, adjusting his sword to lie across the seat beside him. 'Come here, boy.'

He beckoned Crispin. Under the eyes of all de Bourne's soldiers, the castle staff and all the villagers who were taking their dinner with their new master, Crispin could do nothing but obey.

'Musicians are an acquired taste,' de Bourne said thoughtfully, looking Crispin up and down. 'And there doesn't seem to be much meat on your bones, in any case. Instead of having you lightly poached in your own juices, young Crispin, I'm going to be lenient. You'll go upstairs and move every speck and item of my belongings out of lady Rosalind's chamber and into the room that I said she could use——'

'Oh, no, my lord!'

'Oh, yes, my lady!' De Bourne grinned at Rosalind's horror, but his voice was firm. 'Then, Crispin, you will take all my lady's frills, furbelows and trifles back into their rightful room.'

The young musician waited for more instructions, but there were none. De Bourne cuffed him off about his business and sat down for more wine.

'My lord—the lads have spent the whole morning changing the rooms about. What will it achieve?' Rosalind thought of the pointless tasks that Ascelin made them all do. Moving things back and forth until they were weary, restacking the woodpile time and again...

'While I was up in that pretty little room before dinner, I got to thinking. You're used to soft living, sweetbriar. That room of yours is too warm and cosy for the likes of me, brought up to sleep on cold, hard floors. You might as well get the pleasure of it. I'm tough enough for rougher living.'

Rosalind didn't know what to say. It was a long time since anyone had done anything for her. Here was a complete stranger—and a nasty type too, by all accounts—actually claiming to have put her welfare first.

'Don't look so suspicious, sweet! There's nothing in it.'

Rosalind looked at him quickly. His expression was open and honest, as far as she could tell. That was when Rosalind first felt doubt. A terrible uncertainty began as a tiny candle flame within her. From now on she would carry it with her every moment. Though she might try to stifle it, and deny its existence, it remained.

De Bourne had been kind to her, and she had been glad.

Immediately after dinner, Rosalind went up to help Crispin change the rooms about. If de Bourne wanted her to accompany him around the estate that afternoon, he would have to send for her.

The idea sounded well, but Rosalind knew there was a darker truth behind it. She was hiding. From herself, as well as from the new master. She would not go willingly. She would make it as difficult as possible for de Bourne to tempt her again.

A message came, but it was not the one that Rosalind had expected. Marty stuck his tousled head in at the door of de Bourne's new bedroom with some unwelcome news.

'Master says, since you're not allowed to move without the lord Ascelin's say so, he's going out around the estate without you.'

He ducked back through the doorway, but Rosalind called to him sternly, 'Is that all? Did he say where he was going? Is he taking his men with him?'

Marty grinned, his round face folding into soft creases about his small eyes and wide smile. 'Master says you're not to think you can shut him out again, neither. He'll leave plenty behind to keep the place open, he says.'

'He's not going to attack my parents?' Rosalind leapt up and started towards the door.

'He thought of that, too, lady. He's not starting any new 'venturing until the lord Ascelin gets back, and said to tell you as much.'

Rosalind wondered how far she could trust de Bourne's word. Her parents' stronghold was not as well defended as Ascelin had kept his home. Neither was it quite so desirable—but then, that never stopped Ascelin musing aloud about what he would do when he inherited the Carilef estates through Rosalind.

'Tell the lord de Bourne that his message is appreciated,' she said quietly, and returned to sorting clothes.

Marty withdrew, satisfied. He was a good lad, and liked nothing better than to have errands to run or messages to take. Rosalind's first reaction had been to dash downstairs and confront de Bourne. Now she was glad to have sent Marty.

There was something most disquieting about this Black Wolf, apart from his reputation. Rosalind had no intention whatsoever of finding out what it was.

She dismissed Crispin, who was always keen to see departures and arrivals from the castle. Alone in the cool second bedroom, Rosalind looked about her.

She had been surprised to find how neatly de Bourne had ordered his belongings in her room. In the hour or so before dinner everything had been unpacked, set out, hung up or stowed away.

To be here among his possessions seemed a most intimate intrusion. Rosalind hardly dared touch anything. Then she remembered de Bourne's request that everything be ready as soon as possible, and swallowed her misgivings.

She had expected to find nothing but the coarse and obscene among his belongings. In reality, nothing could have been further from the truth.

Clothes were divided carefully into the smart, expensive new and the well worn working varieties. They did not overlap. De Bourne clearly did not just relegate last season's fashions to the hunting field. He had different clothes for every occasion.

That he kept two sets of crusading whites showed optimism, Rosalind thought. Armour was more likely to rust in this climate than need covering up from the sun.

Outside in the yard there came the rush and clatter of horsemen leaving. Rosalind settled down to enjoy an undisturbed afternoon. She was discovering long-forgotten inquisitiveness, and there was no one to stop her.

When all de Bourne's clothes were put away, Rosalind started on his linen. That was a surprise in itself. Most of the towels were thick and new, and he actually had his own sheets. There were blankets, too. And they were clean—no little visitors marching through their herb-scented folds. Things like this had never been used for sleeping on floors.

Hidden away between the blankets there were even several books—a rare luxury. No wonder he kept them hidden from prying eyes.

Rosalind went to the curtain door and fastened it tight shut. Then she took the books and sat down on the bed.

She was in for a disappointment. Ascelin always said that books were wicked things, and only for the dissolute. De Bourne's books certainly weren't. They were deadly dull. Nothing but how to build stupid castles, or object lessons in strategy.

Sighing, she snapped shut a volume of engineering calculations and upended it upon her knees. A parchment page slipped out, fluttering to the floor.

Rosalind nearly had heart failure.

She had ruined one of his books. In a panic she bent and picked up the page, only to have a second slip from the book.

This was terrible. There was no way of knowing where the pages had come from—all the dozens of calculations had looked the same to her, and the pages weren't numbered.

There could be no alternative. She would have to own up, and tell de Bourne what had happened. That wasn't a thought that Rosalind relished. Unpacking was one thing. Breaking a possession was another.

She put the loose pages back into the front of the book and tucked it away in with the others, between the blankets.

The rest of de Bourne's unpacking she completed as quickly as possible. Not even the wonderful array of bits and bridles could tempt her now. She hung them from hooks around the walls as fast as they could be untangled from the hopeless jumble of items that Crispin had made of them.

Rosalind thought for a moment, then decided not to make up de Bourne's bed on the floor, as requested. There was at least one small thing she could do to try and make up for her carelessness.

De Bourne and his men did not return to the castle hall until day was fading. Rosalind was beside the fire, putting the final touches to her masterpiece.

He stopped yelling at his staff. He stopped altogether, and left Crispin to shut the door behind them all.

'Good grief, sweetbriar! What on earth have you been up to?'

'We couldn't be expected to put beautiful linen such as yours straight on to the floor, my lord.'

De Bourne went to watch Rosalind sewing up the final seam of a mattress. Unsettled at having an audience, let alone one to whom she would have to make an uncomfortable confession, Rosalind stopped.

'Carry on.' He gestured cheerfully. 'I'm intrigued, sweetbriar. I never thought one so frail could be so industrious!'

'I didn't do it all, my lord.' Rosalind pulled her twine through a lump of beeswax then carried on stitching. 'The case is an old one—quite good, but in need of some repair. The goose feathers are new, though—fresh this season.'

For the first time de Bourne looked about him, eyes accustomed now to the gloom.

'It looks as though there's been a snowstorm in here! What's been going on?'

'The men you left behind, my lord. They knew what we were doing, but they would keep opening the door to tease the girls. We have spent half the afternoon sneezing.'

'Blizzard conditions.' He smiled, then moved closer to her and further away from his men. 'You have a stray feather in your hair, my lady. I would offer to remove it—but you know what men are...' He cast a meaningful glance over his shoulder at the knot of soldiers talking near the door.

Rosalind's hand went up, brushing through the fine gold of her hair.

'I can't feel anything.'

'Here. Let me cast caution to the wind.' He reached out and brushed away a filament of down. Behind him, his men fell silent. They knew better than to pass comment, but they had seen and would remember.

Harsh words, even violence from de Bourne would wipe away the scene, Rosalind realised. She plucked up her courage and spoke without looking away from her work. 'I have a confession to make, my lord.'

At once he was alert, and all attention was upon him.

'I'm afraid that one of your books was damaged in its journey across the upstairs hall, my lord.'

He swore beneath his breath. That was the sort of language that the soldiers understood, and they waited eagerly for developments.

Rosalind put down her needles and began removing her palm pads.

'It was me. I don't know what happened, my lord— I was about to put a book away when two pages slipped out...'

'Which book?' His eyes had narrowed.

'Calculations—figures and drawings...'

'And what was written upon the loose pages? Did you see?' de Bourne said quietly. His voice might have been gentle, but his expression marked Rosalind as a low miscreant.

'I—I didn't pay any attention, my lord...'

'Are you sure?'

'Writing, perhaps...rather than figures...I don't really know...'

'Do you think it might have been a letter addressed to the Count of Anjou?' His voice rose in volume, though not in anger.

'I suppose it might have been, my lord. The pages simply slipped from the book. I really didn't pay any attention... I was more nervous of what you might say...'

There was the merest whisper of amusement from the soldiers. De Bourne silenced them, then grinned at Rosalind.

'That's it, then. No harm done. You're in the clear, sweetbriar—only my boring old letter of report to Geoffrey. No damage done. Don't look so worried!'

The soldiers went back to their conversations, satisfied at the explanation. Peeling off his gloves, de Bourne studied Rosalind's work as she took up her needles again.

'I've sent a man on to Malmesbury, sweetbriar. To see if they'll let us have a priest. He should be back here tomorrow.'

'Good.' Rosalind was genuinely relieved. 'I don't know how we've managed this long without one.'

'It's as well to have a steadying influence about the place.'

There was no amusement in his voice—no teasing. Rosalind had expected that, but as she looked up at him she saw that he was in earnest.

De Bourne did laugh when he saw her expression.

'I may have done many wicked things in my time, sweetbriar, but old age must be creeping up on me. Reason and right might even be beginning to prevail.'

Rosalind smiled, but looked back at her work. De Bourne wasn't old. He seemed to have a few years more than she did, it was true, but his hair was still the solid blue-black of a raven's wing. He looked as though life had worked his face barely three dozen years.

With a soft clearing of his throat de Bourne put one foot on the rail of her stool. 'Did your husband give any indication of when he was to return, my lady?'

'Oh, no... We don't talk about his work.'

'Then perhaps you and I should talk about it.'

Rosalind secured a final knot and made a great show of looking for her scissors. To answer questions from de Bourne would mean betraying Ascelin. She knew she wasn't brave enough to resist, yet that made what was about to happen all the worse.

'Do your parents own much land, sweetbriar?'

'Enough for their needs, my lord.'

'How much, exactly?'

'That I couldn't say, sir.' Rosalind wound the remaining twine back on to its reel. 'It's been so long since I visited. Mother buys some land—Father sells it.'

She heard de Bourne exhale irritably. He made a sharp movement and she looked up in fear. His arms were folded, and he was glowering down at her.

'You must have some rough idea, my lady.' His voice now was cold and precise. 'People, animals, number of fields...'

Rosalind could put on a chill manner, too. Even if de Bourne was quite capable of extracting information out of a stone, she could at least delay the inevitable.

'As I said, sir. Everything changes. Nothing stays the same——'

'Right!' he burst out, striding to the door. 'I've been patient long enough, lady. If you won't submit to questioning in the normal way, I'm going to have to take a firmer line.'

Flinging the door open he frightened everyone else out into the yard with a roar. As they filed out he leaned against the door jamb, watching Rosalind narrowly.

'You'll tell me, madam. And for your sake it had better be sooner rather than later.'

The last soldier to leave gave Rosalind such a look of pity over his shoulder that she leapt up and bolted for the staircase. De Bourne slammed the castle door shut and reached the foot of the stairs before Rosalind had got out of arm's reach.

'Come down,' he said, but his voice was quite even and reasonable.

With his hand about her ankle, Rosalind could not move without measuring her length up the steps. She stood still, hardly daring to think, much less breathe. The hall was deserted. Nothing but the crackle of the fire and an awakening of mice disturbed it.

'I only want to talk to you, sweetbriar.'

'Then... why did you send everyone else away?'

'I don't want them to know how I work, do I?' He laughed, and shook her ankle gently. 'That would take away all the mystique. It wouldn't do much for my ruthless reputation, either.'

'You're going to hurt me,' Rosalind quavered quietly. 'You're going to hurt me, and I won't be able to stand it, and I'll tell on Ascelin, and——'

'Such a lot of "and"s! Come and sit beside the fire, sweetbriar. We'll sort something out. You can take loyalty a bit too far, you know.'

He let go of her ankle and sprang lightly up the steps to her side. One arm about her shoulder, he led Rosalind gently but firmly back to her seat beside the fire.

'I work for the Empress, sweetbriar, but only as a favour to her latest husband, my friend Geoffrey. The Empress Matilda isn't my idea of a leader—too arrogant, to my mind. Doesn't care who she tramples over to get what she wants.'

De Bourne had one hand on her shoulder, and Rosalind didn't like it one bit. She hunched over on the stool, trying to make herself small beside his overwhelming presence.

'You might not like what's happened here, sweetbriar, but it's as nothing to what might have gone on. Nobody's been killed, or even injured in anger. Yet. Tell me what I can expect by way of a reception at your parents' place, and I can go prepared. If your father's a reasonable chap he'll realise he's outclassed. We'll talk, he'll see reason, and there'll be no unpleasantness. If you don't tell me all that I need to know, things could be a lot worse. Things might even get so bad that my lord Robert of Gloucester gets involved. He might not take such a kind view of those who don't support his sister the Empress.'

De Bourne looked at her steadily, with serious eyes bright in the firelight.

He had Rosalind exactly where he wanted her. Without the information she could give, who knew what might happen to her parents? If she told, there was only Ascelin to worry about.

Only Ascelin? He would see the land and property that he had coveted slip from his grasp.

Rosalind had already lost him his castle. That would be the end. To hand over his inheritance as well would be of minor importance beside that cardinal sin.

'I'll look after you, Rosalind,' de Bourne said quietly. 'You won't come to any harm for speaking to me.'

Rosalind tore herself away from his penetrating gaze.

'I—I don't know what you mean...'

'I'll talk to Ascelin, sweetbriar. It should do both you and I a power of good in his eyes when I tell him what went on in here before I managed to prise any information out of you.'

Once more Rosalind had to face that deep, dark scrutiny.

'When I tell your husband what a valiant struggle you put up to protect his interests...how only my most violent, bloodthirsty persuasions could extract the smallest scrap of information...'

'You *are* going to hurt me!' Rosalind tried to jump away, but he clasped her instantly.

'Of course I'm not.'

'You said...'

'I know what I said. That's what I'm going to tell Ascelin, too, but that isn't *necessarily* what's going to happen.'

He was holding her very close, but very gently.

'Sit down and talk, Rosalind.'

'He'll want to see signs...bruises...' She submitted to being lowered back into her seat.

'Then he'll find out that the court of Anjou teaches persuasions that leave no mark. Ascelin will believe anything I tell him, sweetbriar.'

'How do you know?' Rosalind looked at the mercenary with large, frightened eyes.

'As long as my evil reputation remains intact, he'll believe. Tell him—tell anyone that I've got a weakness when it comes to honest, loyal wives, and my reputation will be gone for ever. Do you understand what I'm saying, sweetbriar?'

'You want me to pretend that you've been cruel to me?'

'That's right, sweet. Mind, if word gets out that all we've done is talk—well, this old *poulain* wouldn't last long amid his young lions, would he? They'd think I'd gone soft. They'd be wrong, of course,' de Bourne said quickly, 'but it does no harm to be merciful now and again.'

Rosalind thought, but not for very long. De Bourne had given her an escape route. It wasn't much, but it was her only chance.

'All right. I'll tell you, my lord.'

'Wonderful!' He pulled up a stool and sat in front of her.

Rosalind told everything, as she remembered it. All the time de Bourne listened in near silence, occasionally nodding at a description or shrugging when she made an estimate of numbers.

During all of her revelations he never wrote anything down, or showed any sign of surprise. Once or twice he even prompted Rosalind about things that she had forgotten, or could not know.

When she had finished, he went to the table and poured them each a goblet of wine.

'Here.' He handed her the drink and went to kick the fire back into life. 'That was well worth it, sweetbriar. One or two little snippets that I might not otherwise have come across.'

Rosalind was offended that her priceless information should be shrugged aside so lightly.

'I was talking for ages, my lord!'

'Ah, yes.' He smiled and raised his goblet to her in salute. 'But you don't think I would rely on your word alone, do you? You could have told me any old rubbish, sweetbriar. Led me straight into a trap! It's not only King Stephen who has his spies. I send the odd one or two out, as well!'

'Oh.' Rosalind watched her fingernails whiten against her goblet. 'Then Ascelin will be upset for no purpose.'

'He's not to know, is he?' De Bourne bent towards her until their heads were nearly touching. 'That's our little secret, sweetbriar.'

He put out one hand to touch hers. Suddenly the atmosphere between them changed. It was charged with a tension that stayed his hand and made Rosalind look up at him sharply. For a fleeting minute she knew what he was thinking. Their minds connected with a single thought, and both held the flame.

Rosalind wanted to cry out, but her voice was only a husky whisper.

'Ascelin——'

The moment burst like a bubble. De Bourne's hand dropped rather too heavily on to hers to have been a romantic gesture, and he laughed.

'Quite right, sweetbriar. No secrets between man and wife. I'll tell him all he needs to know.'

'Will you?' Rosalind bent to pick up her scattered needles and twine from the floor.

De Bourne stood, but did not move away from her.

'My memory's not what it was, Lady Rosalind. Some of the most important things I forget in an instant.'

He strode towards the door, but against his better judgement had to return.

'There should be some signs of our time together...' he said, looking at her with uncertainty. 'A little disarray... you look far too perfect, Lady Rosalind.'

He frowned, as though his last words had been badly chosen.

Obediently Rosalind picked up a little straw and scattered it about her gown. The odd flutter of down clung to her, pure white against the serviceable brown of her work dress.

'Is that enough, my lord?'

He took a pace back towards the door. 'You still look...'

The hopeless shrug and spread of his hands told Rosalind something that she did not want to know. In desperation to spoil and obliterate she scruffed at her hair then snatched at the neckline of her dress.

'No!' De Bourne looked surprised at the volume of his own voice.

'Not that! Do you want people to think I did that to you?'

Rosalind took her fingers from the harsh material and shook her head.

'No, my lord.'

'Well, then.' His air of efficiency had returned, but he had lost any hope of frightening her for the moment. 'And a little bit of untidiness about the place, that's all that's called for. See to it.'

He drew his sword and waved it over the room, but it was no good. De Bourne knew as well as Rosalind that such a display would never frighten her in private again.

He muttered an excuse and went out to try his dubious powers of persuasion on lesser folk.

Rosalind barely had time to put the twine and needles away before distant shouts drifted in from the yard. At first she paid no attention. Better that de Bourne should spend his time and energy in playing soldiers than in more deadly pursuits.

She dragged his new mattress to the foot of the stairs. Marty and Crispin could take it up, and then she would make the bed.

Rosalind paused, and reconsidered.

One of the girls could make the bed. Setting out de Bourne's belongings had seemed intrusion enough, at the time. To go to his room now—even if he had been a thousand leagues away and not just out in the yard—had taken on the status of mortal sin to Rosalind.

She went to the door, looking out for helpers. Everyone was hurrying about their tasks, heads down and busy.

Everyone but de Bourne's soldiers. They were arranged about the outer walls. All heads were turned towards the western roadway.

From the castle steps Rosalind could not see what was approaching, but she guessed. Frost started to work its way from her stomach to her heart and then to every other part of her body.

One shape detached itself from the knot of riders stationed at the castle gate. Rosalind stayed where she was, holding on to the stair rail for support.

'I think you should be seen to be waiting at the gate, lady,' de Bourne said quietly. He leaned forward and pulled at his horse's ears. The animal bobbed and snorted, sensing perhaps that danger was near.

Through the dusk, through that gentle autumn evening, Ascelin Tirold was coming home.

CHAPTER THREE

DUSK was ebbing away into evening. It was a strange light—neither warmed by sun nor entirely cooled by shadow.

Rosalind looked out along the track with fear stifling any other feeling she might have allowed herself. Ascelin was coming home. That he wouldn't be delighted at events was certain. What could not be predicted was what he might do.

'My lord?'

She looked up at de Bourne, who gazed into the distance from the vantage point of his horse.

'Yes?'

The word was drawn out carefully.

'Perhaps we might be safer inside the walls. Ascelin has got quite a few men with him...I for one shouldn't like to get in his way...'

The mercenary backed his horse until he was level with Rosalind, then bent down.

'It's a good job one of us doesn't mind a bit of fun and games, then, isn't it, sweetbriar?'

A torch flared, illuminating his dusky features and showing an ivory-bright smile.

'Go on in, then.' He used the flat of his sword to tap her on the shoulder.

Rosalind was undecided. There was one last request that she ought to make, by rights. Her sinking heart and the thought of the next few hours made the favour impossible to ask. De Bourne sensed her dilemma.

'I won't hurt him, sweetbriar,' he whispered softly. 'And I'll see he doesn't do anything too heroic for his own good, either. You go inside. And remember—I'm the one in charge. I'm the one that comes out with the information now. You've done your bit.'

Rosalind needed no further reassurance. She turned and fled back to the castle hall, calling for Crispin and Marty as she went.

All three were as frightened as one another. Nothing was said, but at each heavy footstep outside the hall or shout from the yard all jumped.

The two lads dragged the mattress upstairs and left it in de Bourne's room. Rosalind couldn't bring herself to make the bed up, even though work was what her nervous hands craved more than anything else.

It was either find work or curl up in a ball of fear in the furthest corner of her room.

She dismissed Crispin and Marty, who were only too glad to lose themselves among the villagers outside. Going into her own bedroom, Rosalind looked about feverishly for something to occupy herself.

There was little left. Ascelin didn't like her writing letters, so she kept no parchment or writing implements. The small piece of embroidery she was working on was nearly finished, and the light from one candle was not enough to sew by.

Rosalind no longer kept large, heavy torches in the room. She had learnt by bitter experience. There was nothing to do but sit down and await the inevitable.

Rosalind did not have to wait for very long. The sound of the door slamming and light footsteps hurrying upstairs soon reached her.

'Lady Rosalind?' De Bourne was out of breath, but at least he had not only knocked at the door but waited, too. 'Your husband wants to see you. We've had to shut the gates against him, temporarily. Are you fit to come up on to the roof?'

She would be an easy target there. There was no knowing what Ascelin might attempt. Rosalind had gone beyond fear now, but there was no point in giving up hope. De Bourne at least might be merciful.

'No.'

'Hurry, then!'

She heard him pacing back and forth, just the other side of the curtain door.

'No. I'm not coming out.'

He murmured something under his breath, then snapped, 'Why not?'

'I'm frightened. I'm scared, my lord—you don't know what he's like . . .'

There was a pause. The pacing stopped, then de Bourne said the very worst thing he could have done in the circumstances.

'I'll look after you, Rosalind——' His voice was low and sweet, a twisting knife between her ribs.

'No! My lord—I won't go out there, and you can't make me . . .'

'I could, Rosalind. There's not a man or woman alive can put up any resistance to me, when I've a mind.' He was firm, but there was a hint of sadness in the voice. 'I'm not going to force you, though. Ascelin only wants a sight of you, to make sure you're all right. That's the least a good wife could do for her husband, isn't it?'

He said no more. For a long time Rosalind sat on the edge of the bed, but her mind had been made up quite quickly. All she had to do was summon up the courage she knew she didn't have.

When at last Rosalind drew back the heavy curtain door, de Bourne watched her with indecision. 'I wonder—my lady, it's a lot to ask—but I wonder if when we go out to face your husband, it might look as though I was ill-treating you a little? For the benefit of the men below . . . to keep them sharp . . . you know . . .'

Rosalind didn't like the thought of that any more than she wanted to be alone with de Bourne.

'I would treat you gently, lady...like this, for instance...'

He caught her hand, and stepping to the side turned her arm behind her back. It only hurt when Rosalind started to struggle.

Instantly, de Bourne let her go.

'You must stand still when we are joined together, lady. I'll whisper what the movements are to be.'

'Not my hand. You're not to hold my hand, lord.' Rosalind rubbed it furiously down her gown as though to rid herself of his warmth.

'How else am I to lay hold, lady, if not by your hand?'

'The wrist. Take a grip on my wrist. Don't hold my hand.'

Despite her fear Rosalind gave the order in a clear voice. De Bourne must have no doubts about what was right and proper. If Rosalind was to aid in any deception, it was going to be on her own terms.

He gave a little bow and indicated that she should go up on to the roof first. As she passed him he spoke again.

'One thing, lady—whatever happens, you must trust me. I wouldn't do anything to hurt you or endanger your life. Whatever I wish the men to think.'

Rosalind gathered her skirts about her and mounted the ladder. Stepping out on to the walkway, she stopped and waited for de Bourne. The wall surrounding the roof was higher here and sheltered them both from view as they readied themselves. This time de Bourne curled two strong dark fingers around her wrist.

Relieved, Rosalind allowed herself to be pushed out to give the onlookers below a good view. There was a semicircle of about two dozen men gathered outside of the castle gates, upturned faces shining by torchlight. Ascelin was at the front.

He was padded and armed enough to meet Roland himself.

Standing in front of de Bourne, Rosalind was alarmed to hear him draw his sword, but a light squeeze on her wrist calmed any fears for a moment.

'Well, well, well.' Ascelin's voice came from outside the gate. 'That's what happens to failures, cherub!'

'You've seen her now, Tirold,' de Bourne called down. 'Now you know she's still alive, how about a bit more negotiation?'

Ascelin might be young in years, but he was old in art.

'Negotiate? Why should I want to talk terms with you, *poulain*?'

'Because I have your wife here on a high parapet, with a sword at her throat...'

He rested his sword harmlessly on Rosalind's left clavicle, the blade a good few inches from her neck.

'And completely at my mercy.'

He gave Rosalind a little push forwards, whispering to her as though with deadly intent, 'When I give the word, fall to the right and cry out. Not too much, mind...'

'You needn't think I'd shed many tears over her, *poulain*! She's no use as a wife. Or anything else, for that matter.'

Rosalind dropped her right knee on command and let out a stifled cry. De Bourne had invisibly loosened his grip on her wrist and dropped his sword arm to take account of the movement. It must have looked an impressively frightening struggle from ground level.

Ascelin Tirold looked up steadily, and did not flinch.

'Your husband made of stone, is he?' de Bourne breathed. Rosalind tried to flick her blonde hair back from her eyes and did not speak. De Bourne could see the answer to that question easily enough.

Ascelin was smiling. To get rid of Rosalind without any expense to himself was exactly what he wanted.

'You might as well give in while you've got the chance, Tirold. I've got everything—your castle, your stocks, your staff—it's all mine, now. What have you got to look forward to out there? A cold night, a wet and foggy morning, no hot food to comfort you. This castle's taken for the Empress, boy. It's all mine, and none of your puny little efforts will get it back.'

'Wrong.'

Ascelin turned aside and called up two men leading pack ponies. Each animal carried a number of small sacks tied over its saddle.

'I've got the one thing that you and your kind can't ever resist, *poulain*.' Ascelin removed his helmet as a gesture of confidence. His golden hair glowed in the torchlight. 'Money. Forty pounds' worth of silver, *poulain*. Straight from King Stephen's personal collection. And all for you.'

Rosalind could hardly imagine such a tremendous amount of money. She had no doubts at all about what it would do to the loyalty of a mercenary.

De Bourne loosened his grip on her. She took care to sink down below the level of the parapet, where she could hear but present no target for Ascelin or his snipers.

'Keep talking, Tirold.'

The mercenary moved to put away his sword, but in a swift movement Rosalind reached forward to touch it. De Bourne looked down at the sharp intake of breath that escaped her.

'To save your own finger another bloodletting, my lord.'

'Idiot girl!' he said softly, but smiled.

'King Stephen will settle all your expenses, *poulain*,' Ascelin shouted, 'And pay you a healthy price if you'll come over to his side.'

De Bourne settled his sword in its sheath, folded his arms and leaned on the parapet.

'How healthy is "healthy"?'

Ascelin didn't answer at once. Rosalind had an evil suspicion that he was working out how he could buy de Bourne yet still keep some of the king's money for himself. It was a wicked thought, and she tried to put it out of her mind.

'What's your rate, *poulain*?'

'Five shillings a week.'

This raised a mutter of astonishment from the onlookers.

'I thought they said you came very expensive, *poulain*?'

'I could always put my price up, if you like...' De Bourne kicked idly at the parapet, his leg brushing against the huddled form of Rosalind until she moved a yard further away.

'No, don't bother,' Ascelin said hurriedly. 'I'll offer you six. And your men?'

'The usual. Just eightpence a day.'

'Then I'll make it ten. Er—how much is that in total, *poulain*?'

De Bourne gave a low laugh. 'I've been around too long to be caught like that. You want me to help you work out the strength of my garrison here, while you're safe out there with the money?'

'Twelve pounds a week should cover it,' Rosalind murmured after working it out on her fingers half a dozen times.

'Bright as well as beautiful, eh, sweetbriar?' de Bourne whispered as he looked down at her through the growing darkness.

'That's as maybe,' Ascelin shouted up after a moment's thought. 'There's plenty of money here. Enough to buy any number of men, and cover their expenses.'

'Then you'll buy us off?' de Bourne called down. 'In that case, come in, my new liege lord. I'll be down directly.'

'He's not very good at sums,' Rosalind said doubtfully as de Bourne ushered her to the top of the ladder. 'Don't confuse him, my lord.'

'I won't take a penny that I'm not entitled to,' he replied, following her down to the upper hall. Here rushlights shivered little flames into the darkness.

'Let me see what you've done to yourself.'

De Bourne's voice was stern and authoritative. Stepping into a pool of the weak light, Rosalind held out her hand. Taking it with nothing but professional interest, de Bourne held it up towards the rushlight.

He turned her hand about between two nut-brown fingers, studying it. The skin was scraped from one knuckle. Tiny pinpoints of blood freckled the surface.

'That'll teach you.'

The words were spoken low and confidentially. For a moment Rosalind thought she saw a gentle look in de Bourne's eyes, but his next words dispelled that awful thought.

'A spit and lick will cure it. Go on, off to your lord.'

That growling tone was used to frighten his men. Rosalind needed no further encouragement, and hurried downstairs to meet her fate.

It was not long before she was looking it in the ice-blue eyes.

'Hello.'

Ascelin was being helped out of his cloak at the door. His pale features gave him a look of frailty in the gloomy room, but Rosalind knew how looks could be deceptive. She curtsyed to him gracefully, remaining with head bowed as her young husband approached.

'No news for me, I suppose?' He pulled off one glove and threw it aside. 'Except, of course, that you've put me in a situation that will cost a lot of money to put right.'

'Surely the King has plenty of money, my lord?'

Ascelin gave a short laugh. 'What would you know about it? It was your job to keep this place secure. You couldn't even manage that, let alone anything more complicated. I suppose I shouldn't be surprised when you can't manage something as straightforward as providing me with a son and heir.'

Rosalind stared at the floor and clenched her fists within the folds of her skirt. Around them the hall was filling up with people, ready for supper. The locals were used to Ascelin, and Rosalind knew they tried not to take any notice when he was taunting her. De Bourne and his soldiers would be laughing instead at her shame, she knew.

'Do I have your permission to retire, my lord?' she asked hopefully, without looking up.

'No, you don't.' Ascelin reached out and raised her to her feet. 'I've just negotiated a difficult deal on behalf of the King. The least you can do is stay, and be civilised over supper.'

De Bourne appeared at his side. 'I don't think so, my lord. Women and the talk of money don't mix.'

Until then Rosalind had been shy in the mercenary's presence. Now his words drew her to her full height.

'There's no call for that, my lord. My husband is your employer now, and in this house his word is law.'

De Bourne bowed to her, but a smile was playing over his lips. 'Lady, I make no secret of the fact that I would rather you were not here to see Lord Ascelin's dealings with me. But, if you are so determined...'

'*I'm* the one who dictates what goes on in my own house, *poulain*. I say she stays.'

De Bourne looked at Rosalind and shrugged, but a smile broke out when he looked back to Ascelin.

'Very well. The decision is entirely yours, Lord Ascelin. Your servant, sir.' With an extravagant bow de Bourne stood back to let his new master take up a seat at the trestle table.

Rosalind was grateful that the two men laughed together over supper. Anything that might dilute Ascelin's rage at the temporary loss of his home was welcome.

She took an extra cup of wine to warm herself, and tried to enjoy Crispin's singing. There would be little enough comfort for her later on.

Ascelin had eaten and drunk well. Flushed with his success at retaking the castle without a fight, he glowed with self-satisfaction. Throwing one arm about Rosalind's shoulders, he grinned at her sunnily before thumping the mercenary leader on the back with his other hand.

'Right, *poulain*. To business.' He looked at the stack of money bags, piled fatly in the centre of the hall. 'I'm agreeing to pay your men ninepence each a day——'

'You said tenpence, my lord.'

Staring hard at the mercenary had no effect. As it was as close as Ascelin intended to come to conflict with de Bourne, there was only one thing to be said.

'Tenpence it is.'

'In advance,' de Bourne cut in quickly.

Ascelin looked a little doubtful, but a quick glance at the reassuring bags of silver convinced him.

'In advance, then. Risky business, war.'

'And expensive.' De Bourne took a slow drink of wine. Placing the goblet down again, he gave both Ascelin and Rosalind an innocent smile. Reassured, Ascelin grinned back.

'We settled on a figure of five and six a week for you, didn't we, *poulain*?'

De Bourne smiled all the sweeter. 'Your memory can be as bad as mine, lord. Six shillings. Also in advance,' he finished slowly.

'Now, to expenses——'

'What time is it, my lady?' De Bourne leaned forward but was not at an angle to see the markings on the candle clock.

Rosalind reached up and twisted the marked candle in its socket. With a sigh de Bourne sat back and folded his arms.

Ascelin was getting into his stride. 'We'll go through the items you've spent on while here, de Bourne, then take off the value of any damage——'

'Sorry,' the mercenary shrugged. 'It's gone eight o'clock.'

Ascelin studied him minutely, but the mercenary did nothing more than pick up a few crumbs from the table.

'What difference does the time make, *poulain*?'

'I don't work after eight o'clock.'

'But this is money!'

De Bourne was looking steadily at Rosalind, who did her best to avoid his gaze.

'For six shillings, lord, I work a four-day week. Eight till eight. Anything else is overtime. Fourpence an hour.'

Ascelin nearly had a seizure. 'I could hire a man for half a day for that!'

'One of your ordinary men, yes. Me, no.' De Bourne grinned wolfishly and called for more wine. 'Don't worry about your silver, my lord. There aren't that many expenses to recount. It shouldn't take long.'

'Very well. Overtime rate it is.'

Ascelin's lips were a tight, angry line. Rosalind recognised the look and knew fear.

Drawing a small, tattered roll of parchment sheets from an inside pocket, de Bourne smoothed them out on the table before him. The top sheet was headed 'Tirold Account' and had the previous day's date in large figures on the top. There were few items upon it, but each had a figure to the right-hand side of the sheet. A subtotal had been inserted in the margin.

'One horse, lost when it slipped on your plank bridge. I'd get that woodwork fixed, if I were you, my lord. It brought you a hefty expense—ten pounds, twelve shillings and fourpence——'

'What?'

'Call it ten pounds twelve, then, and I'm working for the fourpence now...' de Bourne continued blithely. 'Then there's two picks at threepence halfpenny each, broken beyond repair...'

'On my walls!' Ascelin leapt to his feet, but de Bourne gave him a pointed stare that dropped the young lord back into his seat.

'Your turn will come, my lord. And finally,' de Bourne said with a flourish, 'compensation to one sapper, a broken arm sustained in mining the walls. Call that fourpence a day, for a period to be arranged——'

'I'm not paying a man who can't work!'

'If you'd been here doing your duty instead of leaving it to your gallant lady, lord, I doubt he'd have needed to mine the walls. We could have come in more easily.'

'I don't think you should talk to my lord like that, sir...'

'Shut up!' Ascelin snapped at Rosalind, then stood up again. 'All right—all right, then—what do you make your total, *poulain*? Let's see how clever you think you are!'

De Bourne cast an eye down the column of figures, checking his subtotal.

'Giving the boy compensation for, say, six weeks—I make it a total of eleven pounds, six shillings and sevenpence.'

Looking to Rosalind, Ascelin received a quick nod in reply.

'Well, that's a coincidence! Mending the castle walls and making good the gateway is going to cost at least that. And more, I don't doubt!'

De Bourne leaned one elbow on the table, resting his chin on his knuckles reflectively.

'No, I'm afraid I can't quite see that, my lord. My men are careful workers. You won't need to pay out

anything on new materials. What's there can be sal-
vaged, and used again.'

'What about the gates?' Rosalind said, interested to
see how de Bourne would worm his way out of that one.
'They're shattered beyond repair.'

He smiled at Rosalind, but not at her words.

'A day's trimming, a few days of carpentry—that's
nothing. You'll be paying my boys for their time, anyway.
I won't make any extra charge for their expertise. Seeing
as it's you, my lord Ascelin.'

De Bourne slapped Ascelin's arm companionably, but
his young lord wasn't to be mollified.

'I want compensation. It's my right, and my
due——'

The mercenary stood up to join Ascelin, and all his
men were at once attentive.

'Hush, my lord. You don't want to upset my young
lions, do you? They can be very...volatile. I tell you
what.' Ignoring Ascelin's impotent rage, de Bourne put
his arm about the younger man's shoulders. 'Let's go
and start dividing out the cash. Anything that's left over,
we'll call your compensation.'

Ascelin paused in his tirade. He had been under strict
instructions to return to King Stephen every coin that
could not be accounted for. He saw at once how the
mercenary's skill at accounts could be turned to advantage. Under Ascelin's orders de Bourne could be
made to manipulate the figures so that nothing at all
need be sent back.

'Not a word to the King?'

'My lips are sealed, lord.'

De Bourne led his young lord to the pile of money
bags.

'Now, I take first cut, because I'm the senior soldier
here,' de Bourne said loudly to the gathering crowd. 'All
the rest of you can watch, and wait your turn. That'll
see fair play done, too.'

He took a savage-looking knife from his belt and made a gash along the belly of the topmost bag. Silver coins spilled out and glittered in the firelight.

'Right: the compensation, as agreed. Eleven pounds, six shillings and sevenpence.'

The sum emptied one bag and made a distressingly large impact on a second. De Bourne caused raucous laughter when he called out one of the village maids to collect the money in her apron. When it was filled and bulging he despatched her, giggling prettily, to his room.

'Make sure none of those shiny coins catch in your sticky fingers, maid!' de Bourne called after her to much laughter. 'I'll be searching you later, mind!'

The crowd roared, Rosalind blushed, but the girl seemed delighted. She staggered up the stairs with her burden. Rosalind noticed that she did not return.

De Bourne had returned to plunder Ascelin's money once more.

'Now, for my wages. Six shillings per week, four weeks in advance...'

The crowd gasped their enjoyment to see one pound and four shillings disappear into the mercenary's pockets. Ascelin gasped, too, but for quite a different reason.

'Four weeks? You expect me to pay them all a month in advance?'

'Naturally, my lord. Wars aren't won in a day, or even a week. A month...well, that might be tricky, but it gives us a bit of breathing space...'

Ascelin looked aorund at the sea of de Bourne's soldiers. 'There's hundreds of them...'

'No, my lord. Only forty.'

'Rosalind!'

Obediently, Rosalind was already working it out.

'Forty men at tenpence a day for four weeks—forty-six pounds, thirteen shillings and fourpence, my lords.'

Ascelin shot her a look of grim warning. 'Do it again. And get it right, this time!'

'I'm afraid your lady is right, my lord. Coming up to forty-seven pounds. Seeing that you only came in here with forty pounds to start with, and you've paid out twelve and a half already, I reckon that puts you in a bit of a spot, don't you?'

'Cheat! Dirty, filthy cheating *poulain*!' Ascelin leapt for his knife. De Bourne's men leapt for Ascelin. They were far quicker, and he was held fast.

'Looks as if I'm at the reins again, lads!' The mercenary grinned, to the delight of his men. Emptying his pockets back into the money bag, de Bourne growled a warning at anyone creeping too near the silver.

'I'd like to see that so called King Stephen's face when he gets most of his precious money back. It might even make up for losing your support, Ascelin!'

Ascelin struggled against the might of his rough country captors, but it was no use. All he could do was struggle and shout dire threats at de Bourne.

At first the mercenary took his tirade in good part, but soon anger started to darken his features. Ascelin continued to shout the odds, uncaring of the dangerous line he trod.

'Jealous, just because your father couldn't find a decent Frankish girl——'

De Bourne suddenly tore off his tunic and threw it aside.

'Nobody speaks like that and gets away with it,' he spat through clenched teeth, ripping open the laces of his shirt.

'No, my lord—he didn't mean it ... Please, don't hurt him ...'

Rosalind caught at the mercenary's arm as he pulled the shirt over his head. Roughly shaking off her grasp, he confronted the pinioned Ascelin. The younger man had gone quite white at the display of rippling muscle revealed as de Bourne stripped for action.

'Take his knife, then let him go.'

The command had de Bourne's men moving quickly. They released the unarmed Ascelin, then all stood back.

'If you think you can get the better of me, sonny, you're sadly mistaken! If you want to challenge my right to this place, let's get it over with, here and now.'

Rosalind knew that Ascelin could never accept the challenge and survive. De Bourne was a good head taller, with a longer reach. His taut, muscular body had been hardened by years of rough living and foreign wars.

Ascelin liked his home comforts. He was only ever moved to violence when the odds were stacked heavily in his favour.

The Black Wolf circled Ascelin, a look close to delight on his face. He was half crouching, ready to spring. There would be no hope for Ascelin against such determined savagery.

Following a spiral pattern, de Bourne started to move in closer. Trying to keep herself between her husband and his opponent, Rosalind clung to Ascelin and kept her head down. She had to avoid looking at the enemy at all costs.

'Don't fight, my lords...I can't bear it...'

'You heard what she said, de Bourne.' Ascelin desperately comforted Rosalind with a cold, damp hand around her shoulders. 'Only a bully ignores the plea of a lady.'

'And only a recreant hides behind a lady's skirts when it suits him.' De Bourne raised a laugh from his men. 'I know your sort, Tirold. You'll prefer the sort of opponent that can't fight back.'

'There's no difference between the two of you, then.'

Rosalind's voice cut through the confrontation like a knife. De Bourne stopped his advance, but never stopped grinning at Ascelin.

'All right.' He stood up straight slowly. 'As my Lord Ascelin doesn't seem to want to fight, we'll see if anyone will take up the challenge on his behalf. All men as equal.

If someone wants to chance his arm against me on Tirold's behalf for mastery of this place, now's your opportunity. No recriminations.'

All the men in the hall moved uneasily. They looked at the walls, the floor and even the smoke-blackened ceiling. They did not look at each other. Neither did they look at de Bourne. They had seen and heard far too much of his power and ability in the wrestling ring to risk their own necks.

'There's your answer, little Ascelin. You can't expect anyone to fight your battles for you in this life. You have to be prepared to fight your own.'

De Bourne stood back and extended one arm to be handed his shirt. As he pulled it back on, Rosalind felt Ascelin relax.

'Excitement's over.' De Bourne raked a glance over his spellbound audience. 'And time to turn in for the night. Tirold, I'll put you in charge of fixing that money sack and making sure there's the right amount in it. It all goes back tomorrow—minus the bit I've had for our expenses. We're entitled to that. It's the rules.'

Rosalind knew that Ascelin would hardly quibble anyway. De Bourne had reduced him to near panic. It might not ensure his love, but it secured his loyalty.

For the moment.

'I've said you can go, Tirold.' De Bourne looked up as the crowd dispersed. 'Although—leave the girl for a minute.'

He did not look at Rosalind as he spoke, but fastened Ascelin with a glare. Unwilling to cross de Bourne on any terms now, Ascelin thrust his wife forward. He was glad to have at least one bargaining counter left.

'She'll be no good to you.' He backed away with a high-pitched giggle. 'Cold as charity and barren as an empty barrel!'

'Get lost, boy.'

Ascelin slunk to the foot of the stairs with many a backward glance. Around de Bourne and Rosalind, soldiers and servants were finding themselves room on the hall floor to spend the night. The mercenary was refastening the buckles of his protective padded jacket and did not look up at Rosalind as he spoke.

'I want to apologise for that,' he murmured quietly. 'It's not right that a husband should be shamed in front of his wife. I didn't want you there——'

'But Ascelin insisted.' Rosalind smiled. 'I'm sorry, too.'

'It will make things bad for you, sweetbriar. Won't it?'

He flicked a look at Ascelin, who was loitering on the staircase. A frown flitted across Rosalind's face.

'I don't know what you mean, my lord.'

De Bourne turned a look on her so powerful in its unspoken message that Rosalind had to swallow nervously several times before she could speak.

'I—I must go...'

'Yes,' he said softly. 'I think you'd better.'

Ascelin did not speak until they reached the upper landing.

'Some people seem easily pleased,' he said tartly.

'My lord de Bourne wanted to apologise, Ascelin. He was simply sorry that you should have been...put at a disadvantage...'

'Pity he didn't think of that before. Oh, God—what am I going to do now? What must the court think? How am I ever going to be able to show my face there again?'

He pulled at his tunic in agitation. Rosalind knew how much his powerful friends at court meant to him, and when he looked so forlorn she couldn't help but feel some crumb of pity.

'You still have the greater part of the money to return, my lord. Not all is lost.'

Ascelin put his arm around her as they walked towards their room. 'Oh, you are clever, cherub. And at least I won't have to take it back myself. I can send it back by courier. That will put off the embarrassment of facing them all again for a while.'

Rosalind followed Ascelin into their room and sat down on the bed to remove her stockings.

'Of course, my lord. And by the time you feel ready to go back it will all be forgiven, and might even be forgotten.'

'Forgotten?' Ascelin spat, sitting down beside her heavily. 'Fat chance of that. The man whose wife tricked him into handing over a castle?'

In one movement Ascelin had pushed her backwards on to the bed and was swarming over her.

'I didn't...Ascelin—no...' Rosalind managed when she had fought her mouth free from his kiss. 'It's not convenient...'

'It never is, for you.' Ascelin buried his face in her hair, biting her neck and pawing at her clothes with hard, spiteful fingers. 'You refused me the last time. You won't do it again.'

'That was a month ago, Ascelin...' Rosalind pushed at him, trying to lever herself away from his attentions. 'It's too late again, now...'

She had already felt the signs—bone weariness, a dull headache. Ascelin was going to be disappointed for yet another tearful month.

It was no use. Rosalind's struggles had to give way to pleading, then silent repetition of her perpetual prayer.

Please, God. This time. Let the signs be wrong. A baby this time, Lord. Haven't I suffered enough? I'll be good forever—a good wife, but an even better mother.

Please, God. This time.

The torture finished with a vile oath. When no more taunts came and Ascelin rolled away into the darkness,

Rosalind supposed the words had been aimed at the memory of de Bourne, and not herself.

She did not care much.

All it meant was that there was someone else to rouse Ascelin to anger now.

When her fingers could unclench from the bed-clothes, Rosalind sat up slowly. Ascelin was already asleep and silent.

She smeared the tears from her eyes and looked at the pale, wiry shape beside her on the bed. He had found someone else to hate. Rosalind wondered if that would make her position worse, or better.

The only way she would feel better was if Ascelin stopped torturing both himself and her, and packed her away to a convent somewhere.

There was little hope of that. Ascelin lived in fear of her parents reclaiming so much as a blade of grass from his new estate. Rosalind was his warrant of mastery over the castle and its lands. He would never let her go.

Rosalind sat and wondered how things could possibly be any worse.

It wasn't long before she was to find out.

The night was thick and silent when she woke. Everything had an awful familiarity about it. The steady rhythm of Ascelin's breathing. A scatter of mice galloping over the floorboards. The cold pain.

She eased her way out of bed, holding her breath so that Ascelin would sleep on. He did not stir. Dragging on a robe, Rosalind took what she needed and went downstairs.

It was some time before she started back up the stairs. Rosalind had found that it was better to get the crying over and done with. A few minutes completely her own, shut in the garderobe, helped save days of a silent tear now and then.

No one ever disturbed her. Rosalind knew that she had all their sympathy, but there was nothing that anyone could do. The nights were filled with their polite silence, the days with their understanding looks.

Her legs were heavy as lead as she toiled back up to bed. At the top of the stairs, she stopped. Another wave of grief washed over her as she looked towards the door of her room. It wasn't fair. It wasn't right...

Rosalind sank down on to the steps, not caring about the soot and crumbled rushes. She could think of nothing but her failure, and cried as though her heart had broken.

The light footsteps went unnoticed until they were beside her. Rosalind cowered automatically, but it wasn't Ascelin's clipped tones that whispered through the night.

'Are you all right?' De Bourne crouched at the head of the stairs. Despite the village girl, who had never reappeared from his room, he was at least decently dressed in a long robe.

'Yes—yes, it's nothing, my lord. I'm sorry if I woke you...'

'Nothing, be damned.' He stepped down to her level and sat beside her. 'People don't wander about in the middle of the night for no reason. They don't cry, either. What is it? Dear little Ascelin been having another go at you?'

Rosalind hauled herself up into a sitting position and wiped her eyes again.

'I was feeling a little unwell, my lord.'

In the darkness his hand slid across and lay in the small of her back. His finger and thumb pressed either side of her spine and began to move in small, circular movements.

'Is that the place?'

Rosalind nodded dumbly, unable to look at him. He knew. Her shame was absolute now.

'The walls up here are far too thin,' he said in a low voice. 'That's another thing for my list of improve-

ments. We property owners have to protect our invest-
ments.' He laughed softly.

Rosalind put her head in her hands and submitted to
the gentle persuasion of his fingers on her back.

'That's beginning to feel a bit better. Less tense...'
he said after a while. 'Although this always works best
if you're standing up. Do you want to try that?'

Rosalind stood and climbed the last few steps to the
upper landing. Directing her to face the wall and lean
against it for support, de Bourne began to work his
thumbs into the exact spot where pain bit deepest. She
had no thoughts of right or wrong, only of muscles being
warmed and untangled. The relief was unimaginable.

'My lord,' she said slowly, more than half asleep. 'How
did you know what to do?'

'Shamira used to suffer in the same way.'

Rosalind opened her eyes. Nothing more was forth-
coming, and de Bourne continued to work at her back.

'Shamira...?' she murmured, hardly daring to expect
an answer.

'My wife.' The words were muttered as though they
were not fitting for such an occasion.

'I didn't realise that you were married, my lord——'
Rosalind began, but de Bourne cut her short.

'Once upon a time.'

He took his hands away and stood back from her.

'There. Teach young Ascelin how to do it. Make him
do something useful, if he's so concerned with your
innermost workings.'

'Thank you, my lord.' Rosalind moved away from the
wall sleepily. In the quiet of the night their relationship
seemed to have changed. There was an unspoken understanding between them now. Unconsciously, she tried to
take it further.

'You will have been blessed with children, no doubt,
my lord?'

De Bourne did not move as she started off towards her chamber. At once Rosalind realised that the question had been too personal an intrusion and turned to apologise.

To her surprise, the mercenary's look of dark uncertainty faded into a self-conscious grin.

'Two little boys,' he said indistinctly, then added, 'But that's another story. I'd be grateful if...news of that part of my life didn't go any further, Lady Rosalind...'

The Black Wolf a family man? That would certainly blast his ruthless reputation to nothing in the eyes of his soldiers sleeping downstairs.

Rosalind put her hand on his arm purely as a gesture of confidences shared.

'Of course not, my lord. It won't go any further.'

As she spoke Rosalind happened to look along the landing.

Ascelin stood in the doorway of their room. He was watching Rosalind and de Bourne with a look of cruel satisfaction.

CHAPTER FOUR

ROSALIND gasped. Before she could snatch her hand from de Bourne's arm, the Black Wolf held it fast.

'What sort of a loving husband lets his wife wander abroad in the middle of the night?' De Bourne escorted her to Ascelin's side, making a great show of handing her over to him.

'One who won't stand being cuckolded in his own house.'

Ascelin shot a look at Rosalind that would have had her scurrying into their room. As it was, de Bourne had put himself between her and the door.

She stayed where she was. Folding his arms across his broad chest, de Bourne stared at Ascelin so hard that the younger man had to look away. The mercenary laughed—a low, threatening sound in the silence.

'It seems as though I shall have to put you straight on a few things, little Ascelin. I'm in possession of this place. You do as I say—I'm master here. Right now, I'm telling you to take better care of your wife. And what I say goes.'

The briefest hint of amusement still glittered in de Bourne's eyes. Rosalind knew that Ascelin always wanted the last word, and waited for a petulant outburst. Instead, her husband remained ice-cool. Flicking back the curtain door to his room, he matched de Bourne's expression for once.

'You won't get away with this, *poulain*. When everyone gets to hear of this adultery, I can assure you that you'll be ruined in the eyes of every decent person——'

'And you'd be rid of a wife at no expense while securing her inheritance for yourself. That sounds suspiciously like fraud to me, Ascelin.'

With a last, strange look at Rosalind, de Bourne moved to let her pass. He had no fear of either Ascelin or his threats.

'You'll find no sport in trying to frighten me, Ascelin. My reputation's long gone. No woman as loyal and decent as your poor wife would ever look at me twice,' he said slowly, but Ascelin wasn't listening.

He had gone back into his room, where Rosalind was waiting alone.

The next morning, Ascelin ordered Rosalind to stay in her room. Later, there was a knock at the door. She pulled the coverlet over her head, waiting for breakfast to be put down beside her bed.

There was silence. After a while the knock came again. Rosalind called for the servant to enter, but no servant came. Instead, there was the sound of the curtain door being drawn back, and de Bourne's voice.

'Come on, sweetbriar. I want you up and doing— you'll feel ten times worse lying about here in bed.'

His voice was brisk, but soft-edged. When she did not move or reply, he cleared his throat.

'Can I come in?'

'Can I stop you, my lord?'

'No,' he said with a chuckle, and Rosalind heard the curtain fall closed behind him. The next sound was not so welcome. De Bourne was rasping tinder and flint, lighting the smoky rush lights that were set around the walls.

'Don't, my lord...'

'It's pitch-black in here. Can't see myself think,' de Bourne said briskly. As he neared the bed his voice grew softer. 'He's been ill-treating you, hasn't he, Rosalind? And it's far from the first time.'

Rosalind pushed her head into the pillows, willing de Bourne to go away. He was not a man to be easily put off. There came the muffled scrape of his sword on the rushy floorboards. She felt him sit down carefully on her edge of the bed.

'Ascelin's had to go out, sweetbriar. A little matter of some logging that needed doing on the western boundary. It's a nice cold morning. He'll enjoy the walk.'

Rosalind stopped trying to hide herself. 'You made him walk? My lord, it's miles out to that boundary! If he doesn't freeze to death he'll be too exhausted to do anything——'

'I made sure he had plenty of company. If they see he's getting chilly a brisk run will soon warm him up. And a sharp blow with the flat of a sword blade is the best cure for exhaustion that I know.'

'You are a brute,' Rosalind said coldly. 'All the wicked things people say about you must be true, I can see that now——'

'Quite right.'

Rosalind heard him stripping off his gloves. His next words made her go cold with fear.

'I sent dear little Ascelin off on a wild-goose chase so that I could have you all to myself. Now, let's have a look at you.'

Winter-cold air joined his fingers in slipping between her skin and the coverlet. Immediately, Rosalind clutched tightly to the bedclothes, but her fingers were peeled away with professional speed.

'I always mean what I say, sweetbriar, but I don't always say exactly what I mean. Oh, heavens—ssh!'

Rosalind had tried to scream, but de Bourne deftly covered her mouth with one hand.

'We don't want any of that. I only want to see what he's done to you...'

De Bourne had turned the coverlet back from her face and regarded the bruises carefully. Tears had sprung to

Rosalind's eyes at the thought of another assault, but de Bourne only seemed interested in her face.

'I fell...' Rosalind said when he removed his hand from her mouth.

'And Ascelin's fist accidentally happened to be in the way? I wasn't born yesterday, sweetbriar.' De Bourne sat back and picked up his gloves again. He was dressed in a plain grey tunic, cut long and full for warmth at winter work. As he pulled on his fur-lined gloves, he gave Rosalind a slow smile.

'Right. I can't sit around chattering all day. I've got work to do. And you're going to be late if you don't get up, right this instant. I'll have hot water sent up, your breakfast is on its way, and I'll see you down in the courtyard within the hour.'

Leaping to his feet, de Bourne strode to the door in a furl of cloak and tunic.

'My lord...' Rosalind raised herself on her elbow and tried to shake the sleep and confusion from her mind.

De Bourne laughed and clapped his hands in a gesture of urgency.

'Come on! There's no time to lie about. Your parents will be expecting you in time for dinner. Pack enough for a long stay. War and fighting and generally playing the fool is men's work, sweetbriar. You're far too clever to be mixed up in all this!'

'I can't leave, my lord!' Rosalind was astonished. 'My place is here with Ascelin...'

De Bourne shrugged, but looked pointedly at the bruises colouring the right side of her face.

'I'm sure everyone here would agree with you, my lady. They must all marvel at the good care that dear little Ascelin takes of you.'

He walked slowly back to the bed, one hand resting on the hilt of the sword at his side.

'Knowing how loyal you are to Ascelin, sweetbriar, I can't tell you everything that I know. Just be assured that the real war may not be as far from this little haven as you might think. This castle is held for the Empress. I shall fight down to the last man to keep it so, but I have no intention of putting a brave and steadfast lady at risk. Your parents are loyal to King Stephen. You will be quite safe there, so that is where you must go.'

'Then you don't think you can win?'

De Bourne backed towards the door. His mischievous smile had changed to open laughter.

'Sweetbriar, I know full well that I can win.' His dark eyes flashed at her, full of amusement. 'I *shall* win, but no soldier can be expected to concentrate with such a charming diversion on hand!'

He gave a slow, deep bow. When he stood to leave the laughter was still there. Rosalind pulled the bed-covers still tighter around her, and looked away from him.

She found de Bourne not only unsettling now. In these merry moods she knew he was even more of a threat to her than his dangerous reputation had promised.

The early morning was raw with cold. Despite her wearing an extra lambswool shift beneath her overtunic, the cold thrust at Rosalind as soon as she left the warm hall.

A horse was ready and waiting for her in the yard. One of de Bourne's soldiers helped her into the saddle where she sat waiting for the last pack pony to be loaded.

'My lady! My lady!' Crispin ran across the courtyard and caught at the bridle of her horse. His eyes were bright and shining. 'Guess what? The Wolf shouted at me and said I was no use at all to anyone. He said I might as well come away with you—he doesn't want me. I pre-tended I was upset, so that he wouldn't guess...'

'Then I should be careful, Crispin. He's watching us now.'

Rosalind nodded to de Bourne, who was standing outside the kitchen block. He was sharing a joke with two of his men, but his sharp eyes often darted to her.

'I don't like him,' Crispin said through chattering teeth. 'He means us no good, lady.'

'Hmm.' Rosalind unfastened her riding cloak, took it off and laid it across her horse's withers. 'I think I'll reserve judgement for a little while. My lord de Bourne is giving me the chance of going out for a ride *and* visiting my parents. Things I haven't done for nearly six months.'

She put her right hand behind her back. Crispin caught it and vaulted up to sit behind her. When he was settled Rosalind passed the cloak to him, which he arranged over his shoulders. It was large enough to envelop them both during the ride and more practical than Crispin's thin indoor clothes.

Rosalind turned her horse as the little musician's belongings were loaded on to the last pony. She could not help but think of Ascelin, out in the bitter cold. Impetuously she rode over to the kitchen block to face de Bourne.

As her horse halted before him, de Bourne's companions turned and looked up at her. Rosalind pulled her hood round to cover the worst of the bruising. Even so, both soldiers gave a knowing smile before sidling off and leaving their leader alone with Rosalind.

'They said this animal was quiet enough for a lady.' De Bourne paid more attention to the horse than to Rosalind. It nuzzled and snuffed around his cloak, to be rewarded when de Bourne covertly slipped it a morsel.

'I'm worried about Ascelin, my lord.'

'He'll be all right,' de Bourne cut in quickly. 'And so will you. Half a dozen of my best men will make sure that the King's marshal himself would give you no trouble. I'm not sure I like the look of this, though.'

He paced around her horse, scrutinising Crispin. Rosalind felt her friend shrink down behind her.

'Two on a horse? Hardly seems decent for such a respectable married lady.'

'And is what you are doing decent, my lord?' Rosalind said in a loud voice.

De Bourne looked at her innocently. 'What do you mean, my lady?'

'You know very well, sir. Take your hand from my ankle this instant.'

He roared with laughter, but did not do as he was told. Rosalind's attempt to shame him had only made her hot with embarrassment instead.

'Sweetbriar, what does go on in that wicked little mind of yours? I was only about to move your leg, to tighten this girth.' He pushed her foot forward, which spread the many folds of Rosalind's cloak and skirts wide, covering the saddle flap and girth buckles.

'I'm quite capable of doing that myself.' Rosalind stared into the distance as de Bourne busied himself at her side.

The horse shifted its weight as de Bourne tightened the double buckles securing its saddle. He seemed to be taking a long time. Behind her Crispin shivered and clung on, his head buried in her neck. He was no use, as Rosalind had expected.

'Pretty,' de Bourne murmured at last. 'Such a shame that only Ascelin gets to see them.'

Rosalind finally looked down. To her horror de Bourne was inspecting each hem of her many layers of clothing as he arranged it. She swung her leg back in place, and struck out at the Black Wolf with her riding crop as she did so. He caught it before the blow could land.

'Ah—naughty!' With a grin he prised her fingers from the stick and took it away. 'You wouldn't deny me one innocent pleasure, would you?'

'I certainly would!' Rosalind turned her horse. Agitated by her temper, the animal threw up its head, but de Bourne caught at its bridle and soothed it.

'There, look what you've done, sweetbriar! Upset the poor pony. And all because I stole a peek at next week's washing.'

'It's not right—it's indecent...Crispin, do something!' Rosalind flustered.

'Blushing again, sweetbriar? You've got a petticoat as pink as that!' He reached up and slapped Crispin playfully on the back. 'And it's no use expecting great things from our Crispin. The lad and I have come to an understanding—I tell him what to do, and he does it.'

The young musician cringed away, clinging on to Rosalind all the tighter.

'Time for you to go.' De Bourne led Rosalind's horse away from the kitchen doorway, which was growing busy with people. 'See how cruel and heartless I am to your poor husband, sweetbriar? Sending out hot stew and dumplings to him, with mulled wine for his thirst?'

Villagers were bringing two large hayboxes out from the kitchen and loading them on to a cart. Hoods flippered in the icy wind as the villagers blew on their hands. They climbed aboard the donkey cart, nodding farewell to de Bourne with cold pinched faces.

Rosalind had to admit that it was more than she had expected.

'That is a kind thought, my lord.'

'Kind? Nothing of the sort. Cold men can't work.' He led her horse to a column of mounted men waiting near the gateway. 'And these shouldn't be made to wait. They'll come straight back to me, sweetbriar. Don't think your parents will be able to buy them off!'

He laughed again, but Rosalind turned away. When the escort did not move off immediately she looked towards where de Bourne had been, but he had disappeared. A moment later Marty came running from the forge with the Black Wolf strolling along behind him, whistling.

'He says I'm to say goodbye to you, miss...' Marty panted, his eyes wide with terror.

'Is that all? It doesn't seem so very much to be frightened about, Marty.'

She patted his shoulder while he looked up nervously.

'I don't want to be left here on my own, miss. Not with him...'

De Bourne stopped a little way short of Marty. Sticking his thumbs in his belt, he watched the ungainly apprentice dithering at Rosalind's side.

'Don't worry, Marty. Keep quiet, work hard and keep your head down. Do as my lord de Bourne says, and he won't hurt you.'

'I've already told him what the alternative is, sweetbriar. I'll carve your young oak into kindling!'

Marty froze at the laughter of de Bourne's soldiers. The Black Wolf himself merely smiled, and leaned against the gatepost.

Rosalind stared at him insolently, but it only made him smile even wider. In the end she bent down to whisper to her young friend, ignoring de Bourne's amusement. 'Take no notice of him, Marty. Go back to your work and you'll be safe.'

Marty bolted for the safety of the forge. With a nod, de Bourne gave the order for the escort to leave. As the last soldiers rattled over the wooden bridge, he paused in his whistling to call after Rosalind.

'Aren't you going to wish me luck, sweetbriar?'

'You don't need it, my lord,' Rosalind snapped before realising that her words might have been taken as a compliment.

To hear de Bourne's merry laughter, that was exactly the way he had taken it.

* * *

It did not take long for Rosalind's flush of shame to
fade. A ride after so many months cooped up inside was
a wonderful salve to all her feelings. Robins sang early
carols from black-stemmed hazels, whose butter-yellow
leaves hung on in the still, frosty air. Crispin spoke little,
and Rosalind was left with her thoughts.

De Bourne was a terror to all, yet he had been gentle
towards her. And he had been kind—or the nearest thing
to kindness that he could manage. Why did Rosalind
still feel suspicious of him? It wasn't as though he singled
her out alone for special treatment. Ascelin had been
allowed to stay on at the castle instead of receiving a
knife in the ribs or, at best, being thrown out into the
forest. And he would be benefiting from a hot meal when
the donkey cart reached the loggers.

Rosalind sank lower into her cloak. This Black Wolf
had been a surprise. There was no doubt that he could
be ruthless when necessary. Earlier that same morning
Crispin had run to her, terrified, after seeing de Bourne
slice the hand from a man caught stealing.

She looked back along the track. Their passing had
darkened the grass, leaving a broad trail of prints across
the frosted grass.

Rosalind found herself wondering if the Black Wolf
felt the cold after the warmth of his native Levant.

To think about him at all seemed wicked treachery.
Instead, Rosalind took care to centre her thoughts on
the solid wall ahead that enclosed her parents' castle. It
provided a stronghold for King Stephen, safe against
rebellious rascals like de Bourne.

A frown crossed her features, then was gone. If de
Bourne was such a rascal, why was he sending her home
to her parents? It was far too honourable a gesture to
come from a scoundrel.

She rode on, wondering what it could mean.

* * *

Herbert and Joan Carilef were as quiet and unassuming as de Bourne was loud and forthright. While Rosalind was escorted to their castle gate they both stood on the roof-top lookout post and wrung their hands.

'Your mother's been worried sick, Rosalind,' Herbert said in his best indignant voice. 'I hope you haven't been doing anything silly.'

'Of course not, Father. Let me in, and I'll tell you all about it——'

'I'm not having all those filthy traitors in my yard!' Madam Carilef burst out suddenly. 'This is an honest house. We'll have no scoundrels here!'

Rosalind rode forward to the leading soldier. He was only too happy to retreat to a distance that reassured her parents while Rosalind, Crispin and the pack ponies were led in. To the amazement of the Carilefs, not only did he keep his word but he took his men off back to de Bourne when once satisfied that Rosalind was safe.

'They're just like us, really,' Rosalind said to her mother as they sat sewing after dinner.

Her mother was small, sallow and quick in her movements. She reminded Rosalind of a little hedge-sparrow, pecking at her embroidery with a fine, bright needle.

'Your father is worried to death, Rosalind. Look what that evil traitor de Bourne has done to your face! It's all I could do to stop your father going straight over there to give him the—the damned good thrashing he deserves!'

'Mother...' Rosalind said in a firm voice, 'it wasn't my lord de Bourne that did this to me. It was...an accident.'

The thought of her gentle father thrashing anyone, let alone Nerra de Bourne, was quite beyond Rosalind.

'I knew it!' The older woman bit her lip and stabbed at her embroidery again. 'You can't expect Ascelin to be any different. What he must suffer through seeing his wife sullied night and day, at the mercy of that—animal...' Her words shuddered into silence.

'Mother, it isn't like that. My lord de Bourne runs the castle now, Ascelin works for him and I just potter around. Nothing has changed for me since I married Ascelin. Except, of course, that I'm allowed to come and see you again.'

'Don't worry,' her mother continued as though Rosalind had not spoken. 'Help is close at hand. King Stephen is at Wallingford. Your father's sent word to him, asking for men. Help should be at hand for poor Ascelin within the week.'

Rosalind didn't need to wonder why it was always 'Poor Ascelin' and never 'Poor Rosalind'. Her parents were wary of their unpredictable son-in-law, as well they might be. Only the little matter of Herbert's eventual death stood between Ascelin and a large inheritance. The Carilefs were well aware how dangerous life could be when an heir got greedy.

'I wonder why the king is wintering at Wallingford this year?' Rosalind thought of this further snub for Ascelin—he hated the Fitzcounts of Wallingford like poison.

'Oh, he's not there by choice, Rosalind. That awful Brian has thrown his hand in with the traitors. I suppose he thinks he'll get a fat reward for siding with the Germans.'

'They aren't Germans, Mother. They've come over from Normandy and Anjou, like my lord de Bourne.' Rosalind smiled, but her mother's face showed that smiling and the name of de Bourne should not go together.

'Bringing over all their unnatural foreign vices. No wonder you look so pale.'

'Mother, it isn't like that. What more can I say that could possibly convince you?'

Joan Carilef put down her needle to cut another length of wool. Her glance darted over Rosalind, taking in the bird-sharp bones and troubled blue eyes.

'I don't suppose there's been any good news for poor Ascelin?' She moistened the end of a length of cream wool and threaded her needle.

Rosalind shook her head sadly, and tried to concentrate on the work her mother was finishing.

'He'll stray,' Joan said sharply. 'If you don't do something about it, Rosalind, he'll be off to...certain places. Before you know where you are, you'll be expected to bring up the child of some Jezebel, while you're the talk of the country.'

Ascelin had spent their wedding night and many since at the raddle house. That was something Rosalind kept to herself.

'What am I supposed to do?' She threw herself back in her seat in desperation.

'A well-run household and a baby a year, that's what keeps men happy. Look at you! Nearly eleven years married altogether, and not a child to show for it. Eight fine babies I'd had, by the time I was your age.'

And I'm the only one that survived, Rosalind thought bitterly.

Her mother leaned forwards and tapped her on the knee.

'Say your prayers, and always be good to Ascelin.'

Rosalind wondered if this was the sort of advice de Bourne had expected her mother to give. She thought it probably was not.

'My lord de Bourne said that I should ask you for help, Mother. You've left me none the wiser——'

'He tore that shame from you?' The older woman's eyes opened wide with horror. 'The evil blackamoor!'

'Mother! My lord de Bourne hasn't torn anything from me, and he isn't a blackamoor. If you can't be civil——'

'Rosalind! I'm surprised at you, speaking to me like this. You were always such a good girl. I don't know where you've picked it up——'

'Perhaps I've been married to Ascelin for too long already. Mother—I'm sorry, but if you will believe in fairy-tales then you must expect to have a rude awakening. If you must know, when my lord de Bourne puts his mind to it he can treat me with more respect than Ascelin ever has.'

'Then you admit it? That wicked rogue *is* interfering with you!'

Rosalind lay back in her chair and covered her face with her hands.

'Of course he isn't, Mother. I've said he shows me every respect. I could tell you how neat and tidy he is about the house, but that wouldn't make him a housewife, would it?'

Joan Carilef was not satisfied. If anything she became even more agitated. 'He's supposed to have so many women . . . for you to be living under the same roof with him—it's not right, Rosalind . . .'

'He sent me here, to stay with you. That's not living under the same roof as him, is it? He's promised to look after Ascelin, which, considering what could have happened, shows some sort of human feeling. As for the girls—that I couldn't say for certain. My lord de Bourne certainly doesn't conduct his affairs in the open, as some do.' She tried to keep the bitterness out of her voice.

'It seems to me that you know rather too much about this traitor, Rosalind.' Her father had entered the room unnoticed and both women jumped. Herbert Carilef was small, wiry, and never more happy than when he could spend a day out hunting. The war had put an end to his carefree days. It made him nervous, which he tried to cover up with ill temper.

He stood before his wife and daughter, arms folded and rocking back and forth on his heels.

'There has been some news, of sorts,' he began, a frown corrugating his brow.

Joan Carilef clapped her hands. 'The King's on his way!'

'Not . . . quite.' Herbert stroked his chin thoughtfully. 'Now that it's common knowledge Malmesbury is still holding out for the rebels, trouble is breaking out all over. King Stephen will be hard put to it to keep the pot from boiling over now——'

'Herbert!' his wife interrupted quickly. 'How can you say that?'

He raised his eyebrows and looked at Rosalind quizzically. 'I dare say Rosalind will have been told all the reasons frequently, and at length.'

There was a hard edge to his voice that made Rosalind feel uncomfortable.

'If you're suggesting that my lord de Bourne discusses his work with me any more than Ascelin does——' she began hotly, but her father raised his hands for silence.

'I'm not suggesting anything, dear girl. All I'm saying is that it's natural that you should have heard some of the things the rebels are saying. And it is true to say that their case seems most persuasive.'

'Really! Anyone would think that you sided with them, Herbert!' Joan bridled hotly. Her husband pursed his lips and shifted from foot to foot.

'It is true that the Empress Matilda is the late King Henry's legal heir,' he said thoughtfully, 'And Stephen did swear to his uncle Henry to honour her as such.'

'You needn't think that this house is going to change horses in mid-stream,' his wife said firmly. 'Whoever heard of a woman on the throne? And besides, Stephen is anointed and crowned now. That makes the throne his by right, whatever the . . . regrettable circumstances of his accession.'

For the first time Rosalind sensed a genuine difference of opinion between her parents. It made her feel both uncomfortable and uncertain. The atmosphere was unusually tense. She was glad to make an excuse and go to her room.

It was the first time that Rosalind had returned to her old room since her first marriage. There were new tapestries about the wall and a new bed, but the safe feeling was still there.

Shut in with her memories, she sat down. The mattress was much thicker than her own at home. Everything seemed more reassuring. The same patch of sky that she had looked out on as a girl, her first scrap of embroidery still hanging by the bed.

Her thoughts should have been of happy times long ago. Instead, Rosalind found herself thinking of the future. Opinion was swinging to favour the Empress. Meanwhile, King Stephen might be about to gallop to Ascelin's rescue at any minute.

It seemed likely that de Bourne and the other Angevins would win the civil war in the end. Why should there be any more blood shed than necessary?

Rosalind went to find the resident priest. He was delighted to see her, having so recently shouldered the worries of both her parents. Unable to disappoint him, she made her confession, which he seemed to find rather more dull and ordinary than expected. That over and done with, Rosalind asked him for parchment, pen and ink. The priest would have to wait for the next instalment of her confession to find out why.

Returning to her room, Rosalind thought long and hard before starting to write. A curt note served her purpose.

> My lord de Bourne,
> His grace King Stephen has been asked to send a force to help my husband regain our home. They are expected very soon—be ready.

Malmesbury is still held for your comrades, so
you can call to them there for assistance if necessary. While I wish no joy to your enterprise,
sir, I know you will take care of my husband and
while you are in power we will be safe. That is
why I write to you now.

I remain, sir, your loyal servant.

She had worried over the ending for a long time. It
wasn't as though she ever intended to be a loyal servant
of the Black Wolf, but how else could a letter be properly
finished? Finally, she signed the letter hoping that he
took it as it was intended. A formal ending for a formal
letter.

Convincing Crispin to return home with her letter took
all Rosalind's persuasion. Ascelin never let her have any
money of her own, so she could not offer that. Instead
she had to hope that de Bourne would pay well for the
information. Crispin was unconvinced.

In the end, Rosalind had to borrow threepence from
her father. Her embarrassment was almost matched by
her shame at the white lie she had to use. It was certainly
true that she was sending a letter home—she just didn't
tell her father who it was for. He assumed it was to
Ascelin, and Rosalind didn't tell him otherwise.

Her parents' home was a little quieter than her own
castle. When Crispin had been sent off, Rosalind spent
the afternoon following her father about the stables as
he showed off his horses. When the shadows began to
lengthen, she went up on to the roof and looked towards
her own home.

There were no signs of smoke or battle. There wasn't
even a sign of Crispin returning. Rosalind hoped he had
had the sense to go in, and not stay cowering in the
woods. Nothing she could say could convince him that
de Bourne would be glad to receive the letter. Crispin

was sure, as messenger, that it would be the death of him.

After supper the Carilefs spent a quiet evening around the hearth. Joan scolded her daughter for sending the only musician away, and Rosalind was beginning to regret it herself. As she helped her mother wind wool into skeins, she wondered what could have happened to Crispin. If only he could have got back safely to the castle. It was a long way home—almost four miles. November was early for wolves to move towards the settlements, but there were still the dark woods. No one risked travelling alone at night. Anything might be lurking in there.

Rosalind had another day of uncertainty ahead of her. Crispin did not return. Her parents tried to convince Rosalind that he had decided to stay at home. It was no use. Late that afternoon they sent a couple of their own soldiers to find out if Crispin was safe.

It was the next morning before the Carilefs' lookout called a warning of visitors. Rosalind had been in the yard, following the poultry and searching out the last few eggs of the season. She looked up only to see the main gates being slammed shut.

In the distance there was a faint jingle of harness. Rosalind ran inside, and joined her parents as they dashed up to the roof to see who was coming.

It was still very early. A slip of moon rode high in the western sky, which was tinged with finch colours of slate and rose. Mist filled the valley, spilling over hilly spurs like smoke. It sank and collected where the track cut through the trees, making the newcomers unrecognisable until they drew close.

Then Rosalind saw the black banner furling and cracking against the lightening sky.

'It's my lord de Bourne...' she said in a puzzled whisper.

'A black banner to suit a black-hearted demon,' her mother snorted. 'You needn't think I'm going to let him in here, the way he's been carrying on.'

Rosalind shrugged. There was no knowing what horrors her mother had dreamed up. Whatever they were, Rosalind had certainly not suffered them in real life. *Whether I'll have to in the future remains to be seen,* she thought with a shiver.

De Bourne brought his small group of men to a halt a good bowshot from the castle walls. The soldier bearing his standard drove it in the ground, and the horsemen wheeled about, touching it for luck.

'Right.' De Bourne dropped his reins but kept a firm hold on his shield. 'Today is Thursday. I don't work on Thursdays without dire need or copious amounts of overtime, so you'll realise that my journey today has not been undertaken lightly.'

He did not sound in a mood to be trifled with. Rosalind wondered if her warning of attack had come too late. At a nudge from her mother, Herbert cleared his throat.

'I sent two men to you yesterday, my lord. My daughter despatched her musician the day before—nothing more has been heard of any of them,' he said unsteadily.

'Didn't the lady Rosalind tell you, my lord? I eat messengers.'

De Bourne's men laughed, but Herbert shrank back.

'Don't look so worried, lord! You're nice and snug in that castle there, I'm locked out. I'm quite happy with that arrangement. It's my day off, remember. I'm not looking for work. Only your daughter. All you have to do is send her out to me. Quick sharp.'

'Certainly not! How dare you?' Rosalind's mother stepped forward. 'Don't think you can drag my daughter away on one of your evil whims——'

De Bourne removed his helmet and gave a sweeping bow.

'Madam,' he said with a smile, 'if I had my way, the lady Rosalind would remain here with you permanently. As it is, I am sent here by my own priest, with strict instructions to return the lady to her husband. Not even the Black Wolf can defy the Church.'

'That puts a different light on it,' Rosalind's father murmured, but her mother had different ideas.

'Don't be so ridiculous, Herbert!' she hissed. 'It's a trap, of course it is. He's only saying that.'

'Can I speak to my lord de Bourne?' Rosalind risked. Her parents were smiling through clenched teeth at the visitor below.

'Of course not, Rosalind! Your father's sorting it out. Go on, Herbert. Tell him!'

They were settling into their usual pattern. Rosalind knew that her parents wouldn't notice if she slipped away, so she left the roof and went downstairs.

There were no outraged cries from her mother as she crossed the castle yard. No order to return as she reached the little pass door in the gates. The gatekeeper did step forward to warn her, but Rosalind dismissed him with a smile.

A slippery wooden bridge crossed the ditch surrounding the Carilefs' castle. Rosalind had to watch her step. Reaching the safety of the grassland, she looked up. De Bourne was alone beside his standard now. His men had already been sent back out of earshot.

Rosalind walked towards de Bourne, being careful not to hurry too much. As she drew near he leaned on the front of his saddle and looked down at her.

'You must be getting braver, sweetbriar!' He twinkled merrily.

'Or more foolhardy.'

'Coming up?' He reached down as though to lift her up before him, but Rosalind stepped back.

'Certainly not, my lord!'

A scream darted down from the roof. Her mother had seen what was going on, and she didn't like it one bit.

'Rosalind! Come back in here this instant! It isn't safe!'

'It's perfectly safe, Mother.' Rosalind waved up reassuringly. 'My lord de Bourne has more sense than to cut me down in full view of all your staff.'

'I don't think it's murder your mother's worried about,' de Bourne whispered playfully. His horse tossed its head, plumes of steam rising in the cool morning air.

'My letter didn't prevent you venturing out, my lord?' Rosalind looked up warily. He put his head on one side and frowned.

'What letter?'

'I sent Crispin back with a note to let you know that the King was coming to help Ascelin.'

'Oh, sweetbriar...' He gave a heavy sigh and tapped one finger against his teeth. 'Crispin's home, but I never received any letter. When it comes to affairs of the heart, sweet, never—ever—put anything in writing.'

Rosalind felt cold fear crawling over her again. It stifled any outrage she might have felt at his words.

'Ascelin must have taken it,' she said slowly. 'Crispin's not very brave...'

'Then that's why young Ascelin suddenly started making such a fuss. Prostrate with grief at losing you, refusing to eat...that wretched priest made me feel a complete ogre, splitting up the family home. Fetching you back was the least penance I could do. Oh, sweetbriar—fancy putting it in writing! What are we going to do now? Ascelin's jealous enough of me as it is, without you sending me a billet-doux...'

Rosalind shook her head in confusion. 'There was nothing of that nature in the letter, my lord——'

'And you think Ascelin will believe that? Words can mean anything the reader wants. That you sent me a warning would have been bad enough—Ascelin would see that as open treachery. Anything more he could make up for himself.'

'Rosalind!' Her mother's voice came from ground level now, inside the yard. 'Come back in here this instant. That black-hearted devil's bewitched you!'

'I don't think your mother likes me very much, sweetbriar. You'd better go back in to her.' He reached down and took her hand, giving it the lightest of formal kisses. 'I must get back and hold the castle for the Empress if we're to have visitors.'

With a snap of his fingers, his men rode forward. Rosalind was surrounded by a milling throng of horsemen as the black banner of de Bourne was retrieved.

'My lord! What about your penance—collecting me? I shall have to come with you . . .'

De Bourne's horse half reared, eager to be gone. He laughed down at her.

'Far too dangerous for you now, sweetbriar. Ascelin in a fine old bate, the King on his way—and not for wine and white cakes, either! No, you'll be safer here, with your parents.'

Deaf to her mother's frantic cries, Rosalind put her hand to de Bourne's arm. 'You can't leave me here! That would be disobeying the priest's orders, my lord— whatever will happen to you?'

De Bourne calmed his horse, which paced around her irritably as he spoke.

'A few extra hours on my knees? A taste of the lash? Why not? There's no honour in giving out punishment if I'm not willing to take it in my turn.'

'My lord—I'm coming back with you! It's not fair that you should suffer so——'

'Ascelin will hurt you, Rosalind. You're safe here. With the war heading this way I won't be able to watch you every moment. That's what coming back will mean—keeping me between you all the time. Ascelin's afraid of me, sweetbriar. He wouldn't dare hurt you as long as I could be on hand, but when I'm busy...'

'I'll take that risk, my lord,' Rosalind said quietly. She looked up at him, knowing that this enemy of her family understood her husband better than they did.

De Bourne did not seem particularly grateful. His smile was strangely brittle, and the nod of acceptance brief.

Rosalind watched him order two soldiers to remain while the rest started for home at a canter. While de Bourne waited, Rosalind went back to arrange for her belongings to be sent on behind.

'It's madness, Rosalind. Worse than signing your own death warrant.' Joan Carilef wrung her hands in despair. 'What is poor Ascelin going to think when you've been riding around the countryside with that—that creature? Herbert, tell her!'

'Your mother's got a point, Rosalind,' her father muttered. 'The scoundrel's never even returned the two men I sent looking for your boy... Good God!'

His jaw dropped as he recognised de Bourne's remaining escort.

'It's them! And wearing the rascal's colours, too! Whatever happened to good old-fashioned loyalty?'

'It was bought out with good old-fashioned money,' de Bourne called over affably. 'I can never have too many men on my side, my lord.'

Rosalind's horse was led up the gates. Her father went to help her into the saddle, but his wife stopped him. Bullying and pleading with Rosalind had failed. The only hope she had left now was to appeal to her daughter's sense of honour.

'I suppose he's bought you, too,' she murmured grimly.

Rosalind refused to rise to that bait. 'There are more important things in life than money, Mother.' Settling in her saddle, she arranged the folds of her gown and cloak about her. 'And you would be the first to damn a man for disobeying the Church.'

Pushing the horse on into a smart trot, Rosalind clattered out of the castle gates to join de Bourne.

CHAPTER FIVE

'I'D BETTER tell you here and now, sweetbriar—I didn't want you to come back.'

The little party was jogging along the forest track, the escort a respectful distance from de Bourne and Rosalind.

'I won't be any trouble, my lord.'

'You'll be more trouble to me than all of this pointless war, sweetbriar.' He looked down at her with a wry smile. His horse fretted at being made to travel at the pace of Rosalind's mount, but even so de Bourne only held the reins with one hand. The other lay on the hilt of the sword at his side, in case of attack.

When she did not reply he cleared his throat awkwardly.

'You must know, sweetbriar...Rosalind...'

His voice had dropped to an uneven whisper. In a sudden cascade of panic, Rosalind guessed. De Bourne ploughed on.

'Fetching you back was only the start of my penance. To have you near, Rosalind, you must know what that will do to me——'

'I know that I am married to Ascelin, my lord,' she said in a voice that was low and unsteady. 'I would never willingly intend to bring you any—inconvenience.'

She should have listened to her mother, and stayed safe at home. Now all her mother's worst fears were rearing up before Rosalind.

'I had better go back to my parents, lord. If you would be so good as to return me...' She reined in her horse and turned to go back the way they had come.

'It's too late for that now, Rosalind.' He turned too, wheeling his horse to cut off her retreat. 'The damage is done, sweetbriar.'

Her horse stopped, uncertain of her requirements. De Bourne took the reins from her, passing them over the horse's head. He then led it and Rosalind on towards his stronghold.

There was nothing that she could do. The horses travelled on through the chill blue-grey dew that covered the grass. Rosalind could not bear to look up at de Bourne as he rode alongside her.

Jays rustled through the fallen leaves, searching out acorns. A rainbird flew its rise and fall way across the track, landing on a beech trunk before laughing out loud at them.

'Sounds like rain coming,' Rosalind said into the uncomfortable silence.

Her words unleashed a small torrent from de Bourne. 'I spoke out of turn. Forget what I said, sweetbriar. It doesn't matter.'

His rush of words did nothing to ease the situation. Rosalind didn't know how to apologise without making things worse. De Bourne had lost his temper with the hurried speech.

If he spoke at all now, it was only to rebuke his soldiers for their slow pace.

His advance guard had wasted no time in passing on their orders. The castle was being made ready for war. The great gates were being repaired and strengthened with iron straps. Hammers sang out over the furnace roar of the forge.

Everyone bustled to and fro, but there was no panic. Work conquers fear, de Bourne had said. He intended that they should all learn the truth of that.

'Stay there.' Sliding down from his horse, de Bourne ordered the two soldiers escorting her to remain with Rosalind.

He went up into the castle, pulling off his cloak and gloves as he did so. When he reappeared, he was hauling Crispin out of the hall with him.

De Bourne closed the door behind them. After a hurried conversation at the top of the steps he went back into the hall. Crispin fled down to join Rosalind in the yard.

'I didn't mean to, my lady—the lord Ascelin said he'd kill me if I didn't hand the letter over...'

'That's all right, Crispin.' Rosalind sighed and got down from her horse. 'I was reckless, and deserved to be found out. As long as he didn't hurt you.'

Crispin shook his head, and took the reins of her horse. Before he led it away the boy looked at her nervously. 'The Wolf, my lady. He wants to see you in the hall—now. My lord Ascelin is already there...'

Rosalind dismissed the two soldiers and took a deep breath. Walking through the hurrying villagers, rioting children, bleating sheep and panicking poultry, she tried to marshal her thoughts.

There was no defence for what she had done. The enemy, de Bourne, would have been warned of an imminent attack. That could not be denied.

At least the message had not got through. Ascelin might be mollified by that, Rosalind thought, grasping at straws.

Her fingers moved over the still-tender skin near her right eye. The reality would be painfully different. Rosalind's only consolation was that the letter could not possibly inflame Ascelin's jealousy, as de Bourne seemed to think.

She reached the castle door, and found it barred from the inside. Terrified of what might be happening, she beat on it with her fist.

De Bourne let her in almost immediately. When her eyes grew accustomed to the gloom inside Rosalind saw that the two men did at least have the priest with them. He might make one or both see reason.

Ascelin stood in the centre of the hall, holding Rosalind's letter. Dropping the bar across the door behind her, de Bourne went to join the priest at the hearth.

'My lord Ascelin was stating his grievances, Lady Rosalind.' Father Anthony the priest looked grave. 'It seems that you have been most unwise.'

Rosalind went forward and curtsyed to him. 'I only thought to stop further bloodshed, Father. If a surprise attack had been avoided and the castle made ready to repel a siege, the war might be over before my lord Ascelin had cause to fight.'

Ascelin had opened his mouth to shout Rosalind down, but her final words threw him. He hated fighting at the best of times, and much preferred underhand methods of getting his own way.

When no abuse came, Rosalind steeled herself to look at him. The blond curls gave him such a boyish air, quite different to his true character. A petulant frown creased his smooth, pale features. Unwilling to admit that Rosalind might have been acting in his interests, Ascelin scanned the letter for something more sinister.

'Here, then!' He held out the parchment so that all could see and stabbed at it viciously with his finger. 'How are you going to wriggle your way out of this? "I know you will take care of my husband and while you are in power we will be safe."'

Rosalind was mystified, and shook her head. 'It means what I said, my lord—no more, no less.'

'No less than a conspiracy on my life!' Ascelin shook the letter at Father Anthony, who had been looking as puzzled as Rosalind. De Bourne laughed.

'It comes to something when a man fears the loving words of his own wife!'

'My lord,' Father Anthony interrupted crossly, 'I would remind you that you are in quite enough trouble as it is, without making matters worse.'

'Quite.' De Bourne stifled a smile and bowed to the priest. 'Pray continue, Ascelin.'

'He means to murder me,' Ascelin said with a frightening calm. 'Murder me, take my land and set himself up as heir to the Carilef estate.'

'Then...the small matter of my lord de Bourne making off with your wife is not *finally* the point?' Father Anthony said with a quizzical glance.

'Well...' Ascelin showed his first sign of self-doubt. This soon changed to annoyance. 'Oh—of course it is! Don't confuse the matter! When I want empty words I can go to her.' He stabbed a grimy finger at Rosalind, so close that she jumped back in alarm. Glowering at her, Ascelin knew that Rosalind was the only person in the room that he could frighten.

'It all hinges on her. While I'm alive and she's my wife, I get the land. If anything happens to me—or if he gets to marry her...'

The priest strolled forward, took Ascelin's accusing hand and tucked it into the crook of his arm.

'This is easily solved, then, my lord.' He patted Ascelin's hand comfortingly. 'From what you've said, right is bound to be on your side. Agree to meet my lord de Bourne on equal terms and the matter can be settled once and for all.'

Ascelin swallowed hard. 'You mean fight? Him?'

'Why, yes.' The elderly priest smiled broadly. 'With the Lord on your side, Ascelin, it would be a perfectly fair contest——'

'He'll murder me!' Ascelin wrenched his arm away, even frightened of the priest now. 'It's a plot—I knew it—you're all in on it...'

'What about me? Doesn't my opinion count for anything?' De Bourne stepped forward as Ascelin scuttled back a few more paces. 'Nobody's asked me if I want a fight. Well—I don't, and that's an end to it.'

Relief coursed through Ascelin's veins like courage.

'Ha! Coward! Couldn't face the thought of God defending my rights, eh?'

'On the contrary, I've got a much better idea.' De Bourne drew a long-bladed knife from his belt. 'This is sharp enough to split a human hair, and long enough to do twice the damage of your puny knife, Ascelin. I'll hand this into Father Anthony's safe keeping. If at any time you can produce independent witnesses to prove I've been plotting with your wife or leading her astray, you can take this and carve me into as many pieces as you think fit. I wouldn't raise a finger to stop you.'

'I'd do it anyway,' Ascelin muttered, rather more nervously than before.

'But I'd rather you got Father Anthony to give you this, to make a clean job of it.' De Bourne rested the knife tip against Ascelin's small snub nose. 'Equally, mind, if I get to hear the smallest whisper that the lady Rosalind has so much as a broken fingernail while in your care...'

'I think we can guess the rest, my lord,' Father Anthony cut in, taking the knife from de Bourne. 'Now, I don't suppose you will be taking your day off with the times so dangerous. Perhaps you and the lord Ascelin should be out and about, rather than lounging in here?'

Rosalind spent a wonderfully peaceful day. Although Ascelin ignored her pointedly each time their paths crossed, that was better than a sly blow or angry words. De Bourne kept him busy with errands and preparations for the expected arrival of the king's men.

When dusk fell, everything was ready. The villagers were safe inside the castle walls, together with their animals. Everything was as secure as it could be. There was no point in worrying now. All that could be done had been done, so life went on much as usual.

The hall was a warm haven against the bitter weather that had blown up. Once the door was shut and lagged against draughts, everyone could enjoy the sound of wind and rain buffeting around the castle walls.

Supper that night was almost bearable. Ascelin refused to share the same table as de Bourne, and sulked beside the hearth. Rosalind was more practical. She did join her husband, but only after eating a good supper. Ascelin might starve himself on principle, but she wasn't going to.

Rosalind had even dared to start a large piece of embroidery. Ascelin would not be so willing to ruin it if it was kept downstairs in the hall, in full view of de Bourne. The mercenary had even set his men to make a new working frame and stand for it. Rosalind could only hope that he realised what a useful weapon Ascelin found such things.

One of the soldiers set the embroidery frame beside the hearth for her, where the light was best for working. Thanking him with a smile, Rosalind sat down and started to set out her skeins of coloured wool. Ascelin refused to make conversation, so she concentrated on her work.

De Bourne and some of his men had been working late and were still busy with their meal, talking and laughing together. The low murmur of their voices was soothing, and the good fire made Rosalind feel almost peaceful.

That peace was soon to be shattered. A heavy-footed sentry stamped down from the roof-top lookout post and pushed his way to de Bourne's side. The other diners cursed and complained as cold raindrops showered from the sentry, but de Bourne soon silenced them.

After a murmured conversation he sent the lookout back to his post.

'Tirold? You're the only one that's not gainfully employed. Pull the lagging back from the door. We've got guests.'

'Won't you look the fool if it's King Stephen?' Ascelin sneered, and stayed where he was.

'On a night like this? I doubt your man will dare to leave his own fireside this evening. And I don't employ outriders who can't tell our side from yours. Get up and clear the doorway, Tirold. Then you can heat up some wine. Whoever it is will be half drowned, if they're not frozen stiff as well.'

Rosalind leaned across to Ascelin. 'I'll arrange the wine, my lord. You go and see to the door. It's best to do as he says——'

'Yes. You're the living proof of that, aren't you?' Ascelin spat, his eyes narrow slits of hatred.

Rosalind could give no reply. She stepped over supper-stuffed dogs lying about the fireside and started towards the door.

'Sit down, sweetbriar. He'll do it. And before I count ten, too.' De Bourne suddenly shot to his feet. 'Move, Tirold!'

His roar was so thunderous that it catapulted Ascelin out of his seat. The soldiers knew better than to laugh when de Bourne was involved, so they hid their sniggers.

Ascelin was beginning to feel the shame that he had often forced on Rosalind. Despite the treatment she had suffered in the past, she still felt guilty at seeing him tormented. De Bourne was concentrating on his supper once more, so Rosalind went to fetch wine and help Ascelin in that way.

As she reached the trestle table, de Bourne paused momentarily in his conversation.

'Lady Rosalind?'

He stretched out his right hand, pressing the index finger to the edge of the table in front of him. Rosalind went and stood where he indicated.

When de Bourne had finished speaking to his companions, he looked up at her. The twinkling, sloe-black eyes did not match the stern set of his jaw, but still Rosalind hung her head. The memory of his words that morning were still burning into her mind.

'If I tell your husband to do something, then he will do it, lady. I won't stand for defiance from anyone. And disobedience is merely defiance without claws or teeth.' He prodded her, very gently. 'If I say that you are not to help him, sweetbriar, then you will return to your own work and get on with it. Understand?'

Rosalind did not dare look up. 'Yes, my lord.'

She waited for further instructions, but none came. De Bourne rapped his finger on the table, then pointed back to her embroidery beside the fire. At last Rosalind looked up to see that the mercenary was the only person smiling at his own words. All the others had read a much sterner warning from them.

The door burst open as Ascelin was still pulling back the heavy curtains. There was a confusion of draperies and wet cloaks as a dark figure bundled its way in. Ascelin yelled a vigorous oath as he was knocked flying, but the company merely laughed.

De Bourne stood up, beaming at the newcomer. 'Don't worry about that, friend. It's only young Ascelin. He would have had a good hot drink ready for you if he'd been a bit quicker about it.'

The visitor threw back his hood to a laugh of appreciation from the soldiers. He was recognised by most as a former companion, and fielded their jokes amiably.

'You mean to say that you've come all the way from Anjou in this weather?' De Bourne laughed, and, calling for a towel, threw it at the newcomer. 'What news from God's own county?'

'A delivery, my lord. With a few extra men for you, too,' the Angevin said, muffled by the towel as he dried his face and hair. 'And a letter.'

His clothing was so wet and fingers so cold that the Angevin could barely unbuckle his tunic. Ascelin had reached him with a cup of hot wine before the newcomer had found the sealed roll of parchment nestling in the folds of his singlet. The Black Wolf watched with amused curiosity.

'Direct from Count Geoffrey?'

The messenger handed it over with a nod. He took the wine from Ascelin with a grin, but Ascelin only scowled.

'Joined-up writing, too,' de Bourne mused over the sealed letter. 'No wonder it's taken him so long.'

He pushed the parchment back at the Angevin and sat down to finish his dinner.

'You read it out for me. I'm hungry. Oh...' he shot a look across to Rosalind '...and don't bother with the profanities. That should make it a lot quicker.'

The soldiers laughed, and the messenger cleared his throat. De Bourne went back to his roast pork and parsnips.

'"To my loyal vassal, closest friend and respected comrade in arms the lord Mahel de Bourne, currently companion to my lady wife Matilda, who as heiress to the throne of England by birth, Holy Roman Empress through her first husband and Countess of Anjou through her marriage to me, being Geoffrey the fair, son of——"'

'Get on with it!'

De Bourne waved his second-best knife irritably. The messenger shifted, uncomfortable in a growing pool of rainwater around his feet. Taking a deep breath, he began again.

'"Being Geoffrey the fair——"'

'Stop!' De Bourne leapt to his feet and took the letter from the messenger. Tearing off the first two-thirds of the parchment and casting them aside, he handed the remaining slip back to the messenger.

'Do we really want to spend three hours clambering about in the Plantagenet family tree? No. Time is money, lad. Read on.'

'Just this?' The messenger looked at his remaining scrap of parchment. The larger piece curled and rolled about his feet in a draught whipping in under the door.

'A tip for the future.' De Bourne addressed the whole hall. 'Count Geoffrey only remembers to start his letters when he realises that the parchment's nearly filled. All the news is squashed into the bottom corner. The rest is like Genesis—half a page of "begats".'

The messenger wore such a forlorn expression by this time that Rosalind had to smile. When de Bourne ordered him to continue the newcomer's voice was not as cheerful as the message.

'"Dear Nerra. Sounds like good news your end. Well done—I'm counting on you to keep the old lady happy, and, more importantly, well away from this place. Due to a severe attack of my old trouble, things have got a bit hectic here lately—my hands are so full that I nearly had to dictate this letter."' The messenger stopped and looked about. Seeing that Rosalind was listening, he flushed slightly. 'The count goes into some detail at this point, my lord de Bourne. Shall I continue?'

De Bourne savoured a particularly succulent piece of crackling before he replied. 'No. Carry on with the news. I can enjoy the entertainment later, myself.'

The reading continued. '"Rumour has it that you're settled into a good den. It'll be better for the boys to have a proper home at last, not stuck out here in the scrub with someone who's an even bigger scoundrel than their father..."'

De Bourne had stopped eating. Putting down his knife, he studied the messenger intently.

'There—there's a bit more, my lord...' The messenger dripped more rainwater on to the floor as he flattened down his damp, spiked hair.

'Let's hear the worst.'

'It ends "love, Geoffrey," but then there's an addition—"The next one that mentions by—Our—Lady Dog Toby around here gets the sharp end of my boot!"'

Rosalind covered her ears at the escaped oath, but Ascelin was more interested.

'If the Count of Anjou is ill, then his witch of a wife should go back home and tend him,' Ascelin sneered. To his surprise, the remark caused even more laughter than any of de Bourne's jokes over supper had done.

The mercenary leader pushed his plate aside. When the amusement had died down he folded his arms and grinned at Ascelin.

'The only thing that ails young Geoffrey is the same trouble you have, Ascelin. An inability to get out of bed—his own, or anybody else's. That's why he wants his wife to succeed in England. It's a nice long way away from Anjou.'

He stood up and strolled around the table, perching on the edge and taking the parchment from the messenger's hands.

'He's sent another cart-load of money, I hope.' De Bourne scanned the letter, looking for its more amusing parts.

'Yes, my lord. All the bags are verified and still sealed.'

'I wouldn't have accepted less.' Abruptly de Bourne's manner changed. He caught the messenger by his soggy collar, eyes boring into his quarry, who quailed. 'And what about the other small delights that dear Geoffrey thought to send us?'

'Er——'

'Well? You're surely not going to tell me that Geoffrey sent one of his favourites all this way just to tell me he's having a good time?'

'Outside . . .' The messenger jerked his head nervously towards the door. 'In the cart . . .'

De Bourne let go of the Angevin with a sigh. 'Well? What are you waiting for? Christmas? Fetch the little perishers in, if they're coming.'

He returned to his supper as the messenger scuttled back out. When the door crashed open again de Bourne was engrossed in his cooling meal and did not look up. Everyone else did.

Two small figures, overwhelmed in cloaks and hoods were thrust over the threshold by an invisible hand. The door was slammed shut behind them.

After blinking a little in the dull light of fire and candles, two pairs of dark, quick eyes scanned the hall. Ascelin started to laugh, but de Bourne's soldiers knew better than to comment.

'It looks as if your after-supper snack has arrived, *poulain*. Win them in a raffle, did you?'

'Ascelin, how I wish I could give you away as a prize.' De Bourne gave a heartfelt sigh. 'But I'd have no takers. You'll go out with a couple of the others—now!—and help stack away the wages. You all heard what the man said—those bags are all sealed and accounted for. Anyone caught thieving loses their hands.'

Despite the wintery weather several men rushed Ascelin off to do de Bourne's bidding. Work never seemed so arduous when it involved the wages.

The two children huddled together in silence as the soldiers filed past them. Rosalind picked up the towel that the messenger had dropped and went up to them.

A large cloak had been wrapped around them both. Rosalind peeled off this soaked outer layer, then a wet and cold blanket, before reaching the children's own little cloaks and hoods which were barely damp.

She had uncovered twin boys of about four years old, identically dressed in red tunics and woollen stockings. Each clutched a small wooden horse on wheels. There's no mistaking their pedigree, Rosalind thought, even in this light. Coal-black hair and eyes that missed nothing.

'Boys.'

De Bourne acknowledged his sons only briefly. The twins seemed used to the treatment. Rosalind crouched and dried their hands and faces while they watched her unblinkingly, like two little robins.

She smiled, and the twins looked at each other as though wondering what to make of her.

'Would you like something to eat?' she said softly.

'Yes, please, Auntie,' they chorused with beaming smiles.

'Later.' De Bourne had other ideas. Half emptying his goblet of wine in one pull, he wiped his mouth then muttered, 'Don't go to any trouble. They'll pick over what's left here. Leave them, and get back to your sewing.'

He's embarrassed, Rosalind thought as she went back to her fireside seat. The remaining rabble of soldiers must have come to the same conclusion, for amusement whispered through their ranks.

De Bourne cut them all dead with a glare.

Dinner was finished off quickly after that. One by one the remaining soldiers stood and went off out to the stables, or store-room, or raddle house, despite the weather. At last de Bourne was alone at the table. He dug the point of his knife into a last slice of pork and sat back.

'Sweetbriar?'

Rosalind looked up from her sewing. Silently the boys had moved a little closer to their father. They now stood with their backs pressed up against the wall, still some yards from where de Bourne sat.

'Send out to the kitchens for a bit more food, would you? I seem to have worked up quite an appetite.'

She stood up and curtsyed, looking up at him from beneath lowered lashes.

'How much would you like, my lord?'

De Bourne sighed. He put his hands behind his head, looked up at the ceiling, then across at the fire. His glance had covertly taken in the two children, who cautiously moved a little closer each time he looked away.

'Say...four slices of meat—a few parsnips and a couple of those roasted onions. And a bit of stuffing, if there's any left.' He rocked forward in his seat and slapped both hands down on the table. 'And a pitcher of hot milk. I fancy a change.'

'With two mugs?' Rosalind smiled at the twins, who looked back shyly.

'No, thanks. I've got one here. That'll do,' de Bourne said haughtily. He was still staring into the fire as Rosalind pulled on her outdoor things to slip outside.

She had to shelter in the kitchen block for quite a while before returning. When the tray of food was finally ready she hurried back through the rain and crowds. Bursting into the castle hall, she found de Bourne with a child on each knee and pushing one of their little wooden toys across the table. With an oath he half rose, sending the boys slithering to the floor.

'No, my lord—don't get up...' Rosalind entered, then quickly dropped the bar that secured the hall door from the inside. 'You won't be disturbed again for a while.'

De Bourne sank back into his seat, watching her uncomfortably. The children stood and watched her, too. They knew better than to scramble back on to their father's lap before being bidden.

'I've...gone off the thought of more food, sweetbriar. Adrian and Helias might as well have it.'

'Just as well I brought two trenchers, then.' Rosalind smiled and set thick hunks of bread down on the table. Piled high with meat, vegetables, stuffing and laced with gravy, the plates with their appetising smell must have been torment to the two little stomachs, which gurgled in anticipation.

The boys looked at each other nervously. De Bourne studied them, looking from one to another before standing up.

'Well? What do you say?'

Adrian and Helias looked up at Rosalind.

'Thank you, Auntie.'

'And?' De Bourne moved away from the table before the children could see his smile. The two little dark heads had already bobbed down as Adrian and Helias clasped their hands to say Grace.

'They've had a lot of "Aunties" in the past,' de Bourne whispered across the fire to Rosalind. 'It saves confusion if they don't have to learn new names every time.'

Rosalind pursed her lips in disapproval, then realised that he had not intended it as a gibe.

'It was only ever Geoffrey's girls,' he said hurriedly, 'I don't like my boys to see me acting like that.'

She saw his strong features soften as he watched the children.

'Those letters you found,' he said after a while. 'Inside my book. They were to my boys.'

The admission was murmured. He must have felt that writing to children was not the sort of thing he wanted to be remembered for. De Bourne was more than equal to any man, but Rosalind realised that even he had a weak spot. A shiver ran through her. Ascelin was very partial to weak spots. She could only hope that de Bourne managed to keep his a secret.

Rosalind need not have worried. When their prayers were finished, both boys looked up at their father. Instantly his harsh expression returned.

'Go on.'

At the curt command both boys fell on their food. They began munching steadily through everything that had been put before them without a murmur. Only when

Rosalind stepped forward to half fill de Bourne's goblet with warm milk did they hesitate.

Both boys watched as she returned to her sewing. As soon as she looked down at her work there was some urgent whispering.

'Daddy?'

Rosalind smiled to herself, but did not look up. She heard de Bourne cross the room quickly from hearth to table. Then there was more whispering, and the sound of the Black Wolf rapping his finger on the table-top.

'I don't care what Geoffrey lets you have,' he was saying firmly. 'When you're with me, you drink milk.'

That matter settled, de Bourne left them again. He did not go back directly to the fire. Instead Rosalind felt him approach her, positioning himself carefully so that no shadow fell over her embroidery.

Rosalind willed herself to continue working. Ascelin was out in the yard, food had been arranged for the newcomers, out in the kitchen—and the hall door was barred. She had done it herself.

The awful thing was that Rosalind found she was not frightened. De Bourne's presence no longer alarmed her. Instead, feelings stirred that Rosalind found almost as unwelcome in their own way.

The situation had to be defused. Rosalind continued with her embroidery, and did not look up at him as she spoke. 'You and Shamira must be very proud of your boys.'

'Shamira is dead. They're not hers, anyway.'

De Bourne spoke quickly, his voice stabbing the evening quiet as Rosalind's needle stabbed her canvas. A log settled in the fire. One of the dogs raised its head at the disturbance, yawned noisily then flopped down again.

'Then I'm sorry, my lord.'

He remained silent for a long time. Rosalind could feel him watching her intently, as though trying to shred away the last of her resolve. She wished he would make a move while she still had the strength left to repulse him.

Rosalind continued counting threads, pushing her needle down into the cool cream canvas, sewing a green woollen field. As she began yet another stitch de Bourne's warm brown hand slid over hers and clasped it.

'Shamira was taken in adultery, Rosalind——'

'And you think you can use me as revenge?' Rosalind snatched her hand away.

To her amazement there was no resistance. At first she thought de Bourne was unwilling to have an unseemly tussle in front of his sons. Then, when his hand hovered uncertainly before coming to rest lightly on her shoulder, she looked up at him.

Rosalind had intended a glare of defiance. Instead she found herself looking into the same steady, dark-eyed gaze that had hypnotised her so when he had been bringing her back to Ascelin.

There could be no hating that face. No resistance to his wishes, whatever they were. Had he taken her by the hand then and led her away Rosalind would have gone, although hating herself every moment.

'Shamira was stoned to death by her own family...'

A little gasp escaped Rosalind. She found herself touching the hand that lay on her shoulder, feeling the taut muscles beneath winter worn skin.

'That is why you must understand, Rosalind. I couldn't put any man through what I have suffered—not even Ascelin.' His voice dropped bitterly. 'For Shamira to sin was wicked enough, but the pain she left behind was intolerable. It made me bitter and twisted—God knows what it did to the wife of the man I'd called my friend. There's too much pain caused to too many people. That's why I tried to send you away, Rosalind. Seeing you every day—knowing that you're so close—

even at night there's no escape for me. When I see and hear the way that—that—animal treats you ... One day, one day when he starts then I know I'm not going to be responsible for my actions ...'

His fingers tensed. Rosalind had to fight hard to resist the temptation of leaning her head against his arm. De Bourne was the only one on her side likely to put brave words into foolhardy deeds.

'My lord...Mahel...thank you.' Rosalind pressed her palm against his hand. 'I'm sorry to have to disappoint you. I would rather live out a thousand lives with Ascelin than have one breath of suspicion charge you with hurting him.'

The squeeze de Bourne gave her shoulder was more of thanks than passion. Rosalind smiled at him, glad to see that he could still smile back.

'I know exactly the thing to occupy your nights, my lord. You settle the children, while I make them up a bed in your room.'

De Bourne pushed back his thick black hair in a gesture of exasperation.

'No... That won't be necessary,' he said in a low voice. 'I'll farm them out to someone in the village——'

'Whatever for?'

'To see children here... It must be painful for you, sweetbriar——'

Rosalind laughed lightly. 'Not at all. Everyone thinks that, so I'm never offered babies to hold or children to play with. Misplaced kindness is the really painful thing.'

De Bourne's hand fell to his side. His dark eyes searched her face steadily.

'Are you sure you don't mind?'

'Of course not. Their cart must be nearly unpacked by now, if you want to unfasten the door and have their luggage brought in. There are some empty blanket boxes upstairs—they can have one each for their bits and pieces.'

'Hear that, boys?' de Bourne called back to the twins with a laugh. 'You're to sleep in my room. The lady Rosalind says so.'

'Thank you, Auntie,' the children chorused, mouths full. With a smile de Bourne turned back to Rosalind.

'The court of Anjou might be a bit rough and ready, but I have tried with them.'

Rosalind unthreaded her needle and put it away. The intimacy of their moment together was over, and she told herself to be glad. Even so, her small sigh of relief was tinged with regret.

'That's all right, my lord. It's a good job that they're away from it now.'

She looked across at the boys. They were very alike, but not completely identical. Adrian was slightly the larger of the two, his black hair an unruly mop. He had finished his dinner and now helped himself to the food that Helias had left. The smaller boy was lightly built, and altogether neater in appearance than Adrian, who looked dishevelled even though his clothes were plainly new. Helias had laid his head down on one arm and was pushing his toy horse back and forth across the table. His eyelids were drooping by the minute. Rosalind smiled, a little sadly.

'I'll go upstairs and make them up a bed. Then I can take them off your hands and the men will be free to come back in here, my lord. It's not fair to keep them cooped up in the kitchen or out in the wind and rain.'

She rolled up her collection of wools while de Bourne stood by, arms folded. He was busy watching his sons. Although he would not admit to it, Rosalind saw a tinge of pride in his expression.

'I'll bring them up to you.' He put on a stern expression as Adrian scrambled down from his seat, still chewing. 'What happened to manners, Adrian?'

'You're too far away, Daddy,' the little boy said respectfully, his eyes never leaving Rosalind as she put away her work. 'I couldn't ask to get down. Geoffrey spanks us if we shout. It makes his head thump.'

'Especially first thing in the mornings,' de Bourne said to Rosalind over his son's head. They exchanged a smile and she ruffled Adrian's dark hair.

'If you remember that when the lord Ascelin is about, little one, then you should get on very well here.'

Adrian looked up at her strangely, then leaned against his father's thigh. Sensing that it was a delicate moment, Rosalind left father and sons together and slipped away upstairs.

The gap between de Bourne's bed and the wall was just wide enough to take a linen chest. Padded with some blankets, it made a safe bed for the boys until something better could be made.

When de Bourne arrived a few minutes later, he had one child in his arms and the other holding on to his hand.

Helias's small head rolled limply as Rosalind took him and laid him in the new bed. The more independent of the two, Adrian clambered in by himself. Then he held out his arms to Rosalind for a goodnight kiss.

'Night night, Auntie.'

'Goodnight, little one. I'll leave a light in the hall and the curtain pulled back. It won't be long before we all come to bed, too.'

Adrian squirmed in beneath the covers. Pausing only to stop the sleeping Helias sucking his thumb, he lay back and frowned slightly at Rosalind.

'Will you be far away tonight, Auntie?' he asked with touching innocence.

'Only next door. Don't worry—you'll have your father for company.'

'You won't be staying in here with Daddy, then?'

Rosalind realised that the questions were not quite as innocent as they might have been.

'No, little one. You'll have him all to yourselves.'

This seemed to satisfy Adrian, and he let her settle the furs and knitted blankets around him. When she reached de Bourne at the door she found him looking hot and uncomfortable.

'I'm sorry, Rosalind...I don't know why he should have said such a thing. I've never——'

'Daddy?'

Rosalind laughed silently at the fearsome Black Wolf's heavy sigh.

'Yes, son?'

'Tell me about Dog Toby, Dad?'

'Ssh. It's late... Another time...'

Adrian started to whine, disturbing Helias, who wriggled awake noisily.

'Go on, my lord. They're worn out. A few moments and they'll be fast asleep anyway.' Rosalind could not keep the smile from her voice. De Bourne's annoyance was evident. He stalked to the foot of the linen chest in a rattle of chainmail.

'There are some things that a man has to do in private, Lady Rosalind,' he hissed as she made to follow him.

The words had been so sharp that Rosalind bowed to his wishes. She retreated as far as the threshold, and pulled the curtain door closed behind her.

When at last it came, the low rise and fall of his voice was soon interrupted by a sleepy chorus. Rosalind heard de Bourne stride to the door, and she moved back quickly.

'Evidently this torture must be delivered from the bedside. The foot is not good enough. Everything must be exactly as my good friend Count Geoffrey does it.'

He ripped at the buckle of his sword belt and thrust it at Rosalind. Then with much muttering he pulled off his boots before stamping back into the room.

Some time later he emerged, fumbling for his boots in the dim light of the hall. An old hand at anticipating bad temper, Rosalind got in the first remark.

'Thank you for settling them, my lord.'

She held out his sword belt. As he took it their fingers touched, and once more Rosalind felt the tingle of unwelcome excitement.

'The least I can do for them, I suppose,' he muttered angrily. 'After killing their mother.'

Rosalind took a step backward. She knew all about Ascelin's jealous rages, but was surprised that de Bourne should admit the same fault. He sensed her alarm and turned to face her.

'Only indirectly, you understand.' He gave a regretful smile, teeth flashing bright in the candle light. 'She turned up at Le Mans one fine day, on the point of having them. Said I was the father—not that I could remember ever having seen her before, much less anything else...'

Fastening his belt, he started off towards the stairs. When Rosalind did not follow immediately, he turned back.

'Then, in those days there were so many girls, sweetbriar! You must have heard the stories?'

'None told of a man who loved his children,' Rosalind said softly.

This slur on his manhood upset de Bourne. He swung right round and faced her with hands on hips.

'The girl died before they were a week old. What was I supposed to do—leave the miserable little pups to die as well? It opened my eyes to see what suffering a man can inflict on a woman, I can tell you. After Shamira's sin I used women cruelly, as she had used me. But not any more. Not after seeing the struggle that poor unknown girl had to give me my boys.'

'They're a credit to you, my lord.'

De Bourne gave a low laugh and began to go downstairs. 'Then it's as well that Geoffrey sent them here when he did. He'd have turned them into a right pair of ladykillers before much longer.'

Rain lashed at the castle and Rosalind hurried to catch him up. 'You and the count must have made a formidable team, my lord.'

De Bourne reached the foot of the stairs and strolled over to raise the locking bar on the door.

'Geoffrey can charm the birds from their nests. He's got both the looks and the silver tongue. My appeal only ever lay in my novelty value.'

Conscious that Ascelin might return at any moment, Rosalind seated herself primly by the fire again. Once more taking up her needle and threads, she cut another length of green wool.

'I'm sure it wasn't only that, my lord.'

De Bourne nudged a hound aside with his foot and moved to throw more wood on to the fire. In the gloom a soggy birch log was thrown on by mistake. The fire hissed and billowed a flounce of acrid pinkish smoke into the room.

'Don't you be too sure. I can't put together pretty phrases. My looks could only ever be described as unusual, at best. Now I'm nearly forty, they're unravelling fast.'

Rosalind looked up and found him a little embarrassed at the admission.

'I would have put you as being much younger than that, my lord.'

He nudged a good ash log further into the fire where it crumbled into embers.

'I'm nearly thirty-six.'

Smiling, Rosalind threaded her needle and took a stitch. 'Then by your reckoning, my lord, I'm nearly thirty. Quite an old lady!'

'Never in this world!'

He frowned at her, unsure whether or not to laugh.

'I was twenty-seven last month, my lord.'

There was a pause before he spoke again, and Rosalind felt him looking at her intently. 'That's young enough to start again. If Ascelin would give you a divorce——'

'No!' Rosalind jumped as the needle stabbed her finger. 'Not that—I couldn't ever...what on earth would my parents say?'

'What do they say now, when you're not allowed to visit, and when they do see you you're black and blue——?'

'This is madness, my lord! I won't stay here and listen to you saying such wicked things!'

Jumping up from her seat, Rosalind pushed between de Bourne and the embroidery frame, which tipped towards the fire. His hands full trying to save it, de Bourne could only call after her.

'Rosalind!'

The deep resonance of his voice rolled around the room. She could do nothing but stop, almost within reach of the door and safety outside.

In a dozen ringing strides he had reached her side and put a hand to the door. Even if she had had the will to defy him, her way was barred.

CHAPTER SIX

'I'M NOT going to force you, Rosalind. I only want to help you—to look after you...'

Rosalind shook her head, trying to hold back the tears. 'It's no good—there's no future in it, my lord. Ascelin wasn't of my choosing, it's true, but think of the consequences! You're already in trouble about it. The Church would mark us for ever, and my family would disown me—my lord, I'd have nothing——'

'You'd have me,' de Bourne said quietly. 'Your own home here, all the lands that Ascelin helped himself to, and a place of safety where blows and curses are a thing of the past. Well, for you, anyway. I can't guarantee that the men won't feel the sharp end of my temper now and again!'

He seemed incapable of being serious for any length of time. Rosalind tried to lose her temper, but had already realised that humour was his escape from pain.

'No, my lord.' She lifted her head to see him looking down at her with the gentlest of smiles. 'You are good, and kind, and if I were free there would be nothing that could bring me more happiness than—than——'

'Say it, Rosalind. Say that you would consider becoming my wife if anything ever happened to Ascelin——'

'No!' She shook her head violently. 'I can't! Don't make me say such a thing! I heard a story once...about someone who was tricked into saying just such wickedness. There was murder done to suit the circumstances——'

'Oh, sweetbriar, sweetbriar, that hurts.' De Bourne sighed, moved as though to take her in his arms then stopped. Instead he contented himself by stroking her hair. 'I'm not like that, Rosalind. I wouldn't want to win you through trickery. Much as I loathe Ascelin, I won't harm so much as a hair on his head if that's your command.'

'It is.' Rosalind passed nervous fingers over her eyes, praying that Ascelin would see no tears when he came.

De Bourne stepped back and gave a soft chuckle.

'I wish I hadn't been so forward now. What must you think, sweetbriar? The last ramblings of an ageing rascal?'

Rosalind understood the awkward position that he found himself in now. 'No, my lord. Never. It was a beautiful, flattering gesture. One that I am quite unable to accept, but no less appreciated for that. The only gesture I can possibly accept from such a gallant gentleman is this.'

She held out her hand to him. The position had been made clear, and de Bourne acknowledged it with good grace. He took her hand to his lips and kissed it. A cool, formal kiss, it contrasted with the fire that burned in his eyes.

Inclining her head to him gracefully, Rosalind took her cape from its hook by the door and swirled it around her shoulders. Without a word de Bourne opened the door for her, and Rosalind went out into the night with as much dignity as she could still command.

She had to find Ascelin. She had to find her husband, and cling on to the marriage that was at once her despair and her salvation.

'My lord?'

Rosalind found Ascelin in the store-room. He was still stacking Angevin money in the dusty dark. He did not answer, and Rosalind knew that she had to tread even more carefully than usual.

'Ascelin?'

'What?' He whirled around to glare at her.

For once Rosalind did not jump. She was learning fast that Ascelin could only triumph where he saw fear.

'I came to help, my lord. The two of us will finish the task much quicker.'

Ascelin threw down the small sack of silver he held and dusted off his hands. 'I thought you and the *poulain* would have other things in hand.'

'Don't be silly, Ascelin.' Rosalind tried to take his arm, but he jerked away.

'I don't know why you bother pretending. You might as well come straight out with it. Everyone knows about you and the filthy *poulain*...'

'There's nothing to know, Ascelin.' Folding her arms as her mother did when convincing her father of something, Rosalind stood her ground.

'I've seen the way he looks at you!'

'He's Nerra de Bourne, Ascelin. The Black Wolf. I'm sure he looks at every woman. You only notice the times he happens to glance in my direction, because you are my husband.'

Ascelin was openly puzzled by this time. He had turned his back on Rosalind—she had persisted. He had shouted, and she had not flinched. All his arguments were met with plain speech, not the usual frightened silence. Tired, hungry and sick of being treated as de Bourne's skivvy, Ascelin could think of no more insults.

'You did write him that letter,' he grizzled. 'Are you *sure* there's nothing between you?'

'I'm your wife, Ascelin,' Rosalind said carefully. No one could argue with that truth. 'I explained that the letter was to save you having to fight. I know how much you hate it. Come on—we'll hurry up and finish here. There's still some supper left for you in the kitchen.'

'I'm tired.' Ascelin's tone had changed to that of a petulant child. 'You finish stacking the sacks——'

'There are only twelve left. I'll do six for you—that's half.'

Rosalind stacked her share while Ascelin stood and watched. He stuck out his lower lip and tried to will her into finishing his work, but her resolve never faltered. She had proved to herself now that facing up to Ascelin saved her from blows better than cowering ever had.

When her six sacks had been packed away, Rosalind pulled up her hood and went to wait by the store-room door.

'They'll think you aren't coming for your supper, Ascelin,' she said gently. 'Hurry up.'

For the first time in his life Ascelin did as a woman had asked him.

He was amazed—Rosalind was staggered.

Each was careful to hide such terrible emotions from the other.

They splashed across the muddy courtyard to the kitchen. Sulking forgotten in the face of food, Ascelin gorged himself while Rosalind warmed them both some spiced wine.

'What's happened to the wolf cubs?' he said through a mouthful of food.

'They're sleeping in their father's room.'

'Let's hope he remembers to change their napkins!'

Ascelin gave her a knowing laugh. Rosalind realised that her change of attitude had made him wary. Where trying to frighten had failed he was now attempting to win her over against a common enemy.

'Don't worry, cherub. We've got the old dog now. While he's dandling them on his knee, playing "this little piggy" and generally loving his little pups to pieces, King Stephen will be able to stroll in here and take him with no trouble at all.'

'De Bourne hates them.' Rosalind was one step ahead, lying quickly to save the children. 'I had to get their food and make up a bed for them. You'll never see him making a fuss of them, Ascelin,' she finished truthfully. De Bourne would know better than to display any weakness towards them in front of his men.

'We'll see.' Ascelin worked over his supper noisily. 'We'll see about that, cherub.'

It was too much to ask that Ascelin should have turned over a completely new leaf. He did not return to the castle with Rosalind, but stayed on in the kitchen. Whether he continued drinking she did not find out. Ascelin made other arrangements that night, and slept elsewhere.

Without his morning mutterings Rosalind woke late next day. It was still dark outside, but the fattening cockerels were already yelling for their breakfast.

She washed quickly in cold water and pulled on her outdoor clothes. The villagers would be busy, and couldn't be expected to do her work.

The castle yard was full of noise and movement. While there was the danger of attack, the village animals would spend each night within the castle yard. Every morning they would be driven out to graze the rides and woodland close at hand. De Bourne had lookouts posted well away from the castle, so that there would be plenty of time to bring the animals back if an attack looked likely.

Rosalind was glad that most of the animals had been slaughtered with the approach of winter. There were fewer hoofs to churn up the courtyard mud. Less feed was wanted, too, and the villagers would have more grain and roots for themselves.

De Bourne stood on the threshold of the forge, talking with the smith while Marty nervously stoked the fire. The mercenary nodded a greeting to Rosalind as she fetched grain from the feed bins.

'Those birds will have to go, sweetbriar, if there's a siege.'

Rosalind pursed her lips and dipped out a shovelful of rolled barley into the feed pan.

'Whatever else suffers, the horses can't go short of food.' He was watching her scoop out shovels of corn and bran waste. The smith had turned accusing eyes on her as well by this time. As she replaced the lid of the last feed bin de Bourne spoke again. 'I'll be over to talk to you about it in a minute.'

Rosalind said nothing, hoping that poultry was all he wanted to talk about.

She went on to the kitchen. The last cow left in milk was giving less than half a bucket a day now. Rosalind poured just enough into her pan to moisten the feed. There were the children to think about, after all.

Taking the mash out into the yard, Rosalind crossed to the poultry pens. In the first, a drake and two ducks lived together with a gander and two geese left over from Michaelmas. These honked at her gratefully from the green slime of their pen. When their pan had been filled, Rosalind went on to the cockerels. They bounced up and down, chuckling with excitement as she filled a box with food and pushed it into their pen. That was the only thing that kept them quiet.

The laying hens were the last to be fed. Most of them were moulting, and feathers blew about like autumn leaves as she opened the pen gate a crack and pushed in the half-empty feed pan.

A sharp tug at her skirt made Rosalind jump. Expecting de Bourne to have crept up on her, she was on the defensive at once. It was not necessary.

'Auntie?'

It was Adrian. He was neatly dressed for the moment, with a warm winter cape and wooden overshoes saving him from the mud.

'Daddy sent me over.'

Rosalind detected a sullen look in Adrian's eyes as he looked up at her. This vanished quickly enough after a glance back at his father.

'Are there any eggs today, Auntie?'

'You can look.' She smiled and pointed towards the nest box. 'Although it's a bit late in the season, and a bit early in the day.'

Obediently, Adrian went to see. He lifted the nest box lid and felt about. There was only the first effort of a pullet, small and thin shelled.

'Can I have it, please?'

Rosalind crouched beside him and straightened his hood.

'What for, little one?'

'Our breakfast, Auntie,' he said, as though surprised that she had not realised.

'Then of course you can.' Rosalind took him by the hand and they strolled towards the kitchen. She noticed that Adrian forged ahead as they drew level with his father, hurrying her past. De Bourne was deep in discussion with the smith and took no interest in their passing.

'Is Helias still asleep?' Rosalind said, opening the door for Adrian to enter the kitchen.

He was not. Helias stood on a bench, carving chunks off a rock-hard side of bacon hanging from the kitchen ceiling. Dripping sagged in a frying-pan on the hearth while bread and butter stood waiting on the table.

'We can manage, Auntie,' Adrian said stiffly, handing her his egg while he went to help his brother.

Rosalind laughed, but was impressed by the way they were working together. 'Do you do everything for yourselves?'

Adrian nodded, but Helias gave her a winning smile.

'Daddy helped us get ready this morning——' He was interrupted by a sharp poke from his brother.

'Ssh! You *know* you're not supposed to say things like that!' Adrian muttered as Helias jumped down with a handful of bacon.

'Why not? It's true,' the smaller boy hissed. 'Anyway, it was only because you didn't wash behind your ears——'

'I'll pour you out some milk,' Rosalind said, sensing the beginning of an argument.

'Geoffrey always gives us wine and water.' Lifting the frying pan on to the heat, Adrian let Helias throw in the bacon scraps. 'He says it'll make us grow up big and strong, like him.'

They were testing her. Rosalind went to the bucket and ladled out two mugs of milk.

'If Geoffrey had drunk more milk when he was a little boy he would have grown up *twice* as big and *twice* as strong,' she said slyly, putting the mugs of milk on the table.

The boys looked at each other in silent disbelief. Then they left their cooking and without a word went to drink the milk she had put out for them.

Before they had finished, their father entered with the priest. With a nod towards his sons, de Bourne went and settled the frying-pan more securely on the fire. When he strolled towards Rosalind he was smiling, but it was not the ususal predatory look.

'Father Anthony has come to referee,' he said lightly. 'As Ascelin hasn't put in an appearance yet this morning, I thought he might prefer that you and I spoke before an audience.'

'Very wise, my lord.' Rosalind curtsyed without looking up at either man. 'You wanted to speak to me about the poultry, my lord?'

'No—but with the priest here, that will have to do.'

Peeling off his gloves, de Bourne tucked them into his belt and stood watching the twins. They had broken the egg into the frying-pan and while Adrian flicked hot fat over it with a spoon Helias kept well back from any splashes.

'They're good boys, my lord. They'll come to no harm here with me.'

De Bourne shrugged at her words, and turned the dark eloquence of his eyes upon her.

'Are you all right, Rosalind?' he said quietly. Father Anthony looked at the floor.

'Yes, my lord. Ascelin spent the night away from home.'

'I know,' his voice cut in sharply, then seeing the priest's disapproving look he changed the subject.

'I'm sorry to make it so plain, but if it comes to the pinch your little flocks will have to go, sweetbriar. The food they eat would keep a couple of horses on iron rations.' He thought she would be upset at this, so he added a hopeful touch. 'I'll let you get more from Malmesbury market in the spring...'

'My lord!' Rosalind was scandalised. 'I'm surprised that even you are as extravagant as that! Leave me the ducks, the geese and two trio of fowls. They can all live on kitchen scraps and I'll breed them up again from there.' She frowned, wondering how best to arrange things. 'I was saving the cockerels for Christmas, but if the hens have to go too I might as well kill them all at the same time. The meat can be smoked.'

'I thought they were your pets?' De Bourne looked at her in wide-eyed amazement.

'Only until there's meat wanted on the table. Or an emergency, like this.'

'You're more of a farmer than I shall ever be.' Smiling at her, de Bourne could not disguise the true feeling that was in his eyes.

Rosalind guessed his thoughts. She knew that they betrayed the agreement with Ascelin even if the priest's presence prevented him from doing so in the flesh.

'You'll soon learn, my lord. As I have learned to be a good and loyal wife.'

'Well said——' Father Anthony began, but he was interrupted by the rattling chorus of many bells.

Adrian had leapt to his feet, eyes shining. 'Is it the Manceaux, Daddy?'

There was a great commotion out in the yard. Rosalind knew that the loyalist army must have been spotted. De Bourne was already halfway to the door as he called back to his son.

'Not in England, child. We've got different rascals that come visiting here.'

He was gone. In common with every soldier, there was a chance that he might not come back. Rosalind felt a strange pang, and looked towards the priest for comfort.

It came from quite a different direction. A small cold hand slipped into hers.

'I don't like it, Auntie,' Helias muttered when she bent down.

His brother was busy slicing the fried egg in half, quite unconcerned. He piled the bits on to a trencher full of bacon, sat back with pride and licked his greasy fingers. Rosalind wondered at how different they were from each other.

'Everything will be all right if you stay with me,' she whispered to Helias firmly.

There was nothing like someone else's fear for making her feel braver than she was.

Bringing the thick hunk of bread to the table, Adrian put it down and climbed on to the bench. Rosalind seated his brother beside him and they both said Grace.

They ate with less speed than the night before, but equal good manners.

Father Anthony was impressed. 'A shame that such good boys will end up going the same way as their father.'

Finishing a mouthful of food then wiping his mouth, Adrian grinned at the priest.

'Helias wants to be a monk, don't you?'

When prodded, the smaller boy looked from Rosalind to Father Anthony uncertainly. The priest chuckled.

'I don't expect your daddy is very pleased with that, is he? Doesn't he tease you about wanting to do such a silly thing, Helias?'

'It's not a silly thing,' Adrian growled, giving Father Anthony a hard stare. 'My daddy's saving up to buy Helias a place. You'd better not let him hear you say nasty things like that to my brother.'

The piercing glare that the little boy gave Father Anthony had the priest turning away to hide his laughter.

'Every inch his father's son.' He smiled to Rosalind as she opened the kitchen door for him. 'I'll leave them to you, child. If there's to be fighting it won't be long until I'm needed elsewhere—although to look at Crispin I think he needs help right now!'

The young musician was galloping across the yard. When he saw Rosalind in the kitchen doorway he changed course and ran towards her.

'They're only three miles away! They're coming! We're all going to be killed!'

Rosalind met him before he could say such things in front of the children.

'Oh, hush! It wasn't a week ago that you were saying the same thing about my lord de Bourne. You survived his arrival, didn't you?'

'I don't like it, my lady...' His large eyes were wide with terror.

'And neither do the children. If you're to stay with me you'll have to stop being silly, and start being brave for their sakes.'

Crispin gulped a few times, looked at the press of animals and villagers milling into the castle yard and then into the peace of the kitchen.

'I'll try, lady. Can I come in?'

While Crispin cooked bacon and fried bread for himself and Rosalind, she watched over the children. Adrian was excited at the thought of seeing his father working, but Helias was worried. Rosalind had to sit down and coax the remainder of his breakfast into him.

When they had all eaten, Rosalind took the children up to the castle hall while Crispin tidied the kitchen. Helias was happy enough to play with the dogs or sort through Rosalind's sewing box, but Adrian was restless. He roamed about, often looking towards the door. The ring of familiar footsteps outside the door sent him skipping there with a shriek of delight.

The door opened, and Adrian immediately fell silent. De Bourne was not alone. Ascelin slouched into the room after him, small eyes darting about to take in the scene.

'Ever seen the King, sweetbriar?' Ignoring his sons, the Black Wolf walked slowly to the fireside and put his hands out towards the blaze. 'Not a very inspiring sight, but he's out there now if you want to take a look.'

'Can we, Daddy?'

Adrian was halfway to the stairs, but Helias wasn't so sure.

'Please—can I stay here?' he murmured to Rosalind uncertainly, but his eyes were fixed on Ascelin.

'Looks like you've bred a bad 'un there, *poulain*. Takes after your father, does he? Afraid of his own?'

Ascelin smirked, and, picking up a small log from the wood pile, hurled it on to the fire. It was carefully aimed and showered Helias with ash. The little boy jumped like a frog but made no sound.

'Ascelin!' Jerking Helias to his feet, Rosalind brushed him off quickly. 'He could have been burned!'

'Then don't keep him huddled up at the fireside,' de Bourne said evenly. 'Come on—we'll all go up on to the roof and see the fun.'

He strode away and up the stairs, while Adrian dashed on ahead of him. Ascelin and Rosalind were left to follow. Helias hung back, still eyeing Ascelin with suspicion, so Rosalind picked the little boy up.

'I'm frightened, Auntie...' a tiny voice whispered in her ear as she carried him up the stairs.

'You hang on tight to me, little one. I'll look after you.'

They had reached the upper floor. Rosalind crossed to the ladder leading to the roof, and as she did so the little voice trembled again.

'But who's going to look after you, Auntie?'

'Me, of course, sooty!'

Helias twitched as Ascelin pinched his cheek. When she set the child down at the foot of the ladder Rosalind noticed that a red mark had been left behind on his face. Helias made no fuss. He clambered up the ladder, and, crouching below the parapet, called to his brother.

Adrian wasn't listening. He was with one of the soldiers, who was letting him squint down the line of a crossbow.

'He's busy.' Rosalind knelt down in front of Helias and touched his cheek. 'We won't stay up here long. You feel cold.' She held his hands up to her face for warmth.

Leering, Ascelin bent over Rosalind's shoulder. 'I expect you feel the cold, pup, don't you? Being a sooty?'

Rosalind felt Helias tremble beneath her fingers, but he was doing his best to be brave.

Ascelin's angelic curls ruffled in the breeze. He had found a new sport in teasing Helias, and was going to enjoy it to the full.

'What's it like being an infidel, sooty?' He kept his voice low so that it would not carry to de Bourne, on the other side of the roof. 'It must be funny for you to come here and live in a proper house, and wear proper clothes. No grapes for you here, either—or oranges. Poor soots! What can you find to eat? You'll starve, if you don't freeze to death first——'

'Leave him alone, Ascelin. He's only a child.'

'And what would you know about children?' He sneered at her, the favourite accusation never far from the surface.

Turning back to Helias, Ascelin began to sing very softly,

> Sooty by name,
> Soot for a brain...

Here he flicked at the child's shining black hair.

'Watch out, soots! It's leaking!'

Helias could stand no more. With a wail he flung himself at Rosalind. As she comforted him, a dreadful noise cut Ascelin off in mid-chortle.

'That's *my* boy,' Rosalind heard de Bourne say through clenched teeth. He had Ascelin pinned up in a sheltered corner, much to Adrian's delight.

'Nobody sneers at my boys and gets away with it.' The Black Wolf flashed a look at Rosalind. 'Take them downstairs, madam. Ascelin's going to find out exactly what his King Stephen thinks of a man who nearly lost him a lot of money.'

Looking back to Ascelin, he gave a threatening growl. 'And you know how you hated the lady seeing you shamed last time, don't you?'

He grasped Ascelin and thrust him towards the parapet to be shown off. De Bourne used none of the gentleness he had been capable of when Rosalind had been his captive. Frightened for Ascelin, she opened her mouth to protest but the Black Wolf anticipated her.

'It's all right,' he mouthed silently.

Ascelin was too busy cowering to notice. The King's men had set down outside the locked castle gates. A chorus of clapping and whistles had broken out from them as de Bourne pushed Ascelin out into view.

Rosalind carried Helias away. She had no wish to see any exchange between the King and his fallen favourite.

Her instinct was to put Helias to bed and shower him with affection. Sensing that de Bourne would prefer rougher treatment for his son, she dried the child's tears and took him out to see the poultry.

They were looking for more eggs when Adrian ran to find them. Charging through the crowds of soldiers and farm animals littering the yard, he ignored the noise of dogs and other children to catch hold of his small brother.

'Daddy wants you. Upstairs. Right now!'

Helias had been standing at Rosalind's side, and now leaned in towards her protection.

'Is he going to spank me?' he muttered faintly.

Adrian shrugged, picking at weather-splintered wood on the poultry shed.

'Don't know. You're to go up too, Auntie. Ascelin's on the floor.'

'What?' Rosalind had already started across the yard, and the boys had to run to keep up with her.

'He's being a baby!' Adrian laughed as all three ran up the steps and into the hall.

When they reached the upper floor Helias was quick to catch hold of Rosalind's hand again. He pressed himself close to her side as she took in the scene.

The roof-top ordeal over, de Bourne and Ascelin had returned to the upper hallway. Their attitudes could not have been more different. While Ascelin snivelled in a heap on the floor, de Bourne leaned against the doorway of his room, whistling softly.

When he saw Helias he pulled back the curtain of his room and beckoned for the little boy to enter.

'I—I'm sorry, Daddy...' Helias started to whimper, then looked up at Rosalind for support.

Before she could crouch down and reassure him, de Bourne stamped his foot impatiently. Helias scampered into the room without a backward glance.

'You would be better employed in looking to your lord, Lady Rosalind,' de Bourne said darkly. 'He seems to have been a little overcome by circumstances...'

'Oh, Rosalind—wh-what am I going to do?' Raising a tear-blotched face to her, Ascelin wailed piteously.

'He's upset because Stephen evidently hasn't got enough enemies, sweetbriar. We've just been treated to the sight of the false monarch upsetting his ex-best friend.'

De Bourne strolled into the chamber after his little son, the curtain door dropping shut behind them. As Rosalind reached Ascelin's side, the curtain was raised again and the mercenary reappeared. 'You didn't ask me not to hurt the cub, sweetbriar?'

Rosalind crouched beside Ascelin, who had turned to nothing more than wet string.

'Discipline within your family is your own affair, my lord,' she said without looking up at de Bourne.

'Quite so. Then if you good people would be kind enough to excuse me, I must go and ill-treat the babe in the best traditions of tyrants everywhere.'

De Bourne vanished behind his curtain door. He might have given Rosalind a sly wink, but Ascelin had wailed again and grabbed all her attention.

'What am I going to do? I'm disgraced for ever... The King's gone...Malmesbury's still held by the rebels, Cerney's in doubt—God knows what's happening at Trowbridge—Rosalind, we're surrounded...'

He clutched at her, clinging on for support. That the rebels were tightening their hold on the countryside held barely any fear for Rosalind. She had more important things to think about—had she allowed herself to think about them.

'What did the King say to you?'

'Oh, Rosalind—it was h-horrible...'

She patted Ascelin, rather more firmly that she would once have dared. 'What did he say?'

'They were all laughing at me—and the King said...he said...' Ascelin gulped, and his face crumpled into wet pink wrinkles. 'He's got more important things to do than sit about, because I couldn't manage to obey an order. I'll have to wait for the lord M-Miles...'

Remembering the King's words was too much of a crushing shame for Ascelin, who dissolved into tears of hopelessness. Rosalind thought of the way he had taunted Helias. There could only be a small speck of pity left within her for her husband now.

She put one arm about Ascelin's shoulders and heaved him upright. Leading her failing husband to their room, she tried to jolly him along.

'Miles of Gloucester is constable of the King's household, isn't he? Well, then—with a man like that on your side, you don't need the King here in person, do you?'

'The King—the King said that I didn't need to bother following the court any more if I was going to risk his money. Oh, Rosalind, they all laughed at me...'

'Then you'll have to work twice as hard to impress them the next time, won't you?' Rosalind bundled him into their room where he collapsed on to the bed. 'You might not have the money or skill to win the castle back on your own, my lord, but the lord Miles will certainly expect to find you sensible when he gets here, if nothing else. He can't hand the castle back to you if you're acting like this. Wash your face, then get some rest. When can we expect my lord Miles?'

'The King said that he had sent a messenger at first light. The lord constable and two hundred of his best men should be here within the next few days.' Ascelin crawled beneath the bedclothes and curled into a tight ball, like the child he still was. 'Oh, Rosalind—what are we going to do?'

'The only thing we can do,' Rosalind said firmly. 'Wait.'

And worry, she added privately. Miles of Gloucester had a reputation that was as fearsome as that of de Bourne. Any confrontation between them would be to the death.

Rosalind had lost any remaining loyalty to King Stephen that she might have had, after his treatment of Ascelin. Her loyalty to Ascelin was secured only by the bond of their marriage.

The feelings she had for Mahel de Bourne ran deeper than she had imagined. Only now were they beginning to surface.

Rosalind stayed with Ascelin until he fell into fitful sleep. All the while she strained her ears to hear what awful punishment Helias was receiving. Only a low murmur of sounds reached her through the thin partition wall, and they did not include the cries of an injured child.

Finally, she could stand it no longer. Creeping away from Ascelin's side, she went out into the upper hall. The whispered words were no clearer, so she tapped on the door frame of de Bourne's room.

The stream of words hesitated, then carried on afresh. Rosalind drew back the curtain and looked into the room. Knelt on his immaculately made bed, de Bourne leaned on the linen chest where Helias lay. Neither noticed her. Helias had one thumb in his mouth, the other hand toying with the ties at the neck of his father's shirt. The Black Wolf was retelling the tale of bad Dog Toby.

Silently, Rosalind closed the door and edged towards the top of the stairs. It was a while longer before de Bourne was to join her. Arranging the curtain door carefully, he walked towards her with a soft tread.

Rosalind gave a respectful curtsy, determined not to give him any encouragement. Despite what she might feel.

'I hope you didn't beat the child too severely, my lord.'

'Savagely. Flayed half the skin off him.' He raised her up with a twinkle in his eye. 'Learning to be a father has been difficult. Becoming a mother as well—that's a skill that's nearly beyond me.'

Rosalind was stricken by a sudden twinge of suspicion. Perhaps de Bourne's pretty words had been only an attempt to find a mother for his children. That made his flirtation—Rosalind couldn't bear to think of it as anything more—with her even more shameful. She pursed her lips, then said in a small, neat voice, 'You must have employed someone for that when they were tiny, my lord. No small creature lasts for long without a mother's care.'

He had not released her hand, and held it as he escorted her downstairs. When they reached the fireside he let it go with a rueful smile.

'I suppose you want me to tell you about all the other girls that I've...entertained?'

Rosalind's hands flew to her face in horror.

'Certainly not, my lord!'

'Wouldn't it be better to have everything out in the open? With no secrets between us?' He looked puzzled at her increasing agitation.

Rosalind backed away, but he did not pursue her.

'I don't want to know about your wicked ways, my lord! Whatever makes you think I would?'

De Bourne sighed and looked up at the smoke-blackened ceiling. 'I need your respect, Rosalind. I want us to be...close. Perhaps if you understood what I'm really like—behind the picture that the men see—you might realise...'

Rosalind didn't want to allow herself that luxury. She didn't want to watch de Bourne approach her, either, but something stopped her running off for the priest.

'I'm very fond of you, Rosalind.' He had clasped his hands, and now looked down at them with a frown. 'I...love you. There! I've never said those words in earnest to any woman before.'

Suddenly, he looked proud of the fact but at the same time slightly surprised. With the King's constable on his way, bent on the Black Wolf's destruction, it hardly seemed the time for white lies. Even so, Rosalind was wary.

'What about Shamira?' She put her head on one side, expecting him to be evasive and sly. Instead he shrugged and shook his head.

'Her family helped Father bring me up after my mother was killed. Things are different in the Levant. Marriages are often arranged by friendly families rather than for love or social advancement. It was just assumed that we would marry, and, in the fullness of time, we did. I thought we were happy. Though her relatives did all pester Shamira when time passed without any signs of an addition to the family. Until I met you, I thought that was why she looked elsewhere... Now, I'm beginning to wonder...'

His eyes had grown as wary as Rosalind's, and he took a step backward. Rosalind guessed that the difficulty of trying to put words to long-hidden feelings had come as a shock to him.

'We didn't love each other.' Realisation lowered his voice to a whisper. Hugging himself as though cold, he stared into the fire. 'After she was killed, I wanted revenge for the way that she had made me feel.'

One hand dropped to the hilt of his sword and clenched it, the knuckles showing pale in the firelight.

'She deceived me. I wasn't good enough for her, being only a *poulain*...'

'Oh, come...I'm sure that's not true...'

At Rosalind's words de Bourne gave her such an agonised look that it was all she could do to stop from taking him into her arms.

'She made me feel—dirty...' He shook his head, trying to throw off past voices that had come back to haunt him. His voice was low and harsh with loathing. 'I know what the village gossips had been saying. They said that it was all my fault we didn't have a child, because I was a cross breed. A mule——'

At that Rosalind did go to him, putting her hand on his arm. 'Don't say such things! You'll regret it when the moment has passed——'

'I suffered all the taunts in silence. When Shamira was killed I went all out to prove them wrong. I admit it. I was as wicked and immoral as it's possible to be. For years I used women, then cast them aside as Shamira had done me.'

His fingers were digging into the metalwork of his sword hilt. With blazing eyes he stared into the depths of the fire, remembering the shame. Rosalind stood by quietly, her hand still resting upon his forearm. When the inner rage had eased he turned back to her slowly.

'All that changed when the boys came along. I've changed—even more now that I've met you.'

He could not veil the soft light in his eyes now, and Rosalind took her hand from his arm.

'It doesn't matter.' He smiled, speaking softly. 'I know that you are as good a wife as Shamira was faithless. If only Ascelin knew how to appreciate you, I could die happy.'

Rosalind suspected another quick change of his mood, and laughed accordingly. 'Oh, my lord—don't speak of dying! There seems to be almost too much life in the Black Wolf to ever think of that!'

To her surprise, de Bourne did not laugh. Instead he looked at the ashy floor and put a finger to his lips thoughtfully.

'The lord Miles will be here within a day or so. If he is even half the soldier the stories claim, then I am a dead man.'

Easy reassurances died away from Rosalind's lips. She had heard the tales, too. That Miles of Gloucester was the only man capable of putting a stop to Nerra de Bourne. The Black Wolf knew the truth of the matter better than anyone, and he expected the worst.

'Look after the boys for me?' he said casually, a wry smile twisting his mouth. 'I'll get one of my men to hide a bit of the cash away from Ascelin's greedy eyes. For anything extra they might need—Geoffrey needs a lot of badgering, but he's a good lad at heart and generous enough when he's reminded.'

'Don't talk like this, my lord...' Rosalind followed him as he suddenly turned and headed for the door.

'Why not? It's foolish to hide from the truth. Miles is coming here, he's as good as—if not better than—me, I'm likely to be killed within the next few days, you don't love me——'

'That's not true!'

He had slipped it in, sparking an unthinking response from Rosalind. At once she stopped and blushed brightly.

'I—I mean...you might not be killed, my lord. It wouldn't be true to say that you will be...'

She was floundering. He saw, and at once his eyes were thoughtful again.

'You've told me all I have a right to know, sweetbriar. I shouldn't expect anything more.' Laughter flickered in the dark eyes and he smiled down at her kindly. 'King Stephen was kind enough to leave some of his men laying siege to us. He says that the odds will be five to one against me when Miles and all his henchmen arrive. If

that's the case, I'd better go out now and shorten them
a bit before the constable gets here.'

There was an uncomfortable pause. Neither could say
goodbye, but with long practice de Bourne turned the
moment to his advantage.

'Your veil, my lady sweetbriar?'

Rosalind looked at him uncertainly.

'Then if you won't give it willingly, it seems that I
must tear it from you like the evil rogue I am.' He moved
in close and scanned her hair expertly, looking for pins.

'Ascelin will know—he'll kill you. You mustn't, my
lord...' Rosalind spoke quickly, afraid of the feelings
she now craved. With the tips of his fingers de Bourne
removed her veil and laid it, light as autumn air, over
his hand.

'My, what a struggle you put up to stop me taking
your favour, my lady.' Folding the veil into a tiny square
he slipped it inside his shirt. 'Over my heart, so that the
rascals can't harm me.'

Rosalind looked up to find him unruffled and smiling.
Almost certain death in the form of Miles and his men
must be closing in on him every minute, yet de Bourne
looked as wickedly merry as ever.

'There's no mark on it, sweetbriar. Go and find
yourself another. Ascelin's not to know to whom this
one belongs. I'm such a knave that dozens of women
would claim such a veil.' With a wink he went to the
door, but paused once more before leaving.

'You will look after the boys for me, won't you,
sweetbriar? Send them back to Geoffrey before Ascelin
gets his hands on them?'

Rosalind nodded. It was the least and the only thing
that she could promise him.

CHAPTER SEVEN

DE BOURNE'S sortie from his castle was a close-run thing. His men gave a good account of themselves, but they drew back to the castle yard again with few casualties inflicted on the King's men.

Rallying at the thought of a victory for Stephen, Ascelin went to meet de Bourne as he returned to the yard. He had insisted that his wife accompany him. Rosalind could do nothing but obey, although everything warned her that it was asking for trouble.

De Bourne stood in the centre of the yard, watching his horse as it was led back to its stable. The Black Wolf had lost a glove, and held barked knuckles up to his mouth.

'How many men did you lose, *poulain*?' Ascelin sidled up, taking care to keep a cruel grip on Rosalind's arm.

'None.' De Bourne inspected the blood seeping across the creases in his olive-tan skin. 'If I lose a man, then I've failed. The wit of war is to know when to make a strategic withdrawal.'

'When to run away, you mean.' Sneering, Ascelin looked his great rival up and down, wrinkling his nose at the sight of mud splashes and blood smears. 'That won't do you any good when Miles gets here. You're a dead man, *poulain*! Better make your confession now. There won't be time once the King's constable arrives!'

'The only thing I'd like to have on my conscience is being Godless enough to murder you, Ascelin,' de Bourne said mildly. His attention was elsewhere, caught by a flurry of activity among soldiers beside the poultry pens.

'They're after your cock-birds, sweetbriar. I'll choke them off; you come and collect up your pets.'

He stalked off without waiting for an answer. Ascelin watched him go with a satisfied smile. 'He knows he's beaten. Ha! It's only a matter of time now, cherub. Miles will be here and we'll be rescued. The sand of time is trickling away for the high and mighty *poulain*.'

De Bourne summoned Rosalind with a rough shout. Ascelin looked at her through narrowed eyes before thrusting her away.

'I'm watching you, cherub. I'll see anything that might pass between you and that scoundrel. Miles will be very interested to hear about any treachery...'

There was no reasoning with Ascelin when he was in a mood like this. Rosalind knew better than to try. Keeping her head down like a dutiful slave, she gathered up her skirts and picked her way across the yard.

De Bourne had frightened off his men and now leaned against the woodwork of the cockerel house.

'The men know that I won't be testing the opposition again before the dreaded Miles arrives. They were looking for a bit of sport. I stopped them before they let any of the birds go, so there's no harm done.'

Rosalind muttered her thanks, then turned to go. Ascelin's eyes were burning into her and she had to get back. De Bourne had not finished, and spoke out as she retreated.

'I'd like you to have a look at Helias, sweetbriar. I think he may be sickening for something.'

The voice was full of concern, and she looked back quickly.

'You've got more than enough to think of with the lord Miles on his way, my lord. Leave the children to me. I'll look after them for you. You needn't give their welfare another thought.'

Rosalind smiled, hoping to ease him, but the look she received was dark and troubled.

*   *   *

The day dragged on. De Bourne was careful to find plenty of work for Ascelin's idle hands. He took care, too, to remain within sight of Ascelin despite the younger man's continual taunts about the coming of Miles.

Nerves were taut. Regular reports from the lookouts that de Bourne had posted said that the countryside was deserted for miles around. No news was worse than bad news for those who waited.

Only birdsong disturbed the expectant hush that had settled over the castle. Wrens whirred among the leaf litter while robins fought and sang. More than once the cackle of an alarmed blackbird caused eyes to look towards the west. The chortle of jays following a fox in the wood or a quick quarrel among rooks had the nervous jumping to their feet.

Outside, the King's men waited and watched in silence. De Bourne had whispered to Rosalind that it was only a plot to unsettle the castle staff further. It did not mean that an attack was likely. That would wait now until Miles arrived with the reinforcements.

Helias seemed feverish, and was fractious all day. He wouldn't stay in bed but came downstairs, grizzling incessantly. Afraid that Ascelin would lash out, Rosalind wrapped the child in lambskin and sat him between her and the hearthstone as she worked on her embroidery.

'You needn't think I'll let you bother with the pups when he's gone,' Ascelin said as Rosalind gave Helias a tonic of hot milk and honey.

'Where's Daddy going this time?' Helias said crossly, rubbing his eyes and leaning heavily against Rosalind.

'Not far. You must be good, and as quiet as a little mouse, Helias. Ascelin doesn't like noise.'

'He doesn't like orphans, either.' Ascelin strolled over to the fireside and put his hand out to ruffle the little boy's hair. Helias jerked back and started to cry.

'Save your tears for dear "Daddy", cub, soon to be burning in eternal hell-fire with all the other rotten sinners——'

Helias tugged at Rosalind's skirts, tears welling up and spilling from his eyes. 'Daddy's not dead...Daddy's not dead, is he, Auntie?'

'Of course he isn't, sweetheart.' Stroking the fiery little cheek, Rosalind tried to calm Helias. She wondered how she would tell the boys when the time came. 'Ascelin, if you don't be quiet I'll call my lord de Bourne and you can say these wicked things to him.'

'Yes, you'd like that, wouldn't you? A quick assignation out in the stables before bringing him in here to belittle me yet again. God only knows what you two got up to before I came home and put a stop to it. I'm eternally surprised he doesn't expect to couple in public, like the dog he is——'

At that Rosalind leapt up and slapped Ascelin savagely across the face.

He made no sound. One hand went to the angry red mark on his cheek, fingering it thoughtfully. With awful stealth he then turned on a smile of deep satisfaction.

'That's it,' he said calmly. 'That's all I wanted.'

The smile stayed in place. Ascelin carefully picked up the embroidery frame that stood between them and just as carefully dropped it on to the fire. Helias sensed what was about to happen and threw his arms about Rosalind, pressing himself against her.

'Auntie...Auntie!'

The whimper turned into a scream as Ascelin clawed Helias away, hurling him halfway across the room.

'Not the child—Ascelin, don't hurt the child——'

Ascelin wasn't listening. With the same preoccupied smile he was moving forward, backing her into a corner. The screams of Helias went unnoticed. All Rosalind could see was the death in Ascelin's eyes. Her death. His cool pale eyes gloated at the blind fear she knew then.

'Ascelin...no, I promise I've never...I've always been faithful to you——'

With a rasping laugh he lunged forward, fingers clutching at her neck. Rosalind fought, feeling her tongue pushed against the back of her throat. She struggled, trying to cry out but there was no breath left. The blood sang in her ears, forcing one last desperate kick and scrabble at him, then the world went dark.

Dark, and cold—and wet—and noisy all at once. A tremendous roaring waterfall of sound together with intense pain brought the life rushing back into Rosalind. She gasped, striking out in terror as nothing but water flooded into her lungs.

There was thrashing, falling and more pain. Someone was pulling at her, hauling her about. Rosalind coughed and choked and tried to escape, but sense was returning. The hands that held her now were not trying to kill. When she could bear to open her eyes, Rosalind found herself looking up into the face of Father Anthony. A voice came faintly from somewhere far away.

'I *told* you it wasn't safe to leave them together...'

'That's as maybe, my lord, but the less you have to say about this matter for the moment, the better, I think.'

Anthony smiled down at her still, but he was speaking to de Bourne. Rosalind put her hand to the floor and into a great pool of liquid.

Oh, God, she thought. He's killed Ascelin. What will happen to us now?

Footsteps sloshed towards her and with relief Rosalind saw Helias peering down. She struggled to rise, one hand to the bruises at her neck. Too late she realised her hand was wet—with Ascelin's blood? Looking down in horror, she found only water staining the floor and her clothes.

'It's a good job I forbade young Ascelin to carry any weapons. Looks as though he hasn't had much experience at killing barehanded.' De Bourne sauntered over and picked up his son. 'Lucky for us he didn't realise just how hard it is. The barrel gave way before you did, sweetbriar.'

He laughed, but in relief, as Rosalind looked about her. The day's supply of drinking water was dribbling away through the floorboards.

'He didn't hurt Helias?'

'No, child. The little lad ran to find us.' Anthony got to his feet, wringing water from the hem of his gown. 'It seems that I was too hasty in instructing my lord de Bourne to bring you back from your parents, lady. There must indeed be grave doubts about the wisdom of letting your marriage to Ascelin continue, after this exhibition. Be quiet, Mahel.'

Anthony held up his hand for silence before de Bourne had even thought to speak.

'Then Ascelin's still alive?' Rosalind said in amazement.

'He is. He must wait until the King's constable arrives for judgement to be passed. In the meantime, I think you should prepare to leave as soon as the siege is lifted, lady. Whatever happens, I agree with my lord de Bourne. It is no longer safe for you to remain with Ascelin. He must await the justice of Lord Miles—if the verdict is that Ascelin is allowed to live, then you must be put away into a convent for your own safety. If Ascelin is to suffer for trying to take your life, then the lord Miles will doubtless choose another husband for you.'

Rosalind glanced at de Bourne. Both knew that for Miles to be able to make any sort of judgement, the worst must happen to de Bourne. The Black Wolf could find no fine words to jolly them out of that situation.

Rosalind cleared her throat, forcing words past the painful bruising. 'Where—where is Ascelin now? Is he locked away?'

Anthony shook his head. 'As a gentleman, we must respect his feelings, my lady. But you will be quite safe— Crispin and Marty are to have strict instructions to accompany you at all times from now on. The lord Ascelin will be moved from your bedchamber to come and stay with me. There is little else that we can do for the present.'

'It won't be for long, sweetbriar. My bet is that Miles will be here within the day.' De Bourne looked falsely cheerful, then growled at his little son in play. Helias did not feel like playing, and buried his head against his father's neck with a whimper. Rosalind wondered if he sensed that his father's time might be running short.

'Spend some time with your sons now, my lord, if there's nothing more that can be done outside,' she said.

'Everything is as secure as I and forty of Empress Matilda's men can make it.' De Bourne put Helias down and sent him off in search of his brother. 'I was coming in now anyway. To make my confession... and settle things with you... just in case...'

Rosalind could not bear to watch him struggle alone with such unfamiliar tact and diplomacy. Without her veil, hoarse from rough treatment and dripping with water, she knelt down, shivering, on the wet hall floor before him.

'My lord? I'm sorry for causing you all this suffering...'

De Bourne threw back his head and laughed. 'Pah! It's nothing! Wait until this so-called saviour Miles gets here. Then you'll see what suffering is. He'll be so pleased to have me cornered he'll spin out the torture. My fate will serve as an awful warning to those who waver in their support of King Stephen.'

Rosalind shook her head in disbelief. 'You really don't care, do you?'

'It doesn't pay to.' He shrugged, with a wry smile. 'I've had a good run, sweetbriar, but like all good things it has to come to an end at some time.'

A look passed between de Bourne and the priest. Anthony muttered something about going to see where the boys had got to. He went to the door, quickly stepping outside. Leaving the door ajar, he kept one hand to the handle.

'Just to remind us that he's still within earshot.' De Bourne laughed as he led Rosalind to the fireside. 'I'm sorry your work got a bit singed. Will you be able to sort it out?'

The frame had been rescued from the fire. Part of the woodwork had been burnt and a little of the canvas discoloured by smoke. De Bourne plucked at the scorched embroidery, brushing aside flakes of ash. Determined not to meet her gaze, he concentrated upon the work as he spoke into the quiet of the hall.

'I wanted a chance to say goodbye, Rosalind. To be on the safe side—nothing else. I wouldn't want to be taken so suddenly that there wasn't time.' In one sudden movement he caught Rosalind by the shoulders and pulled her towards him. For long moments they looked at each other.

Rosalind knew that the slightest movement from either of them would end in the forbidden kiss. She closed her eyes, waiting for that sweetest sin. After another long moment he laid one cool kiss chastely on her forehead.

'I'm sorry,' he breathed into her wet hair.

'Don't be.' Rosalind felt his arms slip around her waist, but there was no sinister motive behind the movement. It was nothing more than a gesture between friends.

'You understand—about Shamira... Why I can't play the grand seducer?'

'Of course.' A silent smile passed between them, and Rosalind felt his love surround her without the need for more physical contact. 'I wouldn't want you to. In fact, I would rather you were like this. It's good that you can let me see a side of you that no one else knows.'

His hands moved slowly up her back to cup each shoulder in the last remnants of their embrace.

'I would like you to stay, while I spend some time with the boys——' he said at last.

'No, my lord. You'll want to be alone with them.'

She went to the staircase, the cold from her wet hair and clothes gnawing deep into her spirit.

'Rosalind...' He called her back, then seemed uncertain of what to do when she turned. 'What on earth can I say to them?'

She frowned, remembering the panic that little Helias had suffered earlier. De Bourne had troubles enough without having to bear the grief of his children.

'You aren't going out there to come off second best, are you?' she said firmly. De Bourne grinned and shook his head.

'I've never been second at anything in my life!'

'Then why worry them, my lord? You know you're unbeatable. They expect you to win. You have every chance, given their goodwill and that of Father Anthony and myself. We all love you in our own different ways, my lord. We're all behind you.'

Light steps brought him to the foot of the stairs. Looking up at her, his eyes had taken on a strange glow. It lit up his whole face and animated his manner afresh.

'You don't mean that?'

Rosalind smiled down at him, unable to trust herself to speak. In contrast, de Bourne was unable to stop his words escaping.

'Up on to the roof. Go on—hurry! I'll send Marty, and Crispin, and Anthony and the boys up to you...' De Bourne had sprung into action, snatching up gauntlets, helmet and his great black shield. 'Watch this—I'll be back in two shakes of poor puss's ears!'

All the old merriment had returned. With a wave and a laugh he swung out of the door in a rattle of steel links.

There was little point in telling him not to do anything silly. Rosalind guessed that such a word did not exist for de Bourne. He would do his best, which was formidable enough for anyone.

Except the lord Miles of Gloucester.

Rosalind climbed to the upper floor, then mounted the ladder to the roof.

Ascelin had been fizzing with excitement all day about the prospect of Miles coming to the rescue. He had almost convinced himself that the King's harsh words would all be worthwhile, if they meant that he got to walk with the great lord Miles at last. Rosalind had been told over and over again what a brilliant soldier the King's constable was, and how de Bourne would stand no chance against him. Even if the Black Wolf was man enough to stand and fight, which Ascelin doubted. Frequently, and at the top of his voice.

De Bourne never rose to any of Ascelin's words. His own men knew him well enough not to doubt. As for the castle staff, they knew Ascelin too well to pay much heed to his taunts.

The air almost roared with cold as Rosalind climbed out on to the roof. It would be a frost that night. Sounds from the yard sprang up sharp and metallic, carrying in the sharp autumn chill.

Rosalind put a hand to her hair, wishing she had stopped to find a towel. The cold bit fiercely at her wet skin and hair. She felt too weary to go and find anything now, for the sound of footsteps came from the ladder. Adrian scrambled out first, closely followed by Anthony and Marty. The young smith looked petrified, and rushed to Rosalind for reassurance. Crispin showed less alarm. He had found a kindred spirit in gentle, nervous Helias and the two were a comfort to each other. Carrying Helias up the stairs, he set him down safely beneath the parapet, wrapping the lambskin more securely about his little charge.

'There's Daddy!' Adrian shrieked in excitement, taking care to keep within the shelter of the parapet.

Mounted soldiers milled about the castle yard, but Rosalind did not have time to pick out the one she sought. In a flash the castle gates had opened and the force burst out, to the amazement of their enemies.

The besiegers had been taken completely unawares. Rosalind gasped in horror to see unarmed men running about in terrified confusion. De Bourne had told her that the more thoroughly he did his job the less she would like him. It looked likely to be true.

The King's men had been at leisure. Never expecting a second attack that day, they had been taking their ease. Card players were scattered, cooking pots overturned, and the whole camp trampled under the hoofs of de Bourne's men. Men who had been bathing away the grime of campaign ran back and forth in various states of undress.

It was all over very quickly and with no loss of life. In a lightning strike de Bourne and his men had snatched four dozen valuable horses, requisitioned vast quantities of gear and supplies and captured a large flock of deeply embarrassed royalists. Within minutes the loose camp set up outside the castle walls had been reduced to a patch of churned mud and grass.

When the attack was over, de Bourne had his standard set up at a point where he could supervise the rounding up of his spoils from horseback. This he did with brisk efficiency. When the last King's man had been chivvied into the castle yard de Bourne then removed his helmet and executed a deep bow to the watchers on the roof. His lookouts responded with a cheer, but Rosalind took care to remain silent. Only when she spotted a galloping horseman out of the corner of her eye did she call out, and then only to one of the lookouts. He responded with a warning shout to de Bourne.

The Black Wolf turned his horse to face the new threat. It came from the west—the direction from which Miles could be expected.

Without any particular urgency de Bourne pulled a square of cloth from his belt. After wiping his sword clean, he made a few practise lunges and slashing strokes while his horse backed and propped with excitement.

The newcomer could see this exhibition around the mighty black standard from some distance away. He slowed his horse, then bounced on for a little way rather more uncertainly. Finally he stopped, still several hundred yards away from de Bourne.

'Come on, then! Advance, miscreant!'

A woollen hat lay forgotten on the grass. Nudging his horse into position, de Bourne leaned out and flicked the cap high in the air with the point of his sword. As it fell he struck with small, smooth movements and the cap scattered, sliced into half a dozen pieces.

This did nothing to inspire the newcomer, whose sweating horse steamed in the cold and edged away nervously.

'Fancy a bout?' De Bourne pulled on his helmet and spurred on his horse. Eager for work, the great destrier strode out, encouraged by the whistles and cheers of the castle staff. They were hanging over the walls to watch the fun.

The newcomer had no such encouragements. He looked about frantically for somewhere to hide, calling out to play for time.

'No! No, I seek no fight with anyone—my lord, I am unarmed . . .'

De Bourne faltered, but his blood was up and racing. He called for an extra sword to be brought for their guest. Then he cantered on towards the petrified stranger.

'Come on! I won't hurt you—we'll only play for falls. I can be quite gentle——'

'No! No fighting! I've only come with a message!'

'Except when it comes to messengers!'

At this mighty roar, the messenger turned and fled. De Bourne put on a quick spurt, bringing a whoop of encouragement from his men. His destrier sprang across the turf, easily overhauling the terror-stricken messenger and his exhausted horse.

'Oh, no! He's going to kill him!' Rosalind covered her eyes, but Adrian laughed at her scornfully.

'He's only playing, Auntie!'

Helias was less certain. 'Daddy plays too rough when he's been fighting. I don't like it then.'

Rosalind opened her eyes and looked along the ride. De Bourne had brought the messenger to a halt and was receiving a roll of parchment. In return he gave the cowering messenger such a hearty slap on the back that it nearly sent the unfortunate man straight over his horse's head.

Wheeling his horse, de Bourne galloped off into the distance, powering away as the track curved off into the greenwood. Rosalind felt a cool hand upon hers, and realised that she had been unconsciously shredding the plaited belt about her waist.

'He'll be back.' Anthony smiled quietly. 'I expect he needs a little time to simmer down, as Helias suggested.'

Rosalind shook her head in distraction. 'What if he should meet the lord Miles?'

'He'll carve him into kindling!' Adrian yelled, dancing up and down with delight. 'Auntie, can I take Helias down to see the prisoners?'

'I think Helias is better off indoors today.' Rosalind smiled at the boys, unimpressed by Adrian's scowl.

'I think the same should go for you, too, my lady,' Anthony murmured in her ear. 'You have seemed out of sorts for the last day or so. And with the recent shock to your system...'

'I'm all right.' Rosalind took Helias and went with Crispin towards the stairs. All this sudden attention— it's no wonder I feel under the weather, she thought. I must carry on as normal. The priest might have to be told everything, but at least I can be innocent in the eyes of everyone else.

She left Crispin to amuse Helias by the fire while she and Marty took Adrian out to see the prisoners. The castle yard was full of new horses and different voices. Piles of clothing, saddlery and provisions were being checked and catalogued. Over at the stable block the prisoners had been stripped naked and were being herded into a large empty loose-box.

Adrian seemed to lose his eagerness to see the prisoners when he spotted who was at the gate. Galloping off, he taunted the unhappy messenger who waited on the other side of the spiked defence ditch.

'You were frightened of my daddy just then, weren't you?' Adrian swung from the great iron handle of the gates and grinned at the messenger. 'My daddy might have killed you. You were lucky, pipsqueak. I've seen my daddy *eat* people bigger than you!'

'Adrian!'

Rosalind detached the little boy from his stronghold and hauled him across the plank bridge to meet the messenger. Adrian was not so brave when on the wrong side of the defences. He gave the newcomer a troubled look and pursed his lips.

'Apologise, Adrian. I won't have you talking like that to the gentleman.'

Adrian kicked up a divot of muddy grass with the toe of his patten and scowled. It took a lot of persuasion to extract a bad-tempered apology.

'I'm dreadfully sorry,' Rosalind said to the messenger, wondering what he must think of her dishevelled appearance, not to mention his unusual welcome. 'I really don't know where Adrian gets it from.'

'I can guess,' the newcomer muttered as he slid down from his horse. 'Would you be the lady Rosalind Tirold? I was informed by the lord Nerra de Bourne that you are his châtelaine.'

Despite Marty's gasp and Rosalind's speechless nod, the newcomer bowed gravely.

'He called you *that*?' Marty hissed in horror. 'Oh, my lady, whatever sort of shame is that black-hearted villain bringing you?'

'None at all.' Rosalind trod on Marty's foot to drive home the point. 'You know very well the silly things my lord de Bourne comes out with. It must be another one of his jokes.'

The messenger waited politely for this frantic exchange to finish. Then he gave a small cough to remind them of his presence, and spoke. 'I have been sent here direct from my lord Miles of Gloucester.'

'Then my lord de Bourne has ridden out to meet him?' Rosalind felt herself start to panic. She wasn't ready for this...

'No, ma'am.' The messenger had seen many frantic women in his time, and took little notice of her distress. 'My liege lord sent only a directive.'

'A message? Then what is it? When is he coming?'

'Not allowed to give details, ma'am. Your...' he gave Rosalind a sly smile '...bondman took the parchment from me. As I hear that your husband is somewhat "indisposed", I expect the lord Nerra de Bourne wishes to give you the news himself. In...private.'

Rosalind tried to ignore the knowing wink the messenger gave her, and the smirk in his voice. As he had passed de Bourne's scrutiny, he would have to be treated as a guest. His ill manners would have to be tolerated. She took the messenger to the kitchen and cut bread and butter while Marty lowered over him like a thundercloud and Adrian whined to go and see the prisoners.

Finally she put a pot of honey in front of their unwelcome guest and left him to his meal. With the faithful Marty in tow she took Adrian off to see the prisoners, with strict instructions that he was to behave.

They watched the captives burrow down into the thick straw of the loose-box. Food and wine was passed to them through the bars and they settled, sullen with shame under Adrian's watchful stare.

'I'm glad you haven't laughed at these men, Adrian,' Rosalind said as he sat on the empty manger of the adjoining stall.

The little boy shook his head gravely. 'Daddy says that we should know where the money comes from. When he gets the ransom for these we'll get some presents. Well, we might. I hope. We mustn't count on it,' he added as an afterthought. There was a guilty look about him, as though the mere thought had been disloyal.

A clatter of hoofs on cobbles and a rush of sound brought de Bourne bursting into the stable, dragging his gasping horse along in his wake. Adrian shrieked with delight, launching himself from the manger into his father's arms.

'That's my lad!' In greeting de Bourne threw Adrian into the air, then tossed the child into the nearest heap of straw for a rough and tumble. The horse had seen it all before and nosed past Rosalind to its water trough. At once de Bourne wrestled Adrian aside and reached out to grab the reins. Breathless and laughing, he handed them to his son. 'Game's over, Adrian. No more. Walk the horse up and down to cool off, there's a good lad.'

'Oh, but Daddy...'

'Quiet.' The Black Wolf aimed a savage cuff barely a hair's breadth wide of the child's head. Obediently Adrian fell howling as though pole-axed, then scuttled away with his father's horse in tow. De Bourne sat on the straw, carefully picking bits from his clothing. He was watching Rosalind, a slow smile spreading across his face. This soon disappeared as he flashed a look at Marty.

'If I strike my own child so readily, young Marty, what mightn't I do to you? Think on.'

Marty looked from Rosalind to de Bourne's muscular magnificence. Torn between guarding his mistress and blind panic, he stood in the doorway, dithering.

'There's a letter come for your lord Ascelin. Fetch him to the hall, Marty. I'll look to the lady. Go on, or I'll have every inch of your hide flayed off you!'

De Bourne made a quick movement as though to rise and Marty bolted. Unimpressed, Rosalind folded her arms.

'You're nothing but a fraud, my lord. I saw everything—Adrian only pretended that you had hit him. You never touched him——'

Putting one finger to his lips, de Bourne winked and gestured towards the partition and its high grille. Beyond that lay the prisoners. The murmur of their voices was even now being stilled by curiosity.

'Doubt my word, would you, lady?' De Bourne's voice was hard and menacing, but nothing more than laughter danced in his eyes. 'I can see you'll have to be taken in hand—and firmly too, I'll warrant.'

The prisoners had gone suspiciously quiet. De Bourne was enjoying the joke hugely, and wasn't ready to finish it in a hurry.

'Get inside, woman, and be quick about it. I'm not a man to have my private enjoyment watched by the enemy.'

Rosalind thought she heard a sigh of disappointment from the prisoners, but her shame was too great to notice. When they were safely away from the stable block she rounded on de Bourne angrily.

'How dare you? Goodness knows what they'll be thinking! And to have called me your châtelaine, with all that suggests! How can you act so wickedly when at any minute the lord Miles will be arriving to murder you?'

'Ah,' de Bourne murmured thoughtfully. 'Yes...'

He said nothing more as they crossed the yard. Rosalind tried to will him into looking at her, into saying something more, but he would have none of it. Although he was dressed in dark, plainly cut working clothes there was no hiding the natural tinge of arrogance in his bearing. De Bourne was one of the best, and he knew it. With the dark mystery of his looks and honed strength visible in every movement, Rosalind knew that she would never have been able to resist any advances had it not been for Ascelin.

Ascelin. He stood in the centre of the hall, hands behind his back and a look of hatred for de Bourne burning in his eyes.

'Where have you been with my wife, *poulain*?'

'You'll speak when you're spoken to or go out with the other prisoners, Ascelin,' de Bourne said sharply as he went to the table. Sitting down on the edge to face Ascelin, he folded his hands and smiled innocently. 'As a general rule, dear boy, men who beat women get rough justice among even the very nastiest types . . .'

Ascelin shrank back. He didn't like getting his hands dirty at the best of times. To be thrown in with nasty types was the very last thing he wanted.

'I've got a letter.' De Bourne fished inside his jacket and withdrew a scroll of parchment. 'Oh, look—it seems to be addressed to you, Ascelin——'

Ascelin lunged forward but was seized by one of de Bourne's young lions.

'Give it to me! How dare you steal my post?' He struggled and fought, but the soldier held him fast. De Bourne merely smiled.

'I seem to remember that you weren't quite so high and mighty when it came to snaffling a certain letter addressed to me, young 'un?'

Turning the scroll about in his hands, de Bourne affected a look of puzzled amusement. 'Two seals on this. Must be important, Ascelin. This one looks familiar—

I'm sure I'll think of who it belongs to soon. And the smaller one—I'm told that's the mark of the lord Miles of Gloucester. Your friend, Ascelin.'

Ascelin's cherubic looks were contorted with rage. He managed to get one fist free from the soldier's grasp and shook it at de Bourne. 'You wait! You just wait, *poulain*! Your time's measured in moments—when Miles gets here he'll splash your heathen blood from here to Jerusalem!'

'Good chap, then, this Miles?'

'He's worth ten of you, *poulain*!'

De Bourne raised a quizzical eyebrow, then held the scroll out to Rosalind.

'Here, sweetbriar. I don't need to get my enjoyment from reading other people's private correspondence. It might be a touch dangerous to let your dear husband go free at this moment, so you'd better open it and let him read for himself.'

Rosalind did as she was asked. Breaking the seals, she unrolled the parchment and held it up for Ascelin to read, trying to ignore his dreadful curses as he was pinioned by de Bourne's soldier.

His noise soon stopped as he started to read the letter. Confusion replaced anger, with disbelief not far behind.

'You lying infidel! *Poulain*! It's not true—you made it up—you forged this—filthy——'

'Not bad news, surely, Ascelin?' de Bourne asked innocently over a tirade of gutter language.

Rosalind had to see what dreadful thing the letter contained. She turned it around and read it. Then she read it again. The individual words made sense, but the meaning seemed all wrong.

'This can't be right . . .' she murmured faintly at last.

'Oh, yes. It certainly is, sweetbriar. All witnessed, signed and sealed by both Miles and Earl Robert himself.'

'No. No, it can't be true.' Shaking her head with determination, Rosalind stabbed at the letter with an accusing finger. 'You knew what was in this, didn't you, my lord? You must have had a hand in it——'

'I received my own letter, lady. Inside it was that note for Ascelin,' de Bourne cut in smartly. 'And I'm not sure that I take kindly to my integrity being brought into question in that way.'

He seemed genuinely hurt that she had suspected him. Rosalind was crushed.

'I'm sorry, my lord.'

With a nod he accepted the apology, and withdrew a second scroll from his jacket.

'I suspect the words of this might be a little more polite than those addressed to my lord Ascelin.' De Bourne tapped the table beside him. 'Perhaps you might like to read it out to him, sweetbriar. I'm not sure I trust him with my letters.'

Rosalind approached the table warily, but to her relief de Bourne stood and let her take his place. Unfurling the second parchment, Rosalind started to read in a low voice so that only Ascelin could hear.

'"To my lord Mahel de Bourne, known as Nerra: greetings. Our liege lord Robert, natural brother of the Empress Matilda, has assured us to our great and final satisfaction of that lady's rightful claim to the throne of England. The miscreant Stephen, having broken his oath to support the lady and snatched her rightful crown, no longer has our support. We would be greatly pleased, de Bourne, if you would formally accept permanent stewardship of your present position. All principal holdings surrounding your land are held for the Empress. Should help be required, use this letter to secure the aid of any of our vassals at any time. If you have not already done so, the foul and perfidious recreant Tirold..."' Rosalind hesitated. Pausing as he stoked the fire, de Bourne motioned for her to continue. She took a deep breath. '"The foul and perfidious recreant Tirold is to be disposed of as—as you see fit..." It's signed simply, "Miles"...' Rosalind finished with a catch in her voice.

'Well, I don't think there's an awful lot of doubt about that, is there?' De Bourne dusted sawdust from his hands and strolled over to Ascelin. 'Sorry, Ascelin. It goes to show that you should never pin all your hopes on just the one single ally, doesn't it?'

Whether Ascelin believed the letter or still thought it a forgery, he knew it to be his death warrant. All struggling ceased. He hung limply in the hands of his captor, pale face blank now with mindless terror. 'No! No—don't kill me! I'll do anything...my lord, please don't hurt me—Rosalind! Rosalind, please—don't let him touch me!'

As de Bourne approached, Ascelin started to scream. Rosalind thought of the times that Ascelin had cornered her. The times when she had wanted to scream, but had to give in without a fight. Even so, she stepped forward as de Bourne pulled on his heavy leather gauntlets.

'Sorry, sweetbriar. Can't hear your pretty pleas above this racket. Ascelin, will you *shut up*?'

He clapped a heavy hand over Ascelin's mouth, forcing his head back to cut off a last shriek. Putting his face very close to Ascelin's rolling eyes, he spoke in a thunderous undertone. 'I won't kill you, Ascelin, although God knows you deserve it. You're an official prisoner now, and one that the lord Miles won't be too happy to see, by the sound of it. Nevertheless, that's where you're going, first thing tomorrow. Let him deal with you. I loathe you so completely that I can hardly be expected to give you a fair trial. You'll have to take your chance with the justice that the lord Miles deals you. Now, are you going to be a good boy and stay quiet? One squeak and you'll be in with the other prisoners, mind.'

Ascelin's eyes were nearly popping out of his head with fright. When nothing but a few strangled gurgles escaped him, de Bourne removed his hand from the younger man's mouth.

'There. Isn't silence more civilised?' He dismissed the soldier holding Ascelin from the hall. Robbed of support, the prisoner slithered to the ground and lay weeping at de Bourne's feet.

Rosalind knew she should help, but found herself rooted to the spot. Only de Bourne was detached enough from the scene to provide any practical help. He hauled Ascelin to his feet, giving him a good shake to make him stand upright.

'You know full well what I think about you, Ascelin, but that doesn't mean I can't feel some crumb of compassion now. Strong-arm tactics are all very well, as long as you're prepared to take your punishment when the tables are turned. If you haven't got the stomach for your own sort of justice, you should have found other games to play.'

He dropped Ascelin on to a seat beside the fire and went to Rosalind.

'I'm sorry he took it so badly, sweetbriar. I'll have to do my best to rally some sort of sense into him. He can't be sent off like that.' There was a moment when Rosalind thought de Bourne was going to reach out and touch her but he still had too great a sense of honour for that. He smiled slightly, understanding her torment of feelings. 'That pretty gold hair is still dark with the damp, sweetbriar. You should be drying it at the kitchen fire—Ascelin and I have got some serious talking to do.'

She wondered if Ascelin would survive the talking. As though reading her thoughts, the Black Wolf turned and smiled towards her husband. 'I've told you before, sweetbriar—he's quite safe with me. Besides, we won't be on our own. If you could send Father Anthony in to us—Ascelin might find him a comfort.'

Rosalind sighed, looking towards where Ascelin sat slumped before the fire.

'I should tell you if you don't know already, my lord—Miles hates my husband like poison. Ascelin was always trying to buy his favour, and the lord Miles isn't that sort of man. I've heard that he's threatened Ascelin more than once. With Ascelin on the opposing side now—the lord Miles is sure to take terrible advantage of the situation...'

Removing his gloves, de Bourne flexed the fingers of his grazed hand. His face worked over some inner problem, busy turning it this way and that. When he spoke he raised his head slowly to look at Rosalind, as though taking in every last detail.

'Then I am set between Scylla and Charybdis.' He frowned at the thought and shot a dark look at Ascelin. 'He's made your life a misery, and ended up half killing you. My idea of justice for him could never be impartial. If I send him to Miles for justice, it sounds as if he'd get short measure there, too. Miles is now my lord in England—if I were to let Ascelin go unpunished I should be guilty of an act of defiance, however innocently intended.'

He paused to sigh heavily. Whatever decision the Black Wolf made it could mean no good to Ascelin. Rosalind curtsied formally to de Bourne as she saw Ascelin turn towards her. The look of naked hatred in his eyes killed any last flicker of pity that she might have felt for him.

'I'll go and fetch Father Anthony, my lord.'

'Yes.' De Bourne leaned against the wall and studied Ascelin carefully. 'Young 'un will have a good use for him soon.'

Rosalind left the room quickly. The sad finality of de Bourne's tone hinted that a decision, however painful, had been made.

CHAPTER EIGHT

ROSALIND retired to her room, leaving Ascelin downstairs with de Bourne and the priest. She expected her young husband to bolt for safety as soon as he could, but time passed and Ascelin did not appear. Only when the low murmur of voices peaked in anger did Rosalind raise her head to listen.

No distinct words were audible. The floorboards beneath her feet sighed as the hall door below was opened, then slammed shut again.

An empty silence fell. Rosalind got up, smoothed out her gown and went downstairs to hear the worst. Only the usual collection of hounds greeted her in their wide-smiling, fawning way. Apart from the dogs milling about the hearth the room was deserted.

Her cloak hung on a nail beside the door. She hesitated before lifting it down—if a gallows was even now being built out in the yard for Ascelin, did she really want to know?

In the end reason prevailed. Ascelin would need her support, whatever was going to happen. Fastening the cloak about her shoulders, she went out into the yard.

Everything was exactly the same as it had always been. Several of the dogs bundled past her to bounce around grubby children playing in the yard. Marty was drawing water for the smith, while the furnace roared. Soldiers patrolled the wide castle walls or diced and gambled in small, cold groups. The stock cockerel strutted around with his wives, sneering at his brothers in their condemned cell.

Of Ascelin, Father Anthony or de Bourne there was no sign. Rosalind was on the point of going over to Marty and asking him what was happening when there was a disturbance over at the stable block.

De Bourne was ushering the priest out into the chilly evening sunlight. Fearing what might have happened, Rosalind started to run towards them. Both men stopped, but while Father Anthony smiled, de Bourne looked decidedly uneasy. When she reached them, his troubled agitation increased. He was looking at a distant point somewhere over Rosalind's head when he spoke.

'I left Adrian in the kitchen... If you would excuse me, lady, I must go——'

'You've killed Ascelin.' Her voice was level, with no hint of the rising panic that she felt.

'No...no, I wouldn't do a thing like that.' De Bourne moved restlessly under her steady gaze. 'Right...well— I must be off. There's much to do...'

Raising one hand in a half-salute to Rosalind, he walked away towards the kitchen block. His head was lowered, and he did not look back.

'It was an impossible situation, child,' the priest murmured as Rosalind watched de Bourne duck through the kitchen door. 'This way, Ascelin at least gets a chance to obtain some little glint of honour. It seems he had little enough hope of that in life.'

'Then he *is* dead?'

Father Anthony looked towards the stable that the men had just left. 'If not already, then soon.'

'I must speak to him——'

The priest grasped Rosalind's arm as she darted past him. 'No, child! The lord de Bourne has refused you any further contact with him.'

'Oh...oh, that's cruel...' Amazement then sadness filled her eyes. 'That is not fair, Father. I'm a wife who only wants one last chance to convince her husband that I was innocent of what he suspected... You of all people should be on my side! I have to make Ascelin see the truth——'

'You weren't there, Rosalind.' Father Anthony's sad, dark eyes smiled at her kindly. 'I'm afraid I have to agree with my lord de Bourne on this matter. Ascelin wasn't prepared to see you. He didn't even leave you a final message. Things were said that are best not repeated...'

Rosalind could imagine. In their short marriage she had learned that her young husband had little time for anyone but himself. When he was threatened he retreated into insult and savagery. Fear, or even the thought of it, overwhelmed him.

'Let me see him.' She could not bear to think of Ascelin alone at his lowest ebb, with death his only hope of escape.

'The lord de Bourne said no, child.' The priest squeezed her arm companionably, but when he tried to lead her away Rosalind stayed rooted to the spot.

'And this is the lord de Bourne that once said he had no wish to come between a man and his wife?' Her blue eyes glittered in the low sunlight.

Father Anthony thought for a long time. At last he took both Rosalind's hands in his and smiled kindly. 'I can take a last message to Ascelin for you. No doubt there is still time enough for that.'

'Tell him...' Rosalind looked at the priest's dark, reassuring solidity and took a steadying breath. 'Tell Ascelin that my conscience is clear, and that I have nothing to apologise to him for. My only concern is that he should know that I feel sorry for him, and wish our life together and his end could have been different.'

Anthony nodded thoughtfully, then started back towards the stable block. To his surprise Rosalind fell into step beside him.

'No, my lady...you should stay, in case the lord Ascelin has already——'

'He won't, until the last possible moment,' Rosalind said quietly.

'Very well, child, but it might be as well if you were to stay here at the threshold. If my lord de Bourne were to think I had disobeyed his orders and let you enter it would go ill for me, I think.'

He nodded politely, which in his gentle way was a final request to stay where she was. Rosalind watched him enter the stable. The only sound from within was the mutter of the royalist prisoners, and she almost reassured herself that it was finished—that everything was over for Ascelin. She put one hand to the door frame, half for support and half in guilty relief. Then Ascelin's voice rose in anguish.

'Rosalind! Oh, Rosalind—I'm sorry...so sorry...'

Father Anthony's warning had little effect. With rising panic Rosalind rushed forward, stumbling into the noisy gloom. Ascelin was alone, and he was terrified. Despite herself, Rosalind had to comfort him.

'Rosalind!' A hand thrust out between the bars of a corner stall. She faltered, unwilling to disobey Father Anthony who stood guard beside the locked door. Then Ascelin cried out again, and she was lost.

'Don't cry, my lord.' She walked forward. One of them had to keep calm, and Ascelin was incapable of such things.

'They've shut me in here with a knife—they want me to kill myself! Rosalind, he wants me to kill myself so I'll be damned for ever and he'll get this place all to himself...'

'Now, my lord,' Anthony said briskly as Ascelin pressed his tear-swollen face to the bars. 'That's not quite right. You were given the option of a decent way out or despatch to my lord Miles tomorrow. It must be one or the other—if you would rather face the lord Miles...'

'No—no, I can't suffer Miles g-gloating over me. I'd be in his power, and he'd torture me with it... It's no choice at all. Tell them, Rosalind! I love you! Don't desert me now! Don't leave me...'

He was too late with his pleas. Once she might have been taken in by the words, but now Rosalind was beginning to emerge from the shell of guilt that Ascelin had fashioned for her.

'As you have always said, Ascelin, women have no business trying to tell men what to do. If I were to try and plead your case, don't you think my lord de Bourne would take a similar line?'

'Tell him, Rosalind. He'll listen to you...'

'I can't, my lord. If the lord Miles himself says that you must face the consequences of your actions, who am I to interfere?'

Her voice was firm, but not without compassion. Ascelin sagged against the wall of his stall and with a wavering cry sank down into the straw.

'I would have been good to you... It wasn't my fault, Rosalind... I was always so busy, trying to make a living to support us—it's no wonder I got cross at times, but that's going to change—Rosalind, if only you could get me out of here I'd show you how much I really love you...'

He might have changed. The shock might have made him realise the wickedness of his old ways... Father Anthony saw these thoughts flitting across Rosalind's face. Moving quickly, he placed himself between her and a last ditch appeal to de Bourne.

'No, my lady. Say your piece, wish him goodbye and then leave my lord Ascelin to his fate.'

In her heart of hearts Rosalind knew that the little priest was right. That didn't make things any easier to bear. Rosalind was trapped, and now she wanted to escape as soon as possible.

'You must be brave, Ascelin. There's a choice, and you must take it. I'll never forget you, whatever happens.' It was certainly true, if not quite as senti-

mental as she tried to make it sound. Hearing the rustle
of her gown on the straw as she turned to leave, Ascelin
started to wail again.

'Rosalind!'

She stopped, when all her common sense screamed at
her to get away.

'Rosalind ... One—one last kiss? Please? That's all I
ask—that's all...I'll go quietly then...' Ascelin had leapt
to his feet again, scrabbling at the bars of his prison to
reach out to her.

Everything warned Rosalind to pay no attention.
Father Anthony stood aside, eager for her to leave. Despite everything she was drawn back, away from total
freedom.

'There can be no harm in it, Father Anthony.' She
smiled faintly, going to face Ascelin through the bars of
his prison. 'At such a dreadful time my lord wouldn't
dare to——'

The words ended in a strangled cry. Quick as a flash,
Ascelin had thrust his arm through the bars and pinned
her to the wooden partition. She saw a flash of cold steel
as his other arm snaked through to press a knife to her
back.

'Wouldn't dare to what, cherub?' All self-pity gone
now, Ascelin pulled back his lips in a savage smile.
'You—priest! Stop gawping. I want a fast horse waiting
outside the gates. Now! Not next week!'

'Don't leave me!' Rosalind cried out, but she was
pulled closer into the cruel, hard bars. The royalist prisoners yelled in impotent rage, horrified at what Ascelin
had done. In desperation Father Anthony darted out of
the stable, frantically calling for help.

'You needn't think you'll wriggle out of this, cherub,'
Ascelin whispered, his hot breath pouring down
Rosalind's neck. 'I'm on my way to the King. You're
my free pass out of here—the filthy *poulain* won't lift

a finger against me if he thinks it might jeopardise his precious little white slave——'

'It isn't like that, Ascelin! How many times do I have to tell you?' Rosalind was frozen with terror, words spilling out in a desperate flood. 'He won't care about me—he'd rather sacrifice me as an innocent than see you escape from justice——'

Ascelin crushed her even closer to the wooden partition. 'We'll see about that! Now, if you know what's good for you, you'll reach down and unbolt this door. Gently now!' He gave a low giggle as Rosalind tried to reach the bolts. 'We don't want this knife to slip, do we? That would be a pretty mess for the *poulain* to see, wouldn't it?'

Rosalind had no option but to obey. When the door opened Ascelin eased his way to freedom, careful to keep her covered with the knife as one at a time he removed his arms from between the bars. Ascelin had not even manoeuvred her to the stable door before noise and confusion arrived in the yard outside.

'See sense, lad.' The soft reason of de Bourne's voice from outside cut no ice with Ascelin. 'You'll never pull this off. One man against all these soldiers? You'll be cut down before you get anywhere near the gates——'

'Wrong!' Ascelin laughed, clutching at Rosalind as he pushed her out of the stable before him. 'The knife you so kindly lent me, *poulain*, is sharp enough to slice into your doxy before any shot at me could take effect.'

He kicked at Rosalind's heels, his heavy boots urging her on. De Bourne kept a ring of his soldiers at bay around the couple. In their rapt attention, all held their breath as Rosalind did. Powerless to help her, the growing crowd rippled and parted as Ascelin used his wife as a shield to reach the gate.

'If dodging your responsibilities means that much to you, Ascelin, let the girl go. She's never been anything to you before; why keep on tormenting her?'

De Bourne's words had no effect. Ascelin did not take his eyes off the mercenary, but moved with cat-like stealth to keep Rosalind always between him and his great enemy. 'You reckon I'd let my chance of safe passage go? Think again, *poulain*. I've got hold of the one thing that ensures you won't try anything. You've ruined me, taken my land, my castle—everything. You've held me up to ridicule, sat in my chair and feasted on my stores. There's just one thing left that I can cheat you of, *poulain*.' He gave Rosalind a shake. Limp as a rag, she closed her eyes and waited for Ascelin to drive in the knife.

He never struck. Rosalind opened her eyes, praying that it was all a hideous dream. All she saw was reality. De Bourne and his men were within two yards, but none dared make a challenge for fear of risking her life. Inching backwards across the yard, Ascelin had pulled her level with the kitchen block. They were nearly at the gate. When Ascelin reached the horse that had been led out for him, he would have no further use for her.

'I'm off to King Stephen,' Ascelin gloated, pulling Rosalind through the castle gates and on to the plank bridge beyond. 'I'll be welcomed back with open arms, *poulain*, when he hears how you and your lady love have plotted and planned against me. Say goodbye to the love of your life, *poulain*——'

Suddenly, everything happened at once. With a scream of rage a small missile hurtled at Rosalind, hitting her full in the chest. Ascelin stepped back in surprise, but his foot found only the edge of the bridge and beyond it, thin air. Balance lost, he threw out both hands to save himself. Rosalind fell backwards too, but beyond the biting, clawing screams of hate something snatched at her, holding her suspended over the chasm.

'No! No! Let go! Let her go! You love us best, Daddy!'

The words suddenly made sense. Rosalind saw Adrian's face above her, twisted in rage. Below her there were only sounds, thin animal cries that faltered to become feeble gasps, then silence. For down there, where Ascelin had fallen, the deep defence ditch was studded with ranks of deadly sharpened stakes.

'I've got you,' de Bourne said firmly, but his grasp seemed unsteady. 'Don't look down, Rosalind. He's far beyond mortal help now. When they pull Adrian back, just keep looking at me...'

Hands reached out and detached Adrian from her, a weight dragged from her chest. His screams of jealous rage increased. Rosalind wondered if they were blotting out every other sound, or if the scene was unnaturally still and quiet. No one spoke. There was no sound except Adrian and the petulant cries of jackdaws, startled from their roof-top home.

Gently, inch by inch, she was drawn back from the abyss and into de Bourne's arms. Oblivious of the crowds packing the gateway, his men, his reputation and the hysterical rage of his son he held her tightly for a moment, pressing her head into his neck.

'I nearly lost you,' he breathed into her very soul. 'I nearly lost you...'

Adrian jackknifed away from his captors, dashing up to drive himself between Rosalind and de Bourne like a savage little wedge.

'No!' he screamed through gritted teeth. 'You love us, Daddy! Us! Not her! No...'

Striking like a snake, de Bourne bent and snatched Adrian off the ground by a handful of clothing at the scruff of his neck.

'Stop—showing—off!' With each word he gave the child a small shake. Adrian was astonished into silence, then dropped lightly back on to his feet.

'And I don't know what you lot are all staring at!' De Bourne turned to rake the crowd with a dark glare. 'I don't pay you to loiter about. Get moving—sort things out here while I teach this ragamuffin some manners.'

For once Rosalind did not plead on the child's behalf. She was too frightened, too horror-stricken, too tired. As de Bourne hustled Adrian back into the castle yard his soldiers eyed Rosalind uncomfortably. At first she was too numb to move, but soon realised why they hesitated. Ascelin, or what was left of him, would have to be retrieved. They would not want her to be a witness to that.

Rosalind hesitated, almost wanting to see Ascelin for the last time. Try as she might, though, she could not turn around and face the awful scene. Much as he had mistreated her, she wanted only peace, not revenge.

Setting her face resolutely towards the castle, Rosalind went back into the yard. She had only got as far as the kitchen block when an awful unsteadiness attacked her. Unwilling to shame herself in front of all those in the yard, she altered course to find a seat in the kitchen.

De Bourne was already there. He stood with one foot on the bench where Adrian sat, and was leaning down to his son as he spoke. Hearing the door, he straightened up. With a brief smile at Rosalind he pointed at the seat beside Adrian, who was swinging his legs and staring at the table top.

'I'm glad you've arrived,' he said, standing up properly. 'Adrian?'

The little boy looked round at her, his face burning with shame. His lips moved over words, but the words were muffled by resentment.

'You're not getting away with it, lad. You'll say it louder, and mean it.'

'Sorry, Auntie.'

De Bourne patted the child absently. 'Good lad. Now run along—the lady Rosalind and I want to talk——'

'I'd rather Adrian stayed with us, my lord,' Rosalind cut in with a quick look at de Bourne over the child's head. 'I think it's better that he should be with you.'

'We've just been talking about that.' The Black Wolf sat down with a heavy sigh. 'He knows, now.'

Rosalind wondered whether de Bourne would be insensitive enough to renew his courtship right there and then. 'Knows what, my lord?'

'That work and looking after him and his brother means that I haven't had any friends for a long time. Now the time has come, he needn't think he can spoil everything with his tantrums.'

Without acknowledging his words, Rosalind moved a little closer to the child. 'Do you miss your friend Count Geoffrey, Adrian?'

There was no reply. Adrian stuck out his lower lip and frowned, scoring scratches on the table-top with his fingernails.

'Was he your best friend, Adrian?'

'Sometimes,' the child muttered. 'He would say he was, and play with us, and everything was fun. Then he'd find a new auntie, and forget us——'

'That's because he was only your friend, Adrian.' Rosalind took one of his hands. It was stiff and unresponsive, like a bundle of small twigs. 'Your daddy is much more than that to you. He'll never forsake you. He'll always be here, whenever you need him.'

Adrian looked up, but it was at his father.

'You do love us best, though, don't you, Daddy?'

Rosalind nodded her head at de Bourne, who turned his laughter towards his son.

'Of course I do!' With a surprisingly gentle gesture he patted his son's small head.

Adrian pulled away from Rosalind's hand and stood up on the bench to hug his father. With a smile de Bourne returned the gesture.

'I think about you and your brother all the time. Right now, I'm worried that Helias might not be keeping warm by the fire. I shall have to come and see in a minute.

Perhaps you ought to go and sit with him, to keep him company. I expect he's wondering where you are.'

He swung Adrian down from the bench and the child ran towards the door.

'My lord! What if they're still—what if they're bringing Ascelin in——?'

'They'll be careful, sweetbriar,' de Bourne said softly as Adrian hesitated and looked back at her. 'And besides, he'll have to get used to it sooner or later, if he's going to be a soldier!'

Adrian grinned broadly, then dashed off to do his father's bidding. When the door had rattled shut de Bourne sat down beside Rosalind, folding his arms on the table and frowning slightly.

'I didn't think you'd want me to have favourites, sweetbriar.'

'They need you...my lord.' With Ascelin gone the title seemed ungainly, but Rosalind could not bring herself to go further. De Bourne sat strong and self-assured beside her, worrying at the roughened table-top with one fingertip.

'Don't you feel the same for me as I feel for you?' As soon as the words were out he made a noise of disgust. 'That was unforgivable. I'm sorry, Rosalind. To be so insensitive——'

'The children need you, my lord.' She had to stop him following that path for her own sanity. To talk of the children seemed the only safe topic. 'Imagine what they've suffered. Brought up—however well—in a den of ruffians, with a father whose work takes him away for long periods. Then they're brought halfway across the world to a strange place. The security of your love is the only thing they feel safe with, my lord. When they need you most you seem to be showing every sign of doing an "Uncle Geoffrey", and giving all your time to someone else.'

Rosalind heard him stretch out his legs beneath the table, then his hand slid quickly over hers. 'Not just someone else, Rosalind. You. It's too early for you to think about such things, I know, but everything I said in the past still holds true.' The touch on her hand increased slightly. Rosalind could not resist. Even when his arm was laid about her shoulders there was no strength left within her to deny him now.

'I know exactly how you feel, Rosalind. I've been through it all myself. When you lose someone it leaves a gap—a numbness, no matter how badly you may have been treated. Suddenly your whole life changes. After what she had put me through, I no longer...' he hesitated minutely '...loved...Shamira by the time she was killed. That didn't make the loss any easier to bear. Where we had been a couple, I was on my own. The house was silent all the time. I'd got used to getting home and finding that she'd...gone out, but that new, permanent silence——'

'It was all my fault!' Rosalind burst out suddenly. She tried to rise but de Bourne caught at her, forcing her to look into his deep, dark eyes.

'No. Don't ever think that, Rosalind, because it isn't true. I tortured myself like that for more than a dozen years, thinking exactly the same thing about Shamira's death. Going over and over old ground—why did she deceive me? What did I do wrong? What could I have done to stop it—why didn't I realise? It's not worth it, Rosalind. I was here to see how you were treated. I know everything. Ascelin abandoned you at the first sign of trouble, and when he did come back he treated you like dirt.'

His eyes blazed, daring her to deny the truth. Rosalind shook her head but could not look away.

'Things would have been different—if only I could have given him a child...'

'And you think that would have changed him? No, sweetbriar; nothing ever changes a man like that. It was bred into him to be bad, and nothing you or anyone else could have done would ever have changed things.'

Rosalind backed away, trying to free herself from his grasp. Instead de Bourne rose to his feet and advanced. In confusion she tried to wrench away from his hold. At the first sign of her resistance he let her go.

'My lord...my lord, I can't say that my husband and I were happy, but then neither can I say I would have wished him to die like—that... Oh, but I've been so wicked! The times that I have wished...' The memory of what had happened rose up and engulfed her. Putting both hands to her face, Rosalind gave a horrified little cry. At once de Bourne gathered her into his arms. Pressing her to the warm russet of his cloak, he held her in strong brown hands.

'I can guess. Wishing's not the same as killing, Rosalind. Goodness knows I had no love for Ascelin at all. I had every reason to wish him dead, and they all went through my mind at one time or another. In the end what happened was an accident. I'm truly sorry for what happened, but I can't take back the wicked thoughts that I'd been having. There's no use in trying. They're regrettable, but they didn't cause his death. Only Ascelin did that.'

He held her for a long time, still and steady.

'You're hot,' he said at last.

Rosalind felt quite the opposite. She pulled away from him. 'I'm all right. Go and see to the boys. They need you.'

'And you don't?'

There was no denying it. Rosalind nodded, taking in the kind, handsome face with its fine features. He drew her to him once more and she clung to him gratefully.

'Come back to the hall,' he murmured into her ear. 'Sit by the fire with Helias. You need rest.'

Rosalind let herself be led from the kitchen. She had no free will left. Numb with shock and tired to death, she let de Bourne take her back to the castle hall. She barely noticed what was going on in the yard. If Ascelin had been taken there she did not see.

At her insistence, de Bourne went into the hall first. Rosalind stood outside for a moment, waiting until he had greeted his boys. The cold wind sucked away what warmth she still had, leaving nothing but an aching chill.

Glad to get into the warm, she spent the rest of the afternoon crouched over the fire. The blaze roared and there was plenty of mulled wine to be had, but Rosalind could not shake off the cold. She did not move to the table for supper with the boys, but remained at the hearth.

The hall filled with de Bourne's soldiers. Noisy at first, they soon fell into subdued quiet. Rosalind barely noticed. Only when de Bourne himself brought her over a bowl of broth did she look away from the flames.

'You must eat something, sweetbriar.'

The castle hall was almost empty. All but the children and a handful of soldiers had finished their meals and left.

'Thank you. But I'm not hungry, my lord.'

De Bourne pulled up a stool and sat down beside her. He still held out bowl and spoon, and eventually Rosalind felt obliged to take it. The broth was rich and thick, but barely lukewarm after its journey across from the kitchens. She pushed the bowl into the embers of the fire to heat up again, and took another sip of warm wine.

'There's no tactful way of broaching this subject,' de Bourne said quietly. 'I've given orders that Ascelin is to be buried tomorrow. The ground might be frozen hard if we wait too long. I wondered if you might...'

He stopped. Both hands were in his lap and he brushed out the folds of his tunic with sharp, awkward movements.

Rosalind shivered and put her feet on to the hearth-stone for warmth.

'Sweetbriar—Rosalind—I wondered if you'd like to come out and see him...before...'

'No. Oh, no, my lord—I couldn't...' She looked at him with horrified revulsion. De Bourne leaned over and took her hand.

'It's all right, Rosalind. His face is all right, and he's been well looked after. There's nothing to see.'

Tears threatened to spring from her eyes. Rosalind shook her head. 'It's not only that...oh, my lord— without a husband I'm an outcast now. With my home overrun by enemies I've got nothing. Not even a future. I don't think I could bear to look back at the past now...'

The rest of the soldiers straggled out of the hall. De Bourne lifted Rosalind's hand over to his own lap, where he could clasp it in both of his hands.

'I've told you before, Rosalind—you've got me. I'm no more your enemy than you are mine. When you feel ready, I would like to marry you. Even if that doesn't suit, and you won't have me, this is still your home, now and for ever.'

Rosalind smiled through the still threatening tears. 'Oh, my lord—whatever would the neighbours say about that?'

'I'm Mahel de Bourne! I don't care what anyone thinks,' he said, then corrected himself quickly. 'With the exception of your parents. I ought to try and cultivate their goodwill. The only way I can think of is to marry you outright. What do you say?'

A terrible weariness swam over Rosalind. She wanted to accept him so badly, let him shoulder the burden of guilt that she felt. Only the thought of what her mother would say at such indecent haste stopped her.

'Not tonight. Another time, my lord. Some might suspect that Ascelin's death was not such an accident——'

'Everyone saw,' he stated firmly. 'Neither of us was directly to blame. There can be no suspicion whatsoever, Rosalind! Who would be wicked enough to think such a thing?'

'There must be a decent interval, my lord.'

De Bourne's face darkened. He looked across at his children, still busy with their supper. 'If you don't want me, just say it.'

'It isn't that. It's just that I need time...'

'Are you sure that's the only reason? I'm not insensitive enough to want you to marry me right this minute, but can't I have an assurance...?'

'All I need is a little time, my lord.'

'Of course. Of course you do.' He spread her fingers and laced his into them. 'But...might I...hope?'

Gentle words came to him only with difficulty, and he looked at the floor in discomfort.

Rosalind had not dared to give the matter any thought before. Now she was free to make her own way out of Ascelin's shadow. Independence had been drained from her in the last six months, and now the thought of freedom frightened her.

'One day. Perhaps.' That was all she could say. With only his sons to see, de Bourne put her hand to his lips and kissed each fingertip lightly.

'I think perhaps we should go and see Ascelin, before it gets any later,' he said softly.

Rosalind drew back from him, but he squeezed her hand.

'I'll take care of you, my love.'

'It's so cold...'

'Wear my jacket over your cloak. It's not far to the stables.'

There was no arguing with him. Raising Rosalind gently to her feet, he fetched her cloak and fastened it around her shoulders. While she arranged the hood over her hair he slipped his fur-lined riding cape around her for extra warmth. With a warning to his sons to behave, de Bourne took a lighted torch from the wall and escorted Rosalind outside.

The yard was deserted. All the animals had been shut in for the night and off duty soldiers had retreated to the kitchen for warmth. The stable block was well used that night. In addition to the gentle movements of the horses, there was a quiet murmuration from the prisoners' stall as they finished their supper. This fell into silence as de Bourne and Rosalind entered the stable block.

He led the way to Ascelin. Torches flared in the empty stall as Father Anthony moved to greet them. Rosalind had been swallowing hard, trying to force words past the painful obstruction in her throat. As de Bourne swung the stall door open she sprang back.

'No! I can't...'

Father Anthony retreated at once. 'That's quite all right, child. No one will force you——'

'Wait.' De Bourne had been leading her by the hand, but now his grip slackened. Instead he slipped one arm around her waist and drew her gently towards the open stall. 'You must, Rosalind. You might never forgive yourself if you don't.' He paused, unwilling to persist as Rosalind went rigid beneath his fingers.

'I can't, my lord. I don't want to...I never loved him...'

'That matters to you now, but in time things may look differently.' De Bourne's hold changed from restraint to reassurance. 'No one can have—hated quite so much as I did when Shamira was killed. Everyone wanted me to go and see her for one last time. I didn't. I couldn't trust myself. Then, after a long time, I found that I could look back. We did have some good times. She hadn't always been the scarlet woman that I remembered. I found that I was wishing I'd seen her that last time, when there could have been no cruel words between us.'

Rosalind looked up as leaping shadows shrank from de Bourne's face. It was grave and thoughtful. The mouth that was all too ready with a merry grin was pursed and silent. She knew at once that he was speaking the truth.

'I can't imagine ever feeling like that, my lord.'

'That's what I thought, sweetbriar. Things change, given time. Can you really risk missing this last chance?'

Silently, Rosalind went forward. Passing quickly into the stall she was faced by a white shrouded form laid upon a trestle table. She faltered. This couldn't be Ascelin. It was too small—too still...

Without realising it, Rosalind had clasped her hands tightly to take the last few steps to his side. She saw there only the face of a child, asleep. Golden curls escaped from the folds of his cerement and lay on an untroubled brow.

Rosalind knew what would be expected of a loyal wife. She closed her eyes and bent forward. Hot tears splashed on to Ascelin's cold grey skin as she placed one formal kiss upon his forehead. The world swam away before her eyes as she rose. Candlelight splintered into a thousand shards. Her hands found her purse, and a coin, and a cool white candle was pressed into her hands.

The torches reeled and danced, dodging away each time Rosalind tried to light her candle. When the wick did catch a tremendous heat seemed to flow from it, racing over her body in a wave of perspiration. She pulled de Bourne's cape off, trying to cool herself. It worked too well. As she struggled to set her candle up beside the others the ice coldness returned. She was colder than ever now, colder than poor Ascelin—struggling, struggling to stand, to walk...to move...

The world slipped away from her again. In waves of noise and heat and cold she fell, but didn't care. Nothing

mattered any more. All she wanted to do was to rest—
sink into the blackness that enveloped her and go to sleep.

There could be no rest where she was going. Noise
increased, a broken cacophony ringing through her poor
aching head. Suddenly she was being pulled back and
forth, shaken and dragged about. Light turned to
darkness, then back to light again. Rosalind could make
nothing of it. Her eyes only ached less, or more. She
could understand none of it.

The only thing she knew for sure was the formless
noise and unbearable weight on her chest. It was Ascelin,
come back from the dead to crush the life out of her.
His hands were around her throat—pressing down, trying
to take her with him...

Words glittered past, hard and sharp like icicles.
Rosalind could hear the voices, but could not understand. She couldn't even open her eyes to see who it was.
She didn't need to. Without even seeing him, Rosalind
knew that it would be Ascelin. He would be bringing
pain, and fear and torment again, but Rosalind no longer
cared. All she wanted to do was slip into cool sleep.

Even that was forbidden her. It grew hotter and hotter
as the weight upon her increased. She tried to throw off
the stifling cerements that Ascelin was muffling her with.
There was no voice left in her dry, aching throat.

Suddenly there was a greater terror. Ascelin was there
beside her, clutching her to him, holding her close. An
awful truth reared up before Rosalind through a stifling
fog. Even in death she could never escape him. He would
clutch her now through all eternity.

Terrified, Rosalind tried to call out for help. In reply
an ice-cool hand slipped across her face. The blanketing
fog about her increased.

With one last sob she sank into it, and silence.

CHAPTER NINE

ALL Rosalind knew was a darkness that never became day. It enveloped her in a hot, stifling oppression that did not ease. She did try to open her eyes, but the effort was always too much. The dreams were bad enough. Trying to wake brought new tortures, more cold hands pulling at her with muttered undertones of speech.

Then at last the darkness fell quiet and still. Rosalind found herself sighing in deep, restful peace. He had gone. There would be respite for a while.

She tried to stretch out, to ease her aching limbs. It was no use—she was still held fast. A body still lay beside her, enveloping her in an almost overwhelming embrace. The weight crushing her chest seemed to be its head, for she could feel a steady, regular breathing against the side of her neck. Rosalind managed to raise one hand and touch the mystery. She found a silky softness of hair. At least it's not Ascelin, was all she could think. Her fingers rested lightly upon it for a moment.

Slowly, shapes, forms and feeling began to mean something again. That light patch must be the window. She was in bed—in her own chamber. Her arm was growing cold, because a mountain of bedclothes had slipped askew at some time. Her fingers danced over the hair that her hand had brushed. Yes—it was too straight for Ascelin, thank goodness. And it was too thick for Crispin.

There was a sudden movement beneath her fingers, silence, then a warm hand caught at hers. She knew. It was de Bourne. The Black Wolf—he was here in her

chamber, in the middle of the night and—for shame—
they were all alone!

As she cried out he leapt up, pulling frantically at the
bedclothes. Rosalind tried to get away, but had no
strength to struggle out from the tangled covers. He
grabbed her, clutching her so tightly that she could feel
the rough unshaven prickle of his face. To try and resist
now would be useless—he had her trapped.

Rosalind went limp in his arms, and knew no more.

Something small but heavy was moving about at the end
of her bed. Afraid of what she might find, Rosalind kept
her eyes closed and listened.

She heard a little voice say "No", and recognised
Adrian's gruff tone. Small tapping sounds followed, and
Rosalind opened her eyes. Grey daylight was filtering
through the cloth-covered chamber window, but a fire
still crackled on its hearth close to her bed. The room
was unbearably stuffy and close. Her body lacked its
once raging heat but it craved fresh air and most of all,
a drink of cold water.

Dice rattled in a cup, then dropped noisily on to a
board. Rosalind heard Helias cheer, then the tap of
counters as their game continued.

'Daddy's busy,' Adrian said suddenly, his voice di-
rected towards her.

'No, Adrian . . . Daddy said that you were to fetch him
the very instant Auntie woke up. Go on!'

There was a long silence. The cup was shaken again,
and the dice tipped.

'Adrian, go on!'

'No! Daddy's busy. He's got too much to do. Anyway,
he's in here with her all the time. It's not fair . . .'

The squabble continued, and Rosalind closed her eyes
again. There seemed no hope of any agreement, let alone
a drink.

A patter of icy droplets woke her the second time. De Bourne had pulled off his rain cape and was kneeling beside her. He was smiling.

'I came as soon as I could, my love.'

Rosalind shook her head, still dizzy with sleep. 'You were busy...'

'Never too busy to come and see you.' His hand searched deftly under the covers for hers. Taking it, he smiled then leaned forward and kissed her lightly on the forehead. 'What can I get you?'

'A drink. Cold,' she said through parched lips.

He bent towards the hearth and picked up a small cup. 'Try this. Boiled water—it's warm, but there's a little honey in it to give you strength.'

He sat down on the bed, cradling her gently in his arms to help her drink.

'Where's Adrian?' Rosalind said when she could speak more clearly. De Bourne frowned, and, putting down the cup, settled the bedclothes around her more comfortably.

'Up on the roof, watching our visitors. After the scene we had just now he should have been spanked and sent to bed, but perhaps he's not to blame. What with looking after you and the siege I've neglected them both rather too much over the last few days——'

'Siege?' Rosalind struggled to rise, 'Then the King has come back? I can't stay here—I must get up...'

The heaviness in her limbs made all movement stiff and difficult. The damp, prickling heat was too tiring to struggle against. She fell back against him, quite exhausted.

De Bourne only smiled at her, then moved to find a cloth to dry her damp hands. 'Someone further removed from King Stephen could hardly be imagined, sweet. Your father's set down outside with a dozen of his men. I sent word to your mother when things looked bleak—she sent my lord Carilef to fetch you home. I wasn't having you moved to catch your death of cold on top of everything else. The lady Joan didn't think we could take enough care of you. Battle lines were drawn, and your father has spent three days outside the gates!'

'Oh, my lord...he's an old man...' Rosalind looked at the dark tidemarks of rain embroidering the cuffs of de Bourne's tunic. 'He shouldn't be out in this winter weather!'

'Your father spends his nights safe and warm enough.' De Bourne spread her blonde hair out across the pillows. 'He goes home late at night, then rides back at first light. I've told him that both he and your mother would be more than welcome to come in and see you, but he was acting on much higher authority. Your mother is going to prove a tough nut for me to crack, sweeting!'

'I'm sorry to have caused you yet more trouble, my lord...'

He waved aside her apology with a laugh. 'You've been not a bit of trouble since I met you, love. And I shall have to get used to your family and their little ways. If we're to be married eventually,' he finished quietly.

Rosalind blushed and tried to pull the bedclothes more decently around her. 'I thought that you wouldn't mention it again, my lord.'

'Don't you want me to, Rosalind?'

Memories of that moment—so long ago now, it seemed—came flooding back to her. 'I didn't offend you by seeming undecided, my lord? That wasn't my intention—I felt so ill, and so alone. I didn't know what I wanted.'

'But do you want me?' He could not contain the words, which burst out from his indecision.

Rosalind took his hand afresh, feeling its cool, firm grasp hold her safe. 'The truth is,' she began uncertainly, 'the truth is that I don't think I can live without you now, my lord.'

The words did not seem to register with him for a moment. Finally one hand went out and touched her hair, almost as though he thought she might disappear with the dream.

'I've never dared to kiss you properly yet, my love.'

Rosalind felt tired and unequal to any exertion. 'Would it be wise, even now, my lord? When we're alone in my chamber...what would people think?'

'"People" wouldn't know. What I do in the confines of my own home is nobody's business but my own.' This was the Black Wolf speaking. He leaned towards her, sliding his hands beneath her shoulders and raising her up towards him again. 'Resistance is useless now, my little beauty!'

His kiss was gentle and unthreatening. Rosalind sighed, relaxing against the strong hands that held her so carefully.

'Tired?' He smiled and laid her back down. 'You have a rest while I go out to your father. He'll want to hear all the news.'

'Mahel?'

His name sounded strange on her lips. Strange, but somehow comforting. He leaned over her and smiled.

'Yes, my love?' The dark eyes were soft and wondering.

Rosalind stretched out her hand and stroked the dry warmth of his tunic. 'You will—take care?'

'Close your eyes, and I shall be back before you realise I've gone.'

He gave her one last kiss, then waited until she did as she was told and closed her eyes. She was asleep again before he left the room.

Rosalind slept for most of the day. Whenever she opened her eyes either de Bourne, or the children, or more usually both, sat on the bed, stoked the fire or gave her boiled water to drink.

Evening came, and with it the lighting of more torches. A sickly orange glare filled the chamber, making the stuffy heat even more unbearable. Tired of sleep, Rosalind shielded her eyes from the light.

'When can I get up?'

De Bourne was at her side at once. 'Soon. I'm hoping there will be some visitors for you tomorrow. That should help pass the time.'

'Mother and Father are coming in? How on earth did you convince them it was safe?'

'I haven't, yet.' He grinned at her, sitting down to offer her yet more honey water. 'I'm sure they think I'm going to keep them hostage once they're here. As if I'd do a thing like that!'

'If the war depended on it, you might.' Rosalind asked for a comb, and Mahel lifted her into a sitting position so that she could tidy her hair. Her mind felt alert now, but her body was still half asleep. Everything ached, and after a few strokes her hand flopped down on to the coverlet. Without a word Mahel took the comb from her and started running it through her hair, so lightly that Rosalind could barely feel it.

'Shall I tell you how the war is going, or would you like it to come as a wonderful surprise when your parents get here?'

Rosalind bent her head forward for him to continue combing. 'It sounds as though things are going badly for the King.'

Raising his eyebrows quizzically at her words, de Bourne eased an elflock from Rosalind's hair with his fingers before replying.

'Once people heard that Fitzcount of Wallingford had declared for the Empress, the King's supporters have been tumbling like ninepins. When Miles of Gloucester came over to us that was really the last straw. Stephen's only got a few pockets of resistance anywhere in the West now. He's having to dash about like a headless chicken to try and rally support.'

'I suppose Mother and Father are still loyal?'

Sitting back to admire his handiwork, Mahel gave her back the comb. 'Your mother sounds as rock solid as ever. As for your father...' He spread her hair out across the white crispness of her nightgown, watching torchlight ripple over the golden waves like sunlight on the sea. 'I think he would be reasonable enough. Why fight when you can come to some peaceful arrangement? Actually, we've started to get on quite well,' he finished airily.

'Do you really think they'll come in and visit?'

'When your father left this afternoon he seemed *almost* convinced that it might be *nearly* safe.'

Crispin arrived with a dish of whipped egg-white for the patient. It was dull, tasteless stuff—nothing but bubbles. Rosalind would have objected had she not been too weak to resist de Bourne's cajoling.

She was just cleaning her teeth with a sage leaf when Crispin raced in to them with the children at his heels.

'The lady Joan is here, my lady. She wants to come in and see you!'

De Bourne stood up, pulling a face. 'After dark? It's a bit late for visiting. Have the lady brought in—gently, mind!—she can stay the night here, sweet, if that's all right with you.'

'Perhaps I'd better be the one to broach the subject, Mahel. Mother would start a riot if she had the slightest suspicion that you were trying to keep her here!'

With a laugh Rosalind sent Crispin away, but Adrian and Helias lingered at the doorway. They watched their father for any sign that he might evict them, but soon began inching nearer as they had done on that first night.

'Has Helias been ill, too?' Rosalind held out her hands to the boys but only the smaller one ran forward.

'A chill. Nothing more, because he had nothing to do but keep warm while we looked after him. You have had a lot of upset—that's what made your illness so much worse.' Scooping Adrian up in his arms, de Bourne blew into the small sullen face. Adrian did not feel like playing. He scowled at Rosalind, then buried his face in his father's neck.

Laughing broadly, de Bourne sat down on the bed again and swung his little son on to his lap. 'Mark well, rapscallion! Christmastime will soon be here, and little boys who sulk don't get any presents.'

Helias curled up beside Rosalind, working his feet in under the wolfskin coverlets. Thumb in mouth, he began polishing his nose furiously.

'Is it Advent yet, Auntie?' he whispered between sucks. Rosalind noticed that his eyes never left his father and Adrian.

'Not until next week.' She put her arm around his shoulders, gently taking his thumb from his mouth and holding his hand. 'Are you looking forward to Christmas, then?'

Helias ignored the question. He had one that was far more important. 'Will Daddy have to go 'venturing before next week?'

Advent marked the end of the campaigning season. If de Bourne managed to avoid a call to arms before Advent Sunday, he would be free to entertain his boys until after Epiphany. Helias was so apprehensive that Rosalind wondered how many times their father had been called off to foreign parts at the very last minute.

'This is your daddy's home now.' She squeezed Helias comfortingly and put her cheek to his shining black hair. 'If he does have to go away, then he knows that you're here to look after his house, and he'll come back as soon as he can——'

'The lady Joan Carilef,' Crispin announced breathlessly from the doorway. Rosalind's mother swept in, took one look at the scene and tucked her hands primly beneath her fur tippet.

'I'm Mahel.' De Bourne stood up, still holding Adrian and putting his other hand out towards Rosalind's mother. 'And these are my sons——'

'Indeed?' Madam Carilef said shortly, firing a barbed look at Rosalind. 'I'm sorry if I'm preventing them from being put to bed——'

There was no doubt about what the steel in her voice meant. Mahel gathered up Helias and started to make his escape. 'I'll do it. I'll do it right now.' Thrusting Crispin out of the room in front of them, de Bourne and his little family left while they were still able.

'Rosalind!' Joan Carilef took off her tippet, cloak and hood with sharp, angry movements. 'What on earth have you been getting up to? Poor Ascelin murdered, after he's endured nothing but agony over your shame, and with his castle overrun by rebels——'

'Mother, it's not like that at all. Ascelin had an accident—incidentally, while he was threatening to kill me. The lord de Bourne might be a little foreign for your tastes, but he's been nothing but a gentleman. As for the rebels...it's only a matter of time before Stephen has to hand his crown over to the Empress. He can't win, and she can't lose, Mother. Who will be the rebels when it finally happens?'

Placing her outdoor clothes on the linen chest, Joan rolled up her sleeves and advanced towards the bed. Ripping back the bedclothes, she threw them to the floor. Her next words were tinged with cold distaste.

'They say you're sleeping with him.'

Rosalind might have to suffer a blanket bath, but she wasn't going to take that untruth lying down.

'In this condition, Mother, sleeping is about all I'm fit for.'

'Don't be pert, miss!' Joan poured out a bowl of water from the jug at the hearth and sorted soap and towels from among Rosalind's belongings. Removing her daughter's nightgown, she started to scrub Rosalind vigorously. 'It isn't natural. He's a brigand—a—a foreigner! And what about his wife?'

Rosalind screwed up her eyes at the sting of soap and thought it wise not to go into the children's parentage just yet. 'She's dead, Mother.'

'Got rid of her, too, did he?' The flannel flicked over Rosalind's frail limbs with a brisk indignation.

'I'm not going to argue with you, Mother. There's no point. Mahel has been kind to me. He's looked after me when I had no one. You may not be able to like him, Mother, but it isn't fair that you should condemn him out of hand.'

Finishing the wash, Joan towelled her daughter dry with an action she usually reserved for donkey-stoning her castle hearth. When Rosalind was glowing with rough treatment her mother found a clean nightgown. As she shook out the folds a few dried flowerheads of fleabane fell to the floor. Joan took this as a Sign.

'Aha! And that's another thing. Bringing all their foreign pests over here...' Forgetting the nightgown, she knelt on the bed and started inspecting Rosalind's scalp inch by inch.

'Mother, do you mind? None of us has got anything like that——'

'And how would you know? You've been that close, have you?'

They were interrupted by a knock at the door-frame. Through the curtain, Crispin relayed the message that the lord de Bourne would be delighted to entertain Madam Carilef to supper in private. Joan pursed her lips in an expression of deep suspicion.

'He needn't think he's going to get around me that easily!' She bundled up the clean nightdress and pulled it over Rosalind's head.

'That would be lovely, Crispin,' Rosalind answered, despite her mother's horror. 'Tell my lord de Bourne that we would prefer that he took his supper in here with us, though.'

When Crispin's running footsteps had faded into the distance, Joan Carilef shook her head slowly in disbelief. 'I don't know what the world's coming to. In my day a widow would never have dared to speak to another man for six months, let alone entertain him in her chamber!' She remade the bed over Rosalind, turning each sheet and cover to present a cool face. 'Your staff downstairs really are a shambles, Rosalind. They said that there was no clean linen as they haven't been able to get it dry. The rain should be no excuse—my staff manage. Any wet washing should be hung up in the hall to dry in front of the fire——'

'I regret, lady, that the hall here is usually too full of soldiers.' De Bourne's soft country accent came from outside.

'Mahel—come in!'

Joan was just in time to pull the covers up to Rosalind's neck before he lifted the curtain door.

'I've brought you some of my linen, Madam Carilef. I have plenty to spare.'

Coming into the room, Mahel laid a neat pile of sheets on the end of Rosalind's bed. While Joan inspected it, surreptitiously feeling the quality, he was busy wrapping a wolfskin around Rosalind's shoulders. Lifting her out of bed, he carried her to a seat beside the fire. With the wall to support her, Rosalind could enjoy the sensation of watching others working.

'It's the scent of sandalwood. An Eastern spice,' Mahel said simply, catching Joan as she took a crafty sniff at the bed linen he had brought.

There was no doubt that in the Jacob's ladder of her estimation Mahel was some considerable distance beneath the lowest rung. Luckily, he was not so easily put off.

He smiled winningly. 'All the way from the exotic Orient.'

'That's a recommendation, is it? And I'm supposed to find you exotic, too, am I?' Joan said briskly, starting to strip the bed. To her surprise Mahel took the other side and started to help her.

'Not at all, lady. I'm a simple man, new to England it's true, but no less honest for all that. I'm tired of adventuring and ready to settle down.'

'Hmm.'

The sheets had been immaculately pressed and folded. Mahel's willingness and expertise at bedmaking was amazing, but still Joan Carilef was suspicious.

'That doesn't accord very well with the tales we've heard of you and your wickedness, sir.'

Mahel spread his hands wide and twinkled with amusement. 'All right—I confess. Your daughter has succeeded where all others have failed. She's drawn my fangs and filed my claws. How's that?'

Without taking her eyes off Mahel, Joan tucked in the final corner. 'Time will tell, no doubt.'

'No doubt at all.' Lifting Rosalind up to place her back in the bed, Mahel risked giving her a small kiss on the cheek. Rosalind blushed furiously, as did her mother, who was trying not to notice. Arranging the bedclothes around Rosalind to cheat any chill, he sat down on the bed, gesturing that Joan should do likewise. She did so, but on the opposite side to Mahel.

He took one of Rosalind's hands, studying the way its fine pale skin contrasted with the rich weathered tan of his own. Moving close in to Rosalind, he looked up at her mother and tried another winning smile.

'As I've already said, Madam Carilef—I'm a simple man, given to plain speaking. The fact is that I need a mother for my boys, a housekeeper for my castle and someone to look after me in my old age. Your daughter was handy. A bit of a spare part now that poor Ascelin's gone. It's either marry her, or find her a good home. I won't have any dead wood in my castle!'

Joan Carilef's eyes had opened wider and wider as Mahel spoke. She looked at Rosalind in total amazement, which was as nothing to the look that Rosalind was giving Mahel. He carefully avoided looking at either of them.

'Well!' Joan said after a very long time. 'Well! What sort of an animal are you, sir? I swear that the lowest beasts of the field conduct their affairs with more romance than you! How dare you attempt to use my daughter as a mere skivvy?'

'Why not?' Rosalind interrupted hotly. 'Ascelin did, and you gave me to him quite willingly!'

'Oh, Rosalind, really! That was quite different——'

'Ladies—please—it wasn't meant to be a serious suggestion...'

Rosalind and her mother stopped to find Mahel grinning at them.

'Sweet, do you think that your mother would believe how well we've behaved if I had told her the truth? If I had said I'd fallen hopelessly in love with you within hours of arriving? And Lady Carilef—should the time come that either I or my boys need someone to look after us, that's the time they can nail us down!' He squeezed Rosalind's hand, then tucked it beneath the cool, fresh sheets. 'I always try to treat your daughter as though she were made from the very finest spun silver.'

Joan was weakening visibly. Her own husband Herbert treated her as a force to be reckoned with. Every once in a while she felt the need to be treated like spun silver, but Herbert had had all the romance frightened out of him a long time ago.

'I don't know why you're telling me all this, sir.' She threw back her head and marshalled her dignity like a

posturing robin. 'It's my husband who properly deals
with such matters. You'll have to ask him.'

Mahel lowered his head, and Rosalind saw that he was
trying not to laugh. 'Very well, ma'am. Just as you say.
Will your husband be coming to collect you in the
morning, or should I escort you back to him myself?'

'Then…I am only a guest here?' Joan said cautiously.

'Of course! You could go home after supper, if you
wish, but with this rain——'

The rattle of supper approaching made him leap to
his feet and pull back the curtain door for Crispin. To
Rosalind's surprise the tray he carried in was laid with
proper plates, goblets, ewers, Damascene napkins and
small ivory-handled knives and spoons. Meeting a pro-
spective relative by marriage was not the time to be seen
hacking at chunks of meat balanced upon bread. Mahel
handed Joan one of the silvery-yellow plates, then served
her with a genteel amount of thinly sliced meat. In doing
so he seemed to gain the first rung of Jacob's long ladder.

Rosalind received a small portion of poached fish and
a goblet of warm milk. While toying with her own meal
she watched Mahel's immaculate manners as he ate his
meat with a delicacy only matched by her mother.

'Such a change to find someone with real table
manners, Rosalind. I've even got to watch your father
like a hawk. He's only too eager to mash his bread into
the gravy and sharpen his knife on the hearth.'

Mahel—who was no stranger to such barbaric practices when he thought Rosalind wasn't looking—shook
his head in shocked amazement at such awful back-
sliding. He was rising up the social ladder with every
moment. Rosalind cleared her throat meaningfully, and
a silent grin of understanding passed between them.

'What pretty tableware!' Her meal finished, Joan
flipped her cleaned plate over with practised casualness.
There was no maker's mark, only the initials MDB.

Rosalind saw Mahel spot another rung of the ladder within his reach. 'Oh, these old things...I had them made up in Jerusalem.'

'You've been to the Holy City?' Joan Carilef's voice was faint with wonder until she remembered herself. 'Although, I don't suppose that fair city would mean as much to you as it does to us, sir.'

'My father came from Rouen,' Mahel said, a tinge of impatience in his voice so slight that only Rosalind detected it. 'My mother, as you will have realised, did not. While it's true that she was only a convert to our faith, I'm as much a Christian as your good family, madam, and better than some.'

Joan bit her lip and nodded. 'A fair answer. It seems I may have come to a wrong conclusion there, sir.' That was as close as Joan ever came to an apology. Things were not going as badly as Rosalind had feared. In the relief she managed a few mouthfuls of fish. This did at least give Mahel and Joan something to comment on, for conversation had trickled to a halt.

'See that you take only white foods until you've got your strength back, Rosalind.' Her mother pushed the goblet of milk at her as an excuse to lean close and whisper. 'Have you told him about...?'

She left the awful truth unspoken. Rosalind put down her spoon and dabbed at her mouth with one of the Damascene napkins. When she spoke it was in a clear voice, but she did not look at either Mahel or her mother.

'Mahel knows that I haven't managed any children in two marriages, Mother. If he still wishes to marry me then I consider that shows what a gentleman he is.'

'Rubbish!' Mahel took up one of the ewers of wine and refilled Joan's goblet. 'Being a gentleman has nothing to do with it. I've got two fine sons already. I've no need of more—and every need of you, Rosalind.'

'Herbert...has often mourned his lack of a grandson,' Joan murmured nonchalantly. 'To inherit the family estate, reduced though it may be now.'

After the trouble with Ascelin, Rosalind wondered if this was a trick question. Fortunately Mahel was prepared.

'Ah, now that might be slightly more of a problem. One of my lads has his heart set on being a free lance, as I was once upon a time. The other thinks he might like the Church. As a matter of fact I was going to ask you, ma'am, if you thought that they might accept my Helias at school in Malmesbury.' He looked at her enquiringly, but Joan Carilef reached across and actually patted his arm.

'They seemed awfully small to have decided their careers yet, my lord. Let them find their feet here at home first before you send them away.' Joan folded her napkin neatly and placing it on the tray stood up. 'My husband Herbert loves children—he's still one himself at heart, I often think. Perhaps...your boys might like to ride over and visit us one day? Properly supervised and with your approval, of course, my lord.'

She picked up her outdoor clothes from on top of the linen chest, and started to pull on her cloak. Mahel had been so astonished by such a complete change of attitude that her cloak was in place before he had risen to stop her.

'Wouldn't you prefer to stay here this evening, my lady? I was rather looking forward to having your company with us tonight.'

'I'm sure you were.' Joan gave the smallest of smiles. 'There's no need to press the point, my lord. I've discovered all I need to know.'

'I would have helped you on with your cloak if I'd wanted you to go. Stay—Rosalind would be so grateful of your company.'

'A message would have to be sent to Herbert. He's sure to worry...'

'It'll be done straight away.' Mahel darted out of the room and called downstairs to Crispin. When he came back in all thoughts of romance had disappeared, and he was practical once more. 'Give them ten minutes to change the bedding and you can sleep in my room, madam. The boys and I can move downstairs——'

'Oh, pray don't put yourself to any trouble, my lord!' Joan said in a girlish giggle that Rosalind had never heard before. She noticed, too, that her mother did not protest too much and soon agreed to take Mahel's room.

'You could do a lot worse, Rosalind,' Joan confided as Mahel went off to arrange matters. 'I shall send for your father at first light. We'll see if we can't persuade young Mahel to stop all this nonsense about that awful German woman. Then he could turn into quite an acceptable suitor.'

'Mother, you can't expect Mahel to stop supporting the Empress! It's his job—it's what he's paid to do!'

'Paid?' The word echoed around the room like doom. 'He accepts money from that—that pretender?'

'The Empress Matilda's husband is Mahel's friend, Mother. They've worked together for years——'

'What's wrong with farming, like your father? A good home in return for supplying the King with soldiers, and all the produce we can take from the peasants!'

'I expect he'll come around to that in time. He's said that he wants to stop adventuring, Mother. And I believe him.'

'Ah, sweetbriar! You shouldn't set any great store by the promises of rascals! Isn't that true, Madam Carilef?'

To their great surprise Mahel strolled back into the room, but he was smiling. Uncertain of how much he had heard, both tried to think back over their words. Taking an armful of logs to the hearth, Mahel knelt down to stoke the fire.

'I know what you must be thinking, lady. To be honest with you, a few years ago and I would have been thinking much the same thing. Settling down was for other people then—not for me.' He settled an ash log into the brightest part of the fire, pausing to brush flakes of bark from his sleeves before rising. 'There comes a time when everyone must learn the error of their ways, settle down and conform. It may have come a little late in the day for me, but I want to make a new start.'

'We'll see,' Joan said sternly, still unwilling to give him too much encouragement. 'I'm not entirely convinced.'

Mahel was wise enough to give Joan Carilef plenty of time alone with her daughter. He and the boys moved downstairs to sleep with the soldiers, around the hearth.

Enforced idleness made sleep difficult for Rosalind. She was awake long before the sound of Mahel and a rattling breakfast tray came upstairs next morning. He passed her room and went in to Joan first. This gave Rosalind time to wake properly, sit up and comb her hair into some sort of order before he reached her.

'You're looking better already!' Placing the tray down on the linen chest, he went to the window. When the cloth covering was pinned back cold moonlight flooded into the room. 'A clear sky. It looks like a fine day in the offing. I don't know why everyone's so keen to lie in bed—I've been out as far as the western boundary already this morning!'

Rosalind watched him touch torches alight around the walls. 'Trouble? Oh, dear—and Helias was so hoping that you were home now until the new year——'

'An excess of energy, that's all.' Mahel brought the tray to the hearth. The embers were clear and clean, just right for making toast. Kneeling down, despite Rosalind's warning about the dusty floor, he set a pot containing a nugget of bacon fat on the fire. 'A few mild and wet days have had the late mushrooms popping up every-where. I thought you might like a taste.'

A small pile of strangely shaped fungi lurked on one corner of the tray. Their fragrance was redolent of woodland walks, but Rosalind was suspicious.

'Are they safe?'

'Good grief, child—haven't you ever tasted them?'

'William used to let me collect horse mushrooms sometimes, but that was all. I haven't been out any-where to find even them this year,' she finished sadly.

'When you're well, you can come out with me. Your people don't seem to use the woods much for food. There's forest food to find in most months of the year, if the weather's kind. I've been living off the land for years. I know where to look.'

Warmer now, Mahel took off his hat and cape, laying them on the bed.

'I've never noticed that feather in your cap before,' Rosalind said idly as he sliced mushrooms into the pan.

'It's a jay's feather. I picked it up yesterday,' he said casually, before turning to look at her a little uncom-fortably. 'It's exactly the same shade of blue as your eyes.'

'And how can you tell that, if you don't look me in the eyes to see?' she teased him gently.

'Rosalind?'

It sounded serious. A dozen thoughts flashed through Rosalind's mind. Mother's forbidden him to persist . . . I was dreaming, and it was all a mistake . . .

'Rosalind, I was wondering . . . I haven't said anything to the children yet in case they have to be disappointed, but I thought—now that the country around here is safe, perhaps we could take a trip into Malmesbury. Would you like that?'

When William had been alive, Rosalind had accom-panied her mother on an annual trip to Malmesbury. It had been a long time since she had made such a journey.

She stretched out her arms to Mahel and he hugged her joyfully.

'Oh—but it's such a long way... it must be at least twenty miles there and back again! I don't think I could face four hours of travelling in one day just yet——'

'I'm not asking you to. We'll have a nice easy journey there, find somewhere to stay and spend a while there. By the time you're ready to travel the war will have ceased for Advent. In any case, Malmesbury's solidly behind the Empress. It's owned by the Bishop of Salisbury, and he's nobody's fool. We'd be safe there, whatever happened.'

The faintest disquiet stirred within Rosalind. 'Will the boys be coming?'

'I'd like them to—but only if you have no objections.' He held her close, and Rosalind knew that whatever part of him was reserved for his boys, there was plenty of love still for her. 'I had a mind to let Helias spend some time with the monks there, to see how he likes school. If he does like it, I might give him to the Church as an oblate next year, in return for meeting you.'

'And Adrian?'

Mahel kissed her lightly before returning to the sizzling mushrooms.

'I thought the men would see him as a weakness in me,' he said with difficulty, looking away as he set up a slice of bread to toast on the end of his knife. 'It hasn't been like that. They ask me about him. They tell me about their own children, back at home. I never thought they'd realise how hard it is to manage work and a family at the same time. Would you mind if he came too? I'd make sure that the escort looked after him—that we weren't bothered——'

'He's jealous because you're the only thing in his life at the moment, Mahel.' Rosalind stroked his back as he mixed flour and milk into the cooked mushrooms, and turned the toast. 'When he sees that you can be shared

between all of us—him, Helias, your soldiers and me—
he'll improve. If Mother really does agree to entertain
the boys now and again, that will give him something
to think about too.'

Mahel sat back on his heels and sighed. 'Your mother!
I'd almost forgotten—I'm riding back with her this
morning to ask your father's permission for us to
marry...'

'Do you think he won't agree?' Rosalind said as Mahel
piled creamed mushrooms on to the toast for her.

'Oh, no. He already has!' A sudden smile brightened
his face into its usual merriment. 'You don't remember,
my love, do you? There was a time when you were so
very sick that we thought every moment was your last.
I was beside myself. I said a lot of things that were better
left unspoken. It seemed so cruel that we would be denied
the chance to be together...they couldn't take me from
your side. Father Anthony persuaded your father that
even if you could not be saved, some sort of ceremony
might at least save my sanity.'

Rosalind looked down at her hand. For the first time
she realised that William's plain band, used again by the
economical Ascelin, had been exchanged for a ring of
less polished craftsmanship.

'Then you—and I...'

'Not exactly.' He smiled a little shyly. 'It could hardly
be much of a legal wedding with the bride too sick to
make any responses! It was only for my benefit. Anthony
was being kind. He stayed here beside the fire while I
held you in my arms all that night. I was determined to
stay awake—afraid to sleep in case you left me before I
could say goodbye...I remember hearing the first
cockerel crowing, and then the next thing was your hand
on my hair...it was then that I knew you were going to
be all right.'

The confession had taken a lot of courage from one
who liked to seem so detached and carefree. Breakfast

forgotten, Rosalind took his hands and brought him to sit close beside her.

'You needn't worry that I'll ever leave you,' she said simply. 'Whatever Father says in the cold light of day.'

'Oh, it's not that!' With a laugh Mahel slipped his arms around her to keep her warm. 'I'm just worried about what your mother will say if your father lets anything slip!'

CHAPTER TEN

MAHEL came back from the Carilefs' full of delighted good humour. He and Rosalind's father had spent a pleasant hour alone with a good fire and a bottle of wine while Joan fretted in her chamber.

'Your mother was actually worried! She thought that your father might have sprung an objection at the last minute!'

He sat on the edge of Rosalind's bed, warming his hands at the fire. Joan had sent over a wealth of provisions and gifts. While Rosalind sorted through the boxes of dried plums, pickled walnuts and other delicacies Mahel was on hand to sample the things that Rosalind didn't fancy.

'Did Mother find out about this?' Rosalind held out her ring finger with its hastily forged gold band. With a whistle of horror Mahel shook his head.

'Certainly not! That's strictly between us, the priest and your father.' Obediently he stroked the roll of white erminette that Rosalind held out for his inspection. 'Not as soft as this.' He touched her cheek with one finger.

Rosalind rested her head against his hand, feeling his fingers move to her hair. His gentle reticence was such a change, so restful. She sighed almost sleepily, then remembered that there was still work to be done.

'What did Mother send this over for? I'm not to be coated with goose grease and stitched into it for the rest of the winter, am I?'

Mahel laughed and took the bundle of erminette from her. 'Nearly. Your good mother says that a winter wedding shouldn't be all rain capes and pattens. There ought to be a bit of luxury about it.' He was watching her carefully, his eyes even more dark and mysterious than usual. At last he risked coming to the point. 'Would you like to set a date, Rosalind? Heaven knows I've got no great grief for Ascelin, but if you'd rather wait...'

He was uncertain, and irritated by the unusual sensation that it brought. Rosalind knew then that she loved him for all the right reasons. Smiling, she shook her head.

'Let's get married as soon as possible.'

He took her hands with a laugh. 'Today?'

'Mahel! With me looking like this and nothing for either of us to wear? Weddings take preparation, you know!'

'Not if it's to be quiet and private. I haven't told the men. They don't suspect a thing...' he finished uncomfortably.

'I wouldn't be too sure about that.' Rosalind drew up her knees and smiled at him happily. 'It will soon be Advent. I'll be up and about by then, and you can take me on this fabled trip to Malmesbury. We'll have a holiday, Helias can try school, Adrian can play soldiers, and you'll have the chance to get a few things for the wedding. It's a pity I haven't got any money. I could buy the town up and make this the wedding of the century.'

Mahel raised his eyebrows and gave a secret smile. 'That's your wishful fantasy, is it, my sweet? We'll have to see what we can do about that.'

Three days later a small party assembled in the castle yard. The day was as cold and clear as late November could be, the sun low in a brittle blue sky. Adrian and Helias sat in a small ox cart, muffled up in plenty of warm clothing. Rosalind sat beside the driver, swathed in layers of fur and fine wool. With her hood pulled up and hands burrowed beneath her fur tippet she found the cold invigorating, and felt better every minute.

With the exception of the ill-fated stay at her parents', this would be her first trip out of the castle confines since she had married Ascelin. She felt as excited as a child at the prospect.

Four of Mahel's soldiers positioned their horses around the cart, while the Black Wolf himself moved up to ride as close to Rosalind as he dared in front of his men.

The air was clean and crisp as they started out of the castle yard. Ice glittered in every frozen rut and puddle along the way, crackling beneath the print of hoofs.

For most of the way Mahel rode alongside his men. While they laughed and joked together, Rosalind and the children travelled behind in the cart.

'Everybody knows, Mahel.' Rosalind smiled as he dropped back to her side for the hundredth time. 'I don't know why you're still trying to keep it a secret!'

He pulled off one gauntlet, leaned across and reached beneath the coney-skin tippet to find her hand.

'Rubbish. I've told you before—they don't suspect a thing. I have to make sure that our patient isn't getting cold, don't I?'

Rosalind took his hand and held it in both of hers. The feel of her silken skin beneath his workmanlike fingers made him laugh self-consciously.

'That paw's been more used to rough work than a gentle lady's favour these past few years!'

'I don't mind.' Rosalind held on tightly until a restless movement in the cart behind her brought a more long-suffering smile to her lips. 'Although I think someone else needs it more than I do, right this minute.'

Mahel looked puzzled for a moment, then realised.

'That's why I came back,' he said in a voice loud enough to be heard by his men. 'It's time you got used to riding up with us, son.'

To Adrian's delight he was swung over on to the saddle in front of his father. He squealed with excitement as Mahel squeezed into a canter and rocked him up to the front of the line.

The journey passed uneventfully. Rosalind was relieved that they met no other travellers on the road. It was as Mahel had said—everyone was so afraid of meeting trouble, even in Advent, that no one ventured out at all.

Trees were scanty on the chill uplands. Beech trees thrust bony roots into the thin soil, huddling together for protection. It was in the lee of one of these spinneys that they stopped for dinner. The grassland undulated to form a dry, sheltered hollow which trapped the weak winter sun.

Adrian looked glad to be lifted down from his perch, although he would not admit it. As he clambered up to eat his bread and cheese with Helias in the cart, Rosalind noticed that he sat down very carefully.

'He'll be all right, once I've found him a suitable little pony.' Mahel smiled as Rosalind started her dinner. Suddenly a call from Helias alerted him.

'Puss, Daddy?' The child was pointing across the expanse of frost-bare downland. Rosalind could see nothing.

'Well done, my lad. Going to come and help me catch her?'

Rosalind could still see no sign of any hare. As the children scrambled down Mahel searched under the seat of the cart. He pulled out a sling and several large, smooth stones. In answer to her curious frown he pointed out one particular tuft of grass. In a sea of white it was free of frost. A warm body had sheltered there overnight and might still be lying up.

Stealthily Mahel crept towards the tuft, keeping the boys behind him. They were out of the line of shot and would stop the hare breaking back towards the cart.

The hare sensed that something was wrong, and raised itself on its haunches. It suffered for its curiosity. An expertly aimed stone catapulted it into the air, and it fell dead. In that instant a second hare broke cover, only yards from the first. The twins started to give chase, and, startled even more, the hare swerved. Its blind panic sent it headlong into the group of soldiers, who weren't about to let a tasty meal escape. A couple of fine sandy hares were laid in the cart, where the boys spent the rest of the journey stroking the soft fur and wiggling the long ears at each other.

Afternoon shadows were lengthening as the small party rounded the last bend of their journey. A shock was in store for Rosalind. Instead of the tree-girdled hummock packed with houses that she remembered, the settlement of Malmesbury had been razed to the ground. The trees had been torn down or burned where they stood. Nothing was visible of the little village but smouldering ruins and the square solidity of the half-finished abbey.

Only the river seemed the same. It snaked slowly through water meadows hemming the village, circling the hillock where Malmesbury had once stood.

'I doubt that it's as bad as it looks,' Mahel said at Rosalind's anguished disappointment. 'Stephen and his men made a bit of a splash here as a last gesture, that's all. Peasant houses collapse if there's as much as a strong breeze. They're as easily repaired. Anything more substantial will probably be all right. See—what about that building we're approaching now? That looks untouched, even though it's outside the village defences.'

A sturdy single-storey building had been planted squarely beside the track. Its fresh lime wash rivalled the frost for whiteness, and the reed-thatched roof looked thick and weatherproof.

The party drew nearer. Now they could see a large board leaning against the wall of the building. In three badly spelled languages—English, German and the Angevin dialect—it announced proudly: 'No decent guest ever refused!', 'All welcome!' And 'Business as usual— We never close!'

'That's what has saved them.' De Bourne smiled as the cavalcade drew to a halt. 'A classic case of adapt and survive.'

He had insisted that, for safety, his soldiers would bear no identifying mark for the journey. Three of them were sent in to find out tactfully who was in charge of Malmesbury, and whether it would be safe for the party to stay.

The oxen eased forward to take a drink from the river. Beside the stone-kerbed path the water was crazed with ice, and one of the soldiers had to jump down to break a hole for them.

Mahel edged his horse closer to the cart. In the quiet of that winter afternoon the small noises of harness and metalwork rang out clearly. With his men preoccupied, the Black Wolf risked putting out a hand to Rosalind, tucking the sheepskins closer about her and pulling her hood further over her hair.

'You look tired, my love. You should have said if the journey was too hard for you. We could have rested more often.'

Rosalind smiled wearily. Behind them the sun was an orange ball, caught in winter-black twigs scribbled against an ice-blue sky. 'I didn't want to hold you all up. It's late enough already. We would never have reached here before nightfall if I'd asked for a rest.'

'Then it's straight to bed the moment we get in. Bother any thoughts of an Advent fast. You can eat a good hot supper there, in luxury.'

He started off to meet his returning trio of soldiers. Rosalind felt the first cold touch of anxiety. Mahel had been first her protector, then her friend. At no time since their first few confrontations had he ever attempted to compromise her. Now the time had come. He even spoke quite shamelessly of going to bed.

Their friendship was beginning its descent into indignity and discomfort. Rosalind closed her eyes, remembering silent shared embarrassments with William and Ascelin's crude, sudden violations.

'Plenty of room at the inn,' Mahel's voice was whispering close to her ear. 'Not long now.'

He was smiling. Glad that he had interrupted the bad memories but grieved to think of his friendship slipping away, Rosalind could not speak.

Mahel sent the soldiers off to stable their horses and set Adrian to waking his brother. Jumping down from his horse, he handed it into the care of his men then held up his arms to Rosalind.

'I'll carry you. No arguments.'

She was swept into his arms and enveloped within the folds of his cloak. With the children at his heels he strode into the dark recesses of the inn.

The innkeeper was as large and ill-humoured as his wife was small and merry. He dealt with business. With an understanding smile at Rosalind, his wife took the children off to the kitchen for milk and apple cake.

'I'll have rooms for my dear lady, my sons, my men, and last but by no means least—myself,' Mahel stated brightly.

Leaning on the grease-rimed table, the inkeeper put slate and pencil at the ready. 'Fivepence a night for the usual, tenpence with bed and cooking. Towels and linen extra.' Licking the slate pencil, he looked up. His gaze took in Mahel's appearance, then slithered over Rosalind. Eyes red and watery with years of drinking beside an open fire, he blinked several times at the scene, waiting for a complaint at the price. None came.

'Name?' he snapped.

Mahel leaned forward and grinned. 'Think I'd take a chance like that? You might have some of the enemy staying here.'

'And who's to say who's the enemy *this* week? Everyone's the enemy when it comes down to me losing trade. I don't stand for any politicking under my roof.' The innkeeper scratched himself irritably. 'Name?'

'You can call me "sir".' Mahel tossed a handful of silver with his words, which smoothed the innkeeper's wrinkled brow. 'The lads will have the basic, but only the best for my family.'

He kissed Rosalind's cheek lightly. Only once before
had she felt such foreboding at his touch—when he had
been under threat of mortal danger from the lord Miles.
Rosalind wondered if Mahel realised that she was as
apprehensive now as she had been then.

Now that he actually had a hold on Rosalind, Mahel
was not willing to give it up. He would not let her walk,
but carried her all the way to their chambers.

She was set down in a seat beside the hearth. An ash
log fire glittered with welcome warmth. While Mahel
went to see about having the hares cooked for supper,
Rosalind watched the innkeeper's wife making up a bed.
Mahel had been wise enough to avoid extra charges. He
had brought his own linen and towels, and Rosalind
wondered again at their quality and luxury. She would
be sharing in that now.

She did not feel strong enough yet to climb in and out
of a bathtub. Instead the innkeeper's wife put up a screen
beside the fire and brought her a bowl of hot water. A
good wash made her feel better in body, if not in spirit.
She dressed in a crisp white modesty gown, one of the
little decencies that Ascelin had always denied her. Her
life with Mahel could at least start out with good
intentions.

Brushing her hair the required one hundred strokes
made Rosalind realise how weak she still was. It was a
relief to crawl into the bed with its crackling clean sheets
and plump pillows. Despite her intention to lie awake
and worry, she fell asleep almost immediately.

A slight noise and gentle movements woke her. Mahel
was spreading his pelisse over her for extra warmth. The
fur smelled sweet with his fragrance, and a little gasp
escaped Rosalind in her surprise.

'Ssh. The boys are asleep.' He pointed to a cot that
had been set up beside the bed.

'I never heard a thing...'

She saw his smile flash in the firelight. 'We ate ou supper at the fire, too. You've been fast asleep all th time, sweet. I was about to turn in myself, but if yo feel wicked enough to break your fast with a little of th hare then I'll keep you company.'

A bowl of dark stew had been keeping warm on th hearth. He fetched it and rearranged the pelisse abou her as she sat up to eat.

They shared the same bowl. Like true lovers, Rosalin thought, although that was still to come. Mahel coaxe her to eat and her appetite soon returned. When he pu aside the empty bowl and stood up she was surprised t see him adjust his belt and gown as though to leave.

'Call if you need me.' He kissed her brow with th same chaste restraint as before. 'My room is only th other side of the curtain——'

'Mahel?'

Rosalind was confused, uncertain about what wa required of her. He sat down again on the edge of th bed and took hold of her hand.

'Don't frown, my love! What is it?' The soft dar smile worked its magic once more. Rosalind felt strange comforted, and able to put her thoughts into some so of order.

'I thought—I thought that you would want to stay. .

In the shadowy light his expression looked almo wistful. 'Rosalind—it's Advent now, my love . . . we' not allowed to . . .'

Rosalind was thrown into confusion. She saw that sh had managed to surprise him, suggesting such a thin when it had clearly been the last thing on his mind.

'I—I'm sorry, Mahel.' Details were too tasteless revive, but Rosalind felt she had to explain to excu herself. 'It's just that—well, other people weren't qui as obedient to the Church——'

He silenced her words with a kiss. Full on the lips th time, but no less gentle and restrained.

'I thought you would rather wait until after we were married, my love,' he said softly. 'That's why I never started anything before. In case you felt...cornered into something you weren't ready for. I don't want it to be like that with us.'

This time it was Rosalind who started the kiss. He would teach her true longing over the long weeks until their wedding, but for now it was a kiss of gentle gratitude.

Mahel returned it tenderly, drawing her into his arms and holding her close. 'This is how it will be,' he breathed, laying her down into the cloud of pillows. 'Gentle friendship. Everyone already knows how tough and formidable I am. When it comes to *our* life together, Rosalind, I've got nothing to prove. Unless it's how well I can treat my lady.'

Pulling the pelisse and bedcovers up to cocoon her in warmth, he brushed one last kiss against her hair before standing up to leave.

'Sleep well, my love.'

'Good night, Mahel.'

He moved silently towards the curtain door separating their two rooms. Rosalind could not resist one last whisper.

'And thank you. For being so kind...'

He paused, but the shadows were too secretive to show his expression. Rosalind saw only the gesture as he blew her a kiss across the darkened room.

Rosalind opened her eyes to bright sunlight. It streamed through a small grille near the ceiling of her chamber, cold and clear. There were sounds of activity in the street outside, too. It must be very late indeed.

She sat up to find that the boys were missing. Muffled whispers and faint splashes from Mahel's room solved that puzzle. As she threw back the bedclothes, raw cold ran over her, and she was glad to pull the pelisse about her shoulders for warmth.

'Mahel?'

After a little rustling and more whispers he appeared in the doorway with Helias. The child grinned up at her before scampering off to stoke the slumbering fire.

'Whatever time is it?'

Mahel looked at the flickering candle clock, then at the sun glittering through the small window above his bed.

'About ten o'clock,' he said casually. Rosalind was horrified.

'Ten o'clock? Oh, no!' She dashed to the chest where her clothes had been laid, gathering armfuls up in frantic haste. Mahel was delighted.

'What's the hurry? There's no fowls to feed or dairying to do here! You're on holiday—enjoy it!'

'Still in bed at ten o'clock? It's so wicked...slothful... What will people say?'

'*I* say you'll get back into bed and wait for breakfast to arrive. And nobody disobeys my orders.' He tweaked her nose playfully, then sent Helias off to ask for breakfast to be served. 'As a very great treat, I've decided to let Adrian spend the day with the soldiers.'

There was a shriek of joy and Adrian burst out of the room and hurled himself at his father.

'I don't know what I shall do with myself all day without my little shadows,' Mahel said airily, tousling his son. 'Helias will be spending the day at the abbey, so I'll be all on my own.'

Adrian stopped jumping up and down. For a moment he looked exactly like Helias as a worried frown followed dismay across his small face. After a lot of thought he bit his lip, then looked up at his father.

'Auntie could keep you company,' he said slowly. 'I suppose.'

Mahel knelt down and put his arm around Adrian's waist.

'Would you like that?'

This took a lot more thought, then finally Adrian shook his head. 'No, Daddy...but if it means you won't be lonely without us...and you'll still love us best...'

It was time for Mahel to put on a guarded expression. 'You're my boys,' he said carefully. 'Nothing changes that. Not even when you're grown up and sleeping in your own bedroom, like a proper little soldier——'

'I'm grown up now, Daddy!' Adrian pulled himself up as tall as he could and stuck out his chest. 'I'll be a soldier soon!'

Mahel gave a look full of laughter to Rosalind, then shook his head gravely at Adrian. '*I* know that, but my soldiers might not think so if they heard that you still sleep with your daddy. I should keep that a secret from them if I were you, son. You know what they're like——'

Adrian was jumping up and down again, but this time in desperation. 'Can I have my own room, Daddy? You've got a house now, and you said that when we lived in a proper house we could have our own room. All to ourselves——'

'I'll think about it,' Mahel said cautiously.

'Daddy, you promised...'

Adrian's whine was cut short when Helias and the innkeeper's wife arrived with breakfast. Nothing—not even tantrums—came between Adrian and his food. He darted across the room, eager to begin prayers and then the serious matter of eating.

'Mahel! That was nothing short of trickery!'

Rosalind went to his outstretched arms and he laughed in delight.

'It's better known as tact and diplomacy, sweet! A trick I've learned that works well on your mother, too. I've just managed to kill two birds with one stone, that's all. Reassuring Adrian on the one hand, while giving us the chance of some quiet times together on the other.'

He hugged her deep into the wine-red folds of his tunic. The dark gold lustre of his skin and warm aura of his closeness brought Rosalind thoughts of the previous evening. Shameful thoughts, that made her want to snuggle closer while all the time decency and common sense forced her away.

'My lord! Not in public, and with me not even decently dressed!'

'You look fine to me. We're not in public, anyway.' He winked at the innkeeper's wife as she fed the fire. Laughing indulgently, the woman withdrew, much to Rosalind's horror.

'Oh, Mahel—what will she think?'

'That I'm a decent sort of chap who doesn't want his good morning kiss watched by strangers.'

He spoke in a cheerful whisper, drawing closer every moment. Rosalind could fight her instincts no longer. She dissolved in his embrace, eager for his kisses.

'No more...no more...' he breathed in her ear after a long and lingering moment. 'Or I shall never be safe without my two little chaperons today. We've got a lot to do, my little rosebud. After your shameful lie-in this morning we'll be all behind!'

He teased her unmercifully about it over breakfast. When they were finished and all ready to go, Adrian plunged into the friendly throng of soldiers without a backward glance. Helias was a little more subdued.

'There'll be lots to do,' Rosalind reassured him as they climbed into the cart. 'And plenty of new friends. When we come and fetch you, you'll have so much to tell your father that Adrian won't be able to get a word in edgeways.'

'Will you stay with me, Auntie?' Helias slipped his hand into hers. It was cold, and felt very small. Rosalind pulled him on to her lap and covered them both in sheepskin and furs.

'I wish I could, sweetheart, but I've got lots of boring shopping to do. You can tell me all about it later.'

Mahel looked a little doubtful, too, but said nothing as he drove the ox cart up the short steep hill into Malmesbury proper.

Like their host the innkeeper, Malmesbury seemed determined that business should go on as usual. There was barely a building left standing, but awnings had been hastily tied up between the ruins. Amid a criss-cross of guy ropes provisions, dry goods, materials and all manner of other wonders were laid out on the winter-cold cobbles.

The thought of being out and about with the chance of seeing money spent cheered Rosalind considerably. She began to feel better, despite the icy wind that cut through the village like a knife. Even Mahel's slide into apparent ill humour could not distract her.

Malmesbury Abbey was a noisy building site of men and machines. Pack ponies sagged patiently under loads of skinned poles while more scaffolding slowly took shape. Heaps of roughly dressed stone lay all about as though a giant's child had forsaken its building bricks. A winch whined, hurrying on the little donkey that powered its treadmill. Small as insects, men scrambled about the foothills of the mighty building work, scrambling up ladders or inching along crawling boards.

To one side of this sea of construction stood the current abbey buildings. Neatly painted wooden sheds were shuttered tightly against the noise and the cold.

'Go on, then,' Mahel said a little sharply. 'Take him in. And don't be long.'

He was looking down at the handbrake, fiddling with it irritably.

'I think you had better go with him, my lord.' Rosalind tried to tone down her concern with good manners. 'The monks might not appreciate my presence. And besides, clambering across to them looks a little beyond me at the moment.' Rosalind, too, could win by tact and diplomacy. She played her final card by rubbing her chest, apparently without thinking.

At once Mahel sprang down from the cart and strode around the oxen to lift Helias down from her lap. Without speaking he took the little boy's hand and they set off for the nearest wooden building. Helias had to trot to keep up, jumping over discarded shuttering and icy craters on the way.

They disappeared into the hut. Nothing further happened for a long time. For once Rosalind was glad of the layers of blankets and furs that Mahel insisted on heaping upon her. Her wait in the cart was reasonably comfortable. All the villagers that passed her had blue fingers and faces pinched up with cold.

At last the hut door opened and Mahel appeared. He did not start for the cart immediately, but stayed talking to a black-robed monk on the threshold. The monk retreated behind a door that squeezed closer and closer to being shut, but Mahel still remained. Only when the door was finally closed did he start back to Rosalind.

There were many backward glances on the way. When he climbed back into the cart Rosalind took care to leave a little interval before she spoke.

'Did Helias settle in all right?'

'Never even waved when I left.' Mahel snapped the handbrake off and urged the oxen into a fast amble. 'Oh, but I can't spend time thinking about that now. I need a drink.'

Rosalind recognised his tone. She kept quiet while they found a place in a warm corner of a nearby hostelry. After taking a long draught of hot ale, Mahel frowned and stroked his chin thoughtfully.

'I shouldn't have left him.'

'He'll be fine. Stop worrying!' Rosalind nudged him playfully.

'Four years, six months and two weeks—I've been the only one he's known...'

'He's known Adrian. And Count Geoffrey, with all the "aunties". Then there's that little thing called work, which must have taken you away for a lot of the time——'

'He's in there now, all on his own, not knowing anybody...'

Rosalind slipped her hand into the crook of Mahel's arm as he leaned forward for another drink. She knew what was really going through his mind. 'You're his father. He won't forget you, my love!'

'It certainly looked like it, the way he went off with a perfect stranger.' Mahel scowled into the remains of his ale. 'He's too small—I can't abandon him to that sort of life. What if he changes his mind, and he's too frightened to tell me? I for one couldn't take to the life— all that strict fasting, services a dozen times a day... And what about girls? When he's older——'

Rosalind sighed heavily. 'For heaven's sake, Mahel— he's only spending a day at baby school, not taking on the archbishopric of Canterbury.'

A rueful grin turned into laughter as Mahel realised how ridiculous his worries were. He pulled away from her in mock horror.

'You're the first that's ever spoke sharply to me and survived, madam! I hope this doesn't mean you're going to turn into a scold when we're married?'

'I shall, if you're going to come out with such addle-pated twaddle.' She took a sip of ale and smiled to herself at his silence. 'This day is going to pass awfully slowly, Mahel, if all you're going to do is fret. I thought the main reason for our visit here was the chance to do some shopping.'

After a pause he exhaled long and hard. 'You're right, my love. We must talk about money. How much will you want?'

'I'm to have money of my own?' She was incredulous.

'Of course. I can't expect you to work for nothing, can I?'

This was a staggering turn of events. William had used to give her a small sum on the rare occasions she travelled to town with her mother, but apart from that Rosalind had never held her own money.

'The—the amount required depends on what you wish me to pay for... We're careful about the castle—not much more than five pounds a year would cover the cost of things that need to be bought in. If you wanted it to cover staff as well——'

'Rosalind!' He put down his mug and laughed at her openly. 'It's money for *you* we're talking about. Spend it on caged birds, siege engines or bright blue bangles— whatever you like! How much, then? Would three shillings a week sound fair to you?'

She had to think for a moment how best to invest such a vast sum. Mahel took her silence for dismay and immediately offered a further shilling.

'No—stop! Three shillings will be enough to begin with. Until I get used to it,' she added with a grin.

'And how much will cover your Christmas shopping? Five pounds?'

'I don't know what sort of girls you've been used to, Mahel, but it's a good job I'm honest!' Rosalind finished her ale and stood up. 'If you're so keen to spend money we'll go out right now and see how much we can force upon the poor villagers of Malmesbury.'

Taking his hand she tugged him from the hearth and out into the cold, merry, Christmassy, noisy throng of the village.

After a slow start, Rosalind soon found a taste for spending money. Presents for Mahel and the children, exotic dried fruits, spiced wines and herb honey for the Christmas feasts, flower-scented candles and more dried lavender for the hall soon started to fill the cart. There was a new beeswax mixture on sale, guaranteed to bring a shine to oak furniture, and soap with extra lanolin for when the polishing was finished. Sinful extravagances, when the store at home was full of soap and polish, but Rosalind was beginning to enjoy herself.

One stall sold small conceits made from flour and water paste baked hard, painted, then varnished to a sheen. Rosalind bought two dozen, much to Mahel's amazement.

'What on earth are they for?' He picked up one made in the shape of a star and tested it with his teeth.

'You hang them in the Christmas swags and garlands. They're the very latest thing. Mahel, stop biting it! They're not edible!'

'They might have to be, when you've spent all my money!'

He tried to glare at her, but could not continue the pretence. Laughing, he loaded the parcel of paste shapes into the cart.

'Don't forget yourself, Rosalind. I'd hate people to think that I deny my new wife a rag to her back. Even if she spends so much that rags are all I have to wear myself!'

'If you amuse yourself for an hour while I enter into delicate negotiations with the mercer, I'll see what I can do. You could always spend the time in buying yourself a wedding outfit, Mahel!' she added archly.

'I would, if I was likely to have any money left.' He grabbed her quickly, swinging her into the shadows of the market cross for a kiss. Passers-by laughed in appreciation, especially when Rosalind emerged hot, pink and giggling with embarrassment.

'My lord, really! Kissing in the street—whatever next?'

He did not answer immediately, but pulled her back into his arms for another embrace.

'I'll meet you back here at midday.'

Rosalind closed her eyes as he placed another kiss on her brow. 'Don't go looking for any trouble, Mahel.'

'As if I would!' With an impish grin he let her go and set off down the street. More than once he looked back and waved to where Rosalind was watching him.

When Mahel had disappeared into the busy hubbub of the market street Rosalind turned her attention to the stalls of drapers and furriers, haberdashers, hosiers and glovers. There may be a lot still to learn about her fiancé, but Rosalind knew the pride he took in his appearance. New clothing would make excellent gifts.

As a wedding present she bought him a small chess set made of carved fruitwoods. For Christmas presents she purchased a lambswool jerkin, a dozen pairs of leggings in pale shades quite unsuitable for work and assorted garters to adjust their fit, together with fabric in winter tunic lengths for both Mahel and the children. With more than three weeks still to go before the wedding Rosalind purchased an extra length of grey velvet in case Mahel did not get around to buying something to get married in.

Her own wedding clothes took longer to choose. The sun was nearly overhead before the last thread and brooch was accounted for. Mahel had already drawn the cart up at the market cross when she reached it. A small army of apprentice boys trailed along behind her, bearing armfuls of anonymously wrapped bundles and packages.

'I knew it.' He grinned, bending to kiss her in greeting. 'I shall be ruined!'

'It's Christmas, Mahel. Once a year. You offered me five pounds for my shopping, and I can give you nearly three pounds of that back in change—so there!'

'I'm impressed.' He lifted her into the cart then organised the packing of her purchases. Handing a few coins to the apprentices, he climbed up beside her and turned the oxen towards the lodgings. 'I was wondering if I ought to go and see how Helias is getting on——'

'Mahel!'

His dark eyes twinkled at the warning note in her voice. 'Ah, let me finish! Then I thought—no, my lady won't like that. I'll take dinner with her, instead. Purely to take my mind off the dreadful torture my son is having to endure, of course!'

'He'll be having a lovely time, my lord. You'll see— he won't want to leave.'

Mahel put one hand to the brake as they started the steep, slippery descent to the inn. 'That's what I'm afraid of, if the truth were known.'

Putting her hand over his, Rosalind moved closer. That he had made such a difficult admission to her made Rosalind love him all the more.

With their load inching slowly down towards the front of the cart, they reached level ground. Riverside alders still clutched ice between their twisted roots. Overhead, jackdaws tumbled and laughed at kites sailing around the village in search of scraps. Well away from village smells and racket, the inn looked a secure haven. Sheltered by a hazel brake, it sat solidly at the edge of the watermeadows, protected from floods by a slight rise in the ground. Rosalind sighed, knowing for the first time in ages what it was like to look forward to restful days and untroubled nights.

'Tired, my love?' Mahel murmured as he lifted her from the cart.

'A little.' She accepted his arm. One of their soldiers appeared and took charge of the cart and purchases.

'After dinner you can have another rest before the boys come back to us.'

'Mahel, I'll rot in bed!'

'You're still getting your strength back, sweet. I want you hale and hearty by Christmas. There's a lot of serious celebrating to be done this year!'

Rosalind smiled, determined that she would not give in to the weariness she felt. It was no use. Once she had eaten her fill of soup, fresh bread and toasted cheese beside a roaring log fire, sleep felt like a very good idea indeed.

'Rosalind,' Mahel said quietly as she stood up. 'Before you go...'

He produced a sprig of mistletoe and claimed a slow, teasing kiss. Breaking away at last, he laughed.

'The pagans call it a fertility rite!'

'Then it will be of no use to me.'

'Oh, my love...' Instantly he threw the mistletoe into the fire and caught her up in his arms. 'I'm so sorry—I didn't think...'

'Don't worry.' Rosalind stroked his hair, feeling the thick luxuriance that he had passed on to his sons. 'I'm used to it. My only concern is that *you* won't be...that after the first few weeks or months you'll want the one thing that I can't give you——'

'I've got your love.' He sat down at the fireside, drawing her into his lap. 'That's all I want. I've already got two fine boys—I don't want any more. They're all the family we need, Rosalind. And between you and me, though I'd never be without them now, I'm too old to drag myself through all those broken nights, childhood ailments and disgusting cures again.'

She watched the sinister yellow-green wings of mistletoe curl and perish in the flames.

'Are you sure?'

'I've never been more certain of anything in my life.'

After the reassurance of another kiss Rosalind slipped into sleep. Mahel carried her to the bed and settled her in safely before returning to the fireside.

With a kindling stick he thrust the mocking mistletoe deep into the root of the fire.

CHAPTER ELEVEN

THE wedding was set for the day after Saint Stephen's day. Rosalind's mother was a regular visitor all through Advent. To Mahel she kept up the pretence that he was only tolerated to humour her daughter, but Rosalind saw how she relished his gentle teasing. No one had ever teased Joan Carilef before, and it looked as though she was beginning to like the new sensation.

Advent crept past, all fine foods put aside until the Christmas celebrations. The days grew shorter still, and a week before Christmas came the first snowfall of the season.

Rosalind and her mother sprang into panic when they heard the stamp of boots outside. Dashing to intercept Mahel, Rosalind threw herself, giggling, against the door.

'No! No, you can't come in yet!'

'That's a fine tale,' came the deep, well-loved voice amid the children's giggling. 'Deny a man a seat beside his own fire? We've been slaving away, off out at the crack of dawn to fetch in the yule log while you two stay in the warm, toasting your toes!'

Joan gave the word through a mouthful of pins that all the wedding finery was hidden. As the children darted into the room Mahel and two of his soldiers followed, carrying between them what looked like half a tree. Several of the dogs sniffed at it when they stood it up in a corner, but sharp words soon sent them scurrying away.

'Some travellers passed by the woodpile who had very interesting news.' Mahel dismissed his men, then brushed flecks of moss and tree bark from his clothes. 'It seems that the King was last heard of heading for London. I'm afraid that means you've got no more excuses, Lady

Joan. While the cat's away, his mice can be attending weddings. If you should refuse now on the grounds of my politics, I shall send my men over to kidnap both you and my lord Carilef, to bring you here by force. What do you say to that?'

'I say that you're a wicked rascal, Mahel de Bourne!' Rosalind's mother put on a scowl and bent down to tap Adrian. He had lifted a corner of the sheet hiding the unfinished wedding clothes and was trying to attract his father's attention. Rosalind's wail was unnecessary. Mahel turned away pointedly without looking at the surprise. He smiled.

'There's a cart-load of holly and ivy down in the yard, too. That should give the boys plenty of work for their idle little hands. Whereas I've got a much better idea for these...' He caught Rosalind's hands up and kissed them. At that moment two of his soldiers strolled down the stairs, off duty after a spell on lookout.

When they had disappeared out into the yard Rosalind laughed. 'And you still think that we've kept our romance a secret, Mahel? They must have seen us holding hands then!'

In reply he pulled her into a hug. Cold needles of melted snow on his cloak prickled her face. As usual, he was laughing. 'Nonsense! You mark my words—when I stand up on the twenty-seventh and announce that they're going to see a wedding, they'll be absolutely thunderstruck!'

Days began to race past. The hall floor disappeared under mounds of greenery as Rosalind and the children made garlands to hang around the walls. Paste stars and candles brought from Malmesbury glittered in the fire-light almost like the real thing. The hall was warm and fragrant with the smells of Christmas. Outside the air was cold, and smelled only of frost.

On Christmas Eve the Carilefs arrived in earnest. Three chests of luggage and an armed escort accom-panied them. When they were admitted to the castle courtyard, their small party was immediately surrounded by soldiers twice the size and twice as heavily armed. Mahel allowed Madam Carilef her few moments of horrified indignation. Then he strode forward with a laugh to welcome them all.

When the Carilefs had lost their nervousness, everyone settled down to enjoy Christmas. Herbert entertained the children, teaching them to juggle with the less fragile crockery. Joan put a thousand extra 'finishing touches' to the wedding clothes while Mahel and Rosalind complained at being deserted by their guests—but only enough to be polite.

Christmas Day passed in a confusion of ribbons and wrappings. Presents were exchanged after the soldiers had been dismissed from the hall. Only then could Mahel show his delight at Rosalind's choice. For her part, she pretended to be surprised at his gift of singing birds, although their covered cage had been chirruping in the stable for over a week.

The children were given their own surprise. Honeyed almonds and pastry mice were quite forgotten at the news. They were to travel home with the Carilefs after the holiday, and stay with them for a few days. When they returned, their own separate bedroom would be ready for them.

Everyone was happy. The castle hall rang with music and laughter, and there was even a visit by some travelling players. They brought news that the Empress was gaining support every day. This made Joan Carilef purse her lips and worry, but Herbert saw it as a relief. If King Stephen was to be overthrown, then nothing stood in the way of his growing friendship with Mahel de Bourne. Mahel was every inch the man that Herbert would have been, if Joan had let him.

'What time is it?' Rosalind struggled awake in the darkness.

Lighting a candle beside the bed, Joan handed her daughter a breakfast tray. 'About four o'clock. You'll have to hurry.'

'Mother! The wedding isn't until dinner-time—be reasonable...' Rosalind lay back against her pillows and shut her eyes.

It was no use. Joan Carilef was determined to enjoy herself, at whatever cost to her victim. Before the settlement was fully awake, Rosalind had had her hair washed and half dried before the fire. Then Joan tied it all up in rags. As well as putting a temporary curl into Rosalind's fine, silky hair, it also made sure that she would not risk leaving her chamber.

A warm bath, perfumed with lily-of-the-valley, was an experience that Rosalind thoroughly enjoyed. When she was dry there was rose oil to be rubbed into every pulse spot.

At last it was time to get dressed. Joan had brought her a pair of stockings, made of the finest lambswool. Rosalind put them on with great care. For this one day it did not matter that the wool might tickle and would wear thin within hours. Mahel had given her a pair of very elegant garters for Christmas, embroidered with field mice and roses. She tied these on for the first time, much to Joan's amusement.

Outside in the yard things were beginning to move. The animals were being let out to graze and the forge was starting up, just like any normal day. Rosalind had to remind herself that, for everyone else, it was a normal day. Mahel had been adamant that their wedding plans were kept a secret for as long as possible. That they would be seemed unlikely. He had been bursting with good humour for weeks. The evening before, he had even kissed Rosalind goodnight before the hall was empty of his men.

Rosalind heard Mahel and the boys start moving about in the next room as she dressed. Crispin had been given instructions to wake them early, too. As she pulled on her fine linen shift Rosalind wondered whether Mahel's preparations would be as elaborate as her own.

Her wedding gown was of fine woollen cloth in palest green, like a young ash leaf. The tight, high-necked bodice flowed down into a full skirt and train. Long sleeves were bound up in a lattice of golden threads from wrist to elbow.

The overdress was of heavy laurel-green velvet. White erminette iced the hem, low-cut neckline and wide flowing sleeves. Rosalind chose a plain veil to cover her froth of new curls, and secured it with a golden circlet. A gold belt encircled her small waist to complete the picture.

'I think you'll do.' Joan raised her eyebrows as she surveyed her daughter.

'Good. Now can I go and feed the poultry?'

Their laughter was interrupted by a knock at the door frame.

'You needn't think you're going to come in, Mahel,' Joan said in reply to the furious whispers from outside.

'We've got a present,' Adrian's gruff little voice said sharply. At once Rosalind went to the door, pulling back the curtain on the gloomy hall beyond.

The twins were neatly dressed in their new outfits of grey velvet. Pulling at his collar, Adrian looked cross and uncomfortable, but Helias was as proud as a bantam cock. When he saw Rosalind lit by the chamber candles he gasped in wide-eyed wonder.

'Auntie! You're a princess!'

Smiling, Rosalind bent to accept the small pottery bowl that Adrian thrust at her. A clump of budding snowdrops and some twigs of early pink mezereon nestled there in a bed of moss.

Helias whispered, 'Daddy wanted it to be a bunch of flowers, but it's too early.'

'I thought that every bride needed a bouquet.' Mahel stepped out of the shadows and raised her up. 'But it seems that I was wrong. You are exquisite enough.'

For a moment Adrian's complaints and her mother's indignation were forgotten. Mahel stood before her, tall and handsome and resplendent in his wedding clothes of grey velvet. Rosalind knew then that nothing mattered but that they would be together, now and forever. They kissed, without caring what anyone else might think or say.

'Let's go straight down to Anthony now.'

'I thought you were going to spring the surprise over dinner?' Rosalind smiled and stroked the smooth clean plane of his cheek.

'Now that I've seen you like this? I can't wait until then. It's half a lifetime.'

Joan saw then that all her preparations and worrying had been worthwhile. She took charge, whisking the children off downstairs.

'The last few moments before our secret is out.' Mahel took the little bowl of flowers from Rosalind's hands and placed it down on the floor. 'And I have a fancy for putting it to good use.'

With a touch as light as thistledown he slipped his arms around her. Rosalind accepted his kiss, but the old thoughts had already started to resurface. Marriage might change things.

Rosalind knew that she loved Mahel so much that nothing would alter the way she felt about him. She vowed then that whatever happened she would do anything to keep him.

Suddenly, Mahel drew away from her. He looked down into her eyes, the dim light giving him a grim and almost frightening look.

'You don't have to force yourself, Rosalind. It's only a kiss...'

He had sensed her doubts. The fears increased, and Rosalind no longer knew what to say to him. 'Mahel... It's only that—I mean, I wasn't——'

'I know.' He touched her hair, lovingly rearranging the curls that had crept out from beneath her veil. 'You can always say no, Rosalind.'

She threw herself into his embrace again, pressing her cheek against the warm security of his tunic. She felt, rather than heard, a sigh of satisfied amusement escape him.

'Then you haven't changed your mind about marrying me?'

'Oh, Mahel—never! It's just that...' Rosalind still couldn't think how to put it into words. She was only too grateful for the shadows that hid her blushes.

'It's just that when you kiss me you can't help thinking of Ascelin,' he said quietly.

'No—no, not at all. I didn't love him, Mahel—you're the first man that I've chosen to love...the first that hasn't been chosen for me——'

'I didn't mean that, Rosalind. I meant that you always remember the way that he treated you...'

They were both embarrassed now. From the hall below came sounds of laughter as the room filled with soldiers and villagers, eager for a celebration. In the darkness Rosalind found his hand and felt his fingers close about hers.

'I love you, Rosalind,' he breathed into her hair. 'You are the lady of my heart, and soon to become the lady of my life also. There can be nothing rough or violent about that.'

There was a moment of absolute stillness. Rosalind wanted to stay encircled by his arms for ever, but it could not last. Mahel bent and, picking up the little bowl of flowers, handed them to her. Then he led her slowly to the staircase, and they went down together arm in arm.

Rosalind entered her chamber, glad to be away at last from the relentless celebrations downstairs. Her pet greenfinches trilled sleepily as she crossed to their cage below the window. Several stars twinkled in the frosty evening, and Rosalind watched them for a time before lighting the candles.

It had been a very long day. She was half asleep on her feet. Mahel had caught her stifling a yawn and had sent her up to bed. He had claimed to be still worried about her health, but those near enough to hear put quite a different meaning on it. Mahel had silenced them quickly, but it had still wakened the old worries within Rosalind.

She looked around the chamber. During the day Mahel's belongings had been neatly stacked around the shelves by the staff. This was no longer her room. From now on she would be sharing it with Mahel, as his wife.

Rosalind paused to touch one of his tunics, folded away on a shelf. It was green—the colour of love, and the colour of the wedding gowns that she wore now. Suddenly love for Mahel burst like a blossom within her, and she turned to hurry back to his side.

He was in the doorway, watching her.

'I escaped.' He smiled and strolled towards her across the room. 'The lads might have nothing better to do with their time than to dice and gamble, but I have.'

Putting an arm around Rosalind's waist, Mahel drew her close. The fine erminette trimming of her over gown ruffled with his light breath as he kissed the delicate skin of her neck. Uncovering a small, plump softness of earlobe, he nibbled it gently. Tingling fire raced through Rosalind's veins, and at once she moved to stop him.

'Mahel, no!'

Smiling, he caught her hand as it flew to his hair. 'Don't you like it?'

Rosalind blushed all too easily at his amusement, and it always had the same result. Mahel swung her into his arms for a tender kiss.

'I shan't ever do anything that you dislike.' He smiled down at her.

'I didn't exactly dislike it.' Rosalind blushed again as she tried hard to disguise her confusion. 'It's just that...I've never heard of anyone doing such a shameless thing...'

With an intent expression Mahel held her at arm's length. 'Hasn't anyone ever done that to you before, my little sweet?'

Shaking her head, Rosalind looked away, hearing footsteps in the hall outside. Mahel kissed the badly made wedding ring that she had insisted upon keeping. 'Then I insist that the time has come for you to start enjoying yourself. To begin with, here's Crispin.'

The little musician entered at Mahel's call. As well as the psaltery slung over his shoulder, he carried a tray of wine and cakes.

Mahel greeted him, then saw Rosalind's confusion with delight. 'I thought you might prefer a little civilised entertainment, sweetheart, away from the common crowd!' There was laughter in his voice, but Rosalind felt uncertain.

'Mahel! Won't they be expecting you back downstairs?'

'Why? The men have got a good supply of ale and meat to hand—they won't notice I've gone. Some of them are taking your parents and the boys back——'

'But Mother said she was going to come up and help me change——'

'Ah—but as your legal husband of a whole ten hours, I pulled rank on her.' Mahel sat down on the edge of the bed, and patted the coverlet beside him. 'She sends her love, and will see you again soon. Don't look like that, my love! You can change privately enough. There's a screen for you in the corner. I'll only help if you want me to.'

He poured out three goblets of wine. Crispin settled himself beside the fire and began to sing softly.

'Now, isn't this nice and civilised?' Mahel handed Rosalind a tiny almond cake. While she ate and Crispin sang, Mahel stood up and went to a small wooden chest at his side of the bed. Returning to Rosalind, he pressed

a small silver flask into her hand. 'Another present for
you, my love.'

The words had been whispered deep into her ear.
Rosalind turned to find Mahel grinning at her mischievously. She looked at the little silver bottle with its en-
graving of vine leaves.

'What is it?'

'Magic oil. One of those wicked foreign indulgences
I expect your mother's warned you about!' He tipped
his head in the direction of Crispin, who was too busy
with his music to notice. 'When he's gone I can show
you properly, but just as a first temptation...'

Mahel took the bottle from her. Unscrewing the top,
he shook a few drops of oil on to the back of her hand.
At once Rosalind was surrounded by a warm fragrance.
Bittersweet yet subtle, its perfume mixed the sweetness
of flowers with a heady tang of ripening fruit.

'It must be warmed gently to work.' Mahel smiled,
putting the bottle on a shelf close at hand. 'May I?'

Without waiting for a reply, he began massaging the
oil into her hand. With slow, gentle strokes he manipu-
lated each tiny bone and muscle. Combined with the
exotic perfume, the feeling was delicious. A little sigh
of regret escaped from Rosalind when he stopped work
and sat back.

'Would you like me to do the other hand?'

She nodded, eager to relive the sensation. Lubricated
by the oil, Mahel's fingers slid over her skin, the well-
worked firmness of his palms contrasting with the silky
smoothness of hers.

'It works best when applied to the pulse spots,' he
said at last. 'Would you like to try?'

The scent was so delightful that Rosalind would have
willingly bathed in it. She took a tiny droplet on to her
finger and dabbed behind each ear.

'No—like this...' Mahel slipped his hands up to her
neck and began stroking the oil into her skin. A warm
wave of love rose over Rosalind. She leaned forward and

kissed Mahel with an intensity she had never experienced before. The music stopped, Crispin crept out of the room and Rosalind didn't even notice.

'Oh—I didn't think!' Mahel murmured when she freed him for a moment. 'How are you going to change your clothes now? It would be a shame to get oil on your pretty dress.'

For the first time in her life, Rosalind felt totally shameless. 'You can help me—we can manage together.' Suddenly, some half-remembered modesty swam into the back of her mind and she blushed. 'I—I'm quite decent in my shift...'

Mahel smiled, and slowly but surely unlaced the gold threads at her wrists and released the golden belt.

'This first, I think.' With a delicate touch he removed her circlet and veil. Rosalind closed her eyes as he stroked her flagging curls back into place.

'Ah—I still have the veil you gave me as a favour, sweet. See?'

Rosalind opened her eyes. Half in a dream she saw that Mahel had pulled off his tunic. He was reaching inside his shirt to withdraw the small square of gossamer that he had taken from her. As his shirt fell open she caught another glimpse of the finely tuned muscles she had seen when he had challenged Ascelin.

'That's a heavy sigh, my love? Is there anything I can do?'

Mahel was smiling at her. His wide, dark eyes were as innocent as those of the children. He would never take cruel advantage of her. Rosalind sighed again.

'I wish—I wish that you would hold me close, Mahel...and kiss me again...'

He bowed to her command. Rosalind felt the moulded firmness of his body beneath her fingers and was borne along on a restless tide of her own passion. A strange but delightful feeling rippled over her. Then his kisses were no longer enough.

Mahel had already sensed as much. Unhurriedly, with tiny kisses and the lightest caress of his fingertips, his encouragement continued. When at last he lifted her on to the bed she still wore her shift, but had shed all the old feelings of guilt and fear with her finery.

'I should have warned you what that magic oil is capable of, my little sweetbriar! You never asked...'

Rosalind reached up to pull him close for another kiss. He nibbled her ear again playfully.

'It's dangerous, you know!'

'Mahel...I want you...'

With a smile he lay down beside her. Candlelight danced over the sweep of dark curls shading his chest.

'That special oil,' he murmured, one finger lifting a blonde curl away to expose her ear again, 'is the most powerful love potion known to man. That's why it's so dangerous, sweeting. It makes women feel totally wanton...'

Rosalind gasped as the tip of his tongue delicately traced the outline of her ear. 'You don't need to tell me...' she breathed softly before dissolving into the embrace of Mahel's love.

Rosalind's previous knowledge had only stretched as far as William, then Ascelin. Nothing had prepared her for Mahel, and the way that he made her feel. He was gentle, and funny, and treated her as a thinking, feeling person. Not as an occasionally useful household appliance.

'Mahel?'

There was only one candle still left burning. Soft shadows shed in the late evening dark rippled over Mahel's body as he lay beside her. He did not pause in the kissing of her fingers.

'Mmm?'

'Have you used that oil on many women?'

It was too dark to see him clearly, but she felt a slight movement beneath her hand.

'No one but you, my love.'

'Oh, Mahel! You expect me to believe that, with all the stories of your wicked life?'

They were lying across the bed, and he wriggled up to start kissing the tip of her nose.

'That was then, this is now,' he said between kisses. There was a definite smile in his voice. Then he stopped kissing and pulled back a little, laughing. 'Oh, but I can't fib to you any more, sweet! There's no magic in the oil—I made it up. A few drops stolen from each of your perfumes, mixed together...'

In her amazement Rosalind forgot to be cross. 'Mahel—it worked so well...'

She felt him shrug and laugh again.

'I didn't want you to feel nervous. It was a way of breaking the ice...I got the idea from one of the men. He was telling us about some trickster who did the same thing and made himself a fortune. It just goes to show that there's no limit to the power of the mind!'

Rosalind's smile was not quite as genuine as his laughter.

'Did you tell them, then—what you were going to do?'

'Certainly not! Nothing in the world would make me talk about our private life, my love!' He stroked her hair and accepted another kiss.

'Are you sure, Mahel?'

'Of course I'm sure. Get into bed and I'll tell you all about it!' Kneeling up, he caught hold of the bedclothes and began pulling them back, beneath Rosalind. 'As long as I'm not ordering the men about, they neither know nor care what I'm up to. See how amazed they all were at the wedding! I told you they didn't suspect——' He stopped suddenly, distracted by a strange arrangement of the bedclothes beneath his hand. While he lit an extra candle Rosalind crawled up beside him to get into bed. Soon, she too was feeling about in the half-dark. She drew two neatly wrapped packages from beneath the pillows as Mahel pulled a handful of dried flower petals from between the sheets.

'Flowers in the bed—and they've done something to the sheets...an apple pie bed! I'll kill them!'

'You won't,' Rosalind countered, holding the larger of the two parcels out to him. 'Not after they've been to so much trouble.'

'I wondered why they'd all been acting oddly since we went to Malmesbury,' Mahel chuckled, sitting back on his heels to unwrap his present. 'You told them, sweet!'

Rosalind put aside her present and looked at him meaningfully.

'I certainly did not! It was you—you've been bouncing about for weeks. They didn't need to be told.'

Mahel stopped her laughter with a kiss, then sat back again to start fiddling with the wrappings of his parcel.

'You aren't going to open it now, Mahel?'

'Of course I am! Although...perhaps it might be better done first thing tomorrow. Then I wouldn't feel duty bound to go straight downstairs and thank them all at once...' Indecision crossed his face, and to Rosalind's delight he actually seemed to blush. 'Tomorrow, at work, I'll be able to thank them a few at a time.'

Rosalind took the half-opened parcel from his hands and placed it down next to hers. Gifts and tricks forgotten, she went to Mahel and wound her arms about his neck. 'Yes. Leave it until morning,' she said with a sweet softness of tone she had never had cause to use on anyone else. 'They'll understand.'

For long moments they kissed, while the greenfinches fidgeted and a low murmur of merriment drifted up from the hall below.

'I do love you so,' Rosalind murmured at last.

'I know,' came the gentle reply. 'I know.'

Winter was slow to lose its grip that year. The civil war idled to a halt, crippled by roads either bottomless with mud or frozen solid. Mahel and Rosalind had all the time in the world to linger over their love.

When the weather improved a little, Mahel had the men build themselves a separate guard house in the castle yard. New privacy in the hall allowed him to keep up his ruthless reputation in front of the men outside, while inside he could let the mask slip a little. Only Rosalind, the boys and a few of the indoor staff saw his true nature.

Whether spending a quiet evening by the fire with Rosalind or mending the children's toys, Mahel grew more loving and attentive with each passing day.

Spring slipped into summer. If the campaign season had not interrupted them, they would barely have noticed. All Rosalind knew was that Mahel's work prised him away all too often. The only consolation was the sheer delight of his homecomings.

Autumn soon loaded the hedgerows for another winter banquet. Mahel learnt the simple pleasures of a land-owner. In return, he showed Rosalind how to appreciate the wilder countryside that they owned. When they took the boys for a ride through the woods and downs, they returned with baskets of rosehips, brambles and wild mushrooms.

The year 1140 trickled to its close. Once more, Advent's abstinence ended in magical Christmas cele-brations. Every soldier and villager crowded into the holly-decked hall for a riot of food and wine.

Madam Carilef and Mahel had long since come to an unofficial truce. There were frequent visits between the two estates, and Rosalind's parents stayed with them for a few days over the festive season. Mahel's party manners and hospitality knew no bounds. Any lingering doubts that the Carilefs might have had about their new son-in-law had been completely put aside. They had been even more delighted with Adrian and Helias, who were spoiled outrageously.

Days passed in a haze of songs and simple enjoy-ments. The Carilefs went home in very good spirits after celebrating Mahel's and Rosalind's first wedding anni-versary. The villagers and staff were more reluctant to leave their new stronghold in the hall. Only when Mahel put on his best stern manner and threatened them all with extra duties did the castle begin to empty.

At last, in the early hours of the morning, Rosalind and Mahel were alone together.

Bolting the hall door behind the last reveller, Mahel took Rosalind by the hand. They made their way to the fireside through all the party ruins—mistletoe sprigs, cake crumbs, holly leaves and discarded crockery. The yule log still glittered on the hearth. Rosalind sat down within its glow while Mahel stoked the fire carefully.

She looked down on Adrian and Helias, who were curled up and sleeping with the dogs. Both boys had settled well and grown fast. Within the next few months they would go their separate ways. Mahel had finally decided to send Helias to live at school, if only for a trial period. Adrian, too, would be leaving home. He was soon to enter the household of the Earl of Gloucester as a page.

'Oh, I shall miss them both,' Rosalind murmured with regret. 'Even though it means I shall have you all to myself when they're gone!'

'Can this be the same little sweetbriar who used to make any excuse to avoid me?' Mahel sat down and slipped his arm about her waist. 'Hmm...not so little any more! There's certainly more of you now than there was back then!'

Leaning into Mahel's protective embrace, Rosalind gave him a look of mock dismay. He teased her with a smile.

'You were far too thin then, sweet. Nothing but skin and grief. Now I've got plenty to love.'

His light touch strayed from Rosalind's cheek to her neck. Sipping kisses from her lips, his fingers began the gentle teasing that delighted her so much.

A warm languor crept over Rosalind. The fire crumbled to ashes and an owl quavered faintly outside. She began returning his love with growing desire.

'Not here!' Mahel murmured, chuckling softly in her ear. 'It's our anniversary, remember! I had some good wine and sweetmeats sent up to our room earlier... We can put the boys to bed and then linger over our own, more private celebrations...'

Rosalind looked up into Mahel's deep, expressive eyes. Drinking in his exotic dark looks, she rose from her seat, but could not bear to let go of his hand. Mahel was unwilling to lose her, too, even for a moment.

He stood, then swept her into his arms. Another lingering kiss burned like fire on her lips.

'Happy anniversary, my darling,' he breathed, holding her close and warm. Then he stopped, and laughed. Even when empty the public hall often had that effect on him. A little reserve would return, embarrassing any more words of love away for a moment.

More than half asleep, Rosalind smiled up at him. She had learned to sense what Mahel could not always say. His love for her was far more than whispered words in evening shadows.

Unlike Ascelin, Mahel was gentleman enough to move out of her room for the necessary days each month. In January he slept with the children for a week, as usual. Things were not quite as usual with Rosalind. Her pile of clean linen remained untouched. She never thought to mention it to Mahel. After all, it wasn't worth the mentioning.

He was due to return to her side on the Monday after Epiphany. As a surprise on that first morning he woke her by bringing breakfast in bed. That turned out to be a mistake. Rosalind could smell the hot milk he brought even before he crossed the threshold.

Her smile disappeared. Mahel immediately put down his tray and went to the bed.

'You're very pale, my little sweetbriar.' Sitting down, he gathered her into his arms. 'You'll need feeding up——'

'Oh, no...' Rosalind interrupted faintly. He smelled of cold winter air and outdoor things, which revived her slightly. 'I—I think my stomach is still trying to decide what to do with last night's roast kid...'

Mahel held her away from him, searching her face with loving eyes. 'Are you sure? Everyone else seems all right this morning, and they had twice as much as you. I know—it's a cold and frosty morning, set fair for more snow. Spend the day in bed.' He enveloped her in the silken sheets and furs. 'And I'll come in every so often— just to make sure that you're all right...'

Rosalind knew the mischievous twinkle in his eyes too well. It meant that she would get little rest, and for the first time she felt less than enthusiastic.

'I think... I'll get up, Mahel. If you don't mind...'

His face fell, and Rosalind saw how he tried to hide his disappointment.

'Fresh air will soon cheer me up,' she said hopefully, stroking his hand. 'Take me out with the boys. We'll ride across the downs, and that will soon make me forget all this nonsense.'

It didn't always feel like nonsense. There were plenty of times during the next few weeks when Rosalind could tolerate nothing more than beef tea and dry bread. Sometimes she lost that, too.

I must be ill, she thought to herself time and time again. After all, it can't possibly be... *that*...

She hardly dared even think the word. Mahel had made his feelings on that matter very plain in the past. Often as they watched the boys at play he would squeeze her hand and say that two was the right number for a family. He always maintained stoutly that he had quite finished his duty in that department.

Rosalind hid the sickness from Mahel as much as she could. It would be silly to upset him for no reason. After all, she thought, I'm losing weight, rather than putting it on.

It had to be something else. There must be some sickness that brought with it the strange fizzing and prickling feelings that had started. It was a mystery that Rosalind half hoped she didn't know the answer to.

Time passed. Shrove Tuesday came, heralding the beginning of forty days of abstinence. Mahel moved in with the boys once more.

Rosalind was left alone to long, lonely nights of puzzling. And a pile of linen that stayed resolutely spotless.

The only thing missing from her wonderful life was a child. It was also the only thing that Mahel did not seem to want.

If only there were a way of pleasing them both.

Day after day, Rosalind hoped and prayed. She forced herself to try and resent the one thing that she had always wanted.

It was impossible.

Rosalind woke very early on the morning of St Valentine's day. She lay still in the darkness, trying to fight off the usual feeling of sickness.

When she could bear to get up, Rosalind washed and dressed quickly. Slipping out of her room, she found that all was still quiet. There were no sounds from Mahel and the boys in their room next door.

She crept downstairs and out into the early morning.

Reaching the village huts unnoticed, Rosalind entered the last shack in the rank.

An hour later, Rosalind returned to the hall carrying a small parcel. Looking up from his breakfast, Mahel forced a smile.

'A Valentine's day present for me?'

The pain in Rosalind's eyes was quickly mirrored in his. He stood up, but did not come forward immediately. Lately, there had been a new caution in his manner. It worried Rosalind, but he never spoke about it.

'My love—what is it? Whatever is the matter, Rosalind?'

At the mention of presents the boys had jumped up too, and ran forward. Rosalind knew that they could not be allowed to see their father's rage at her news.

'I—I must speak to you alone, Mahel...'

There was a silence, and he looked down at the table. 'Of course.'

The sharpness of his tone was unknown. He must have guessed. Gathering her wits, Rosalind busied herself boiling a small pot of water. That way she could not see his expression.

'I would be grateful if you could come up to my room, Mahel. The matter should not be discussed here. If you could give me ten minutes to prepare...'

Rosalind loved Mahel so very much that she could not walk away without looking at him. The expression in his eyes was haunting. Pain and disappointment mingled until she could bear it no longer. Pouring herself a cup of hot water, she left him in the hall and went upstairs.

It was a long time before Mahel arrived outside the room. The wise woman's herbal infusion had started to take effect, and Rosalind's nausea was ebbing. All that was left now was her own fear.

Mahel entered slowly, ducking to avoid the low lintel. He was holding his gloves, turning them about in his hands. The action would have made a lesser man seem nervous. It merely made Mahel look uncomfortable.

'I don't think I want to hear this,' he said indistinctly, strolling to the window grille. Rosalind saw it as a calculated action. In looking at her birds or out of the window he had an excuse not to look at her, and it hurt.

'I'm truly sorry, my lord.'

Mahel was silent for a long time. His strong fingers were still pulling the gloves this way and that. It was the only outward sign of his agitation. When he spoke it was with a cool detachment.

'I thought we were so happy——'

'Oh, but we were...' Rosalind cut in quickly. 'We are—and we could be still...'

'When did it happen?' he said abruptly as her voice faded away.

She shrugged. 'It's hard to tell. During Advent? And to think—we thought it such a little sin at the time...' She tried to raise a smile, but the effect upon Mahel was disastrous. He swung around, and the pain spilled from his eyes and words.

'Rosalind—oh, Rosalind, how could you? I thought you loved me as much as I love you...'

His arms spread wide in a gesture of hopelessness. Rosalind could bear it no longer. She threw herself into his arms, willing to surrender herself to any penance as long as it stopped him hurting.

'Mahel, I know what a shock this must be to you, but I have to tell you now that I can't find it in myself to be sorry. I don't know why it should have happened after all this time...' Words tumbled out. She tried to cover his face with the kisses he so loved to receive. Now he only turned his head away. She tried again, desperately. 'It won't affect the way I feel for you, Mahel—it's just made me love you more——'

'How can you dare to say that?'

He raised his hands as though to push her away. Rosalind clung to him, anger making her brave.

'How can you dare to think otherwise? This baby is part of you, Mahel! It was made with your love and mine. How can a poor, innocent little mite be anything but a sign of that love?'

His hands fell to his sides. Suddenly he was very still in her arms. Rosalind eased her grip upon him, afraid of some new manifestation of his rage. There was none. Mahel de Bourne, the Black Wolf, looked like a man who had been hit over the head by a quite unexpected truth.

He had gone almost pale. When he raised his hand again it was with an uncertain, mechanical action. He stroked Rosalind's hair as if expecting her to shatter beneath the lightest touch. 'I thought...oh, Rosie, I thought you'd found somebody else——'

'Never, my love.'

'You've changed towards me...over the past few weeks. I was sick with worry, certain that you were about to leave me——'

'I've been sick, too.' She leaned against him and this time was greeted tenderly. 'Not just with the worry, either. That's been the reason for any change in me. I'm only sorry that you'll be so disappointed——'

'Oh, Rosie, never!'

After the first staggering shock to his system, he had gathered his wits. Sweeping Rosalind into his arms, he carried her to the bed and laid her down with a kiss.

'Will you be all right?'

'You're not cross?'

He was beaming with such delight that he did not even need to shake his head. 'As long as you can be kept safe, my love, it's the answer to all my prayers.'

'Mahel! You've always been so determined that you didn't want any more children!'

'Your feelings have always been, and always will be, more precious to me than my own, sweet. I'd rather have cut my tongue out than let you know how I've wished for this.' He gathered her up in his arms with pleasure undisguised. 'I'll want my chance to look after it, mind. When there's no one else about to see, of course! I'm very good with babies—it's the appalling amount of practice I've had. It's just a matter of getting used to living without sleep all over again!'

'Oh, Mahel...are you sure you don't mind?'

His expression clouded for a moment, then he was all smiles once more. 'All I'm worried about is you, my love. If the same thing were to happen to you as happened to that poor girl——'

'It won't. I've got a good clean home with plenty of food—when I can take it!' She laughed and pulled at his ears playfully. 'I haven't had to drag around the countryside until I'm worn out. Besides, my mother's survived lots of babies. Old Meg says that means I'm from "good, substantial stock"!'

'I love you,' he said simply. 'If anything were to happen to you——'

'It won't. You shouldn't even think such things, Mahel. It's tempting fate!'

There was a sudden confusion of happy noise down in the yard. Until that moment Mahel would have been the first at the ready. Now he barely noticed the uproar.

'Then is it safe to ask when...?' he said, a little uncertainly.

'Around harvest time.' She laughed and kissed him again. 'Don't worry—I'll take care not to interrupt the work! A nice dry nest under a tree, where the women can keep an eye on me in between driving the oxen and filling the carts——'

'You'll hold court in here with the best attention that money can buy! The very thought of it—no daughter of mine is going to be born anywhere near a grain waggon! I'll borrow somebody from the infirmary at Malmesbury, and you'll be watched every minute.' Starting to enjoy himself again, he pushed her back gently into the pillows. 'From now on, if I find you doing anything more than resting up and waxing healthy, I'll lock you in here. Nothing but sweetmeats to eat and dressed only in the finest frills. How's that for punishment?'

'Better order the frills in an extra enormous size if you're going to feed the two of us on sweetmeats.' Rosalind put a hand to the part which showed precious little difference yet, despite all her secretive measuring.

'And who brought you safely through the fever? Unless you let me spoil you totally, madam, I shall cast you out into the ice and snow like the scoundrel I once was!'

Rosalind put her hands to his face and cupped it, feeling the smoothness of his dusky skin.

'My lord! My lord—lady Rosalind!' Crispin came galloping up the stairs. Rosalind let her fingers slip from Mahel's cheek with a sigh of regret.

'More work to take you away from me, I suppose.'

'Not now. Nothing will ever take me away again...' Mahel bent forward with a smile and kissed the tip of her nose. At that moment Crispin burst into the room.

'Get out!' Mahel roared good-naturedly, but Crispin stood on the threshold, waving his arms as he caught his breath. Rosalind laughed at the musician's strangled gasps.

'No, Mahel—don't shout at him again. It must be serious!' She started to rise, but Mahel stopped her with another kiss.

'The King...' Crispin managed, bending forward to rest his hands on his knees. 'The King—he's been captured! The Empress has won!'

The war was over, for the present. For a while there would be no more calls to arms in the middle of the night, no more skirmishes. Rosalind, Mahel and the children could concentrate on becoming a proper family, without an ever-present threat hanging over their heads. Nothing mattered now but their own happiness.

Oblivious to the celebrations down in the courtyard, the thunder of Adrian and Helias coming up to find them and even Crispin laughing in the doorway, Rosalind and Mahel kissed again, for sheer joy.

Look out for the two intriguing

OUTRAGEOUS FORTUNE
Marion Carr

Lady Caraddon was a persistent matchmaker for her grandson, Sir James, but he really thought she had gone too far when he had to accompany her to Cornwall to meet Miss Charlotte Forbes. Ambitious, James was intent on carving out a political career in Pitt's government, and he certainly didn't want a wife just yet.

First impressions were not favourable, and James was even more perturbed when he discovered that Charlotte's background held a scandal that could rebound even now in 1786! On her eighteenth birthday, Charlotte was to be told the truth of her parentage, and that she was an heiress – but delegated to break the news, James had no idea of the turmoil that would ensue, or that he would be so thoroughly embroiled in trying to keep Charlotte safe!

LOVE'S INTRIGUE
June Francis

In the troubled times of Henry V's attempts to take the throne of France, Louise Saulnier and her sister Marguerite became separated. Believing Marguerite to have been taken by an Englishman, Louise was determined to travel to England to rescue her.

For safety's sake, Louise became Louis, but her attempts to feed herself resulted in her capture by John Milburn – the man who had abducted Marguerite! But unknown to Louise, she had the wrong man, for John had an identical twin, Harry. She also didn't know that John had rapidly discovered her secret, she only knew that John seemed intent on taking her under his wing – and as he was her only lead to Marguerite, Louise had no choice but to reluctantly acquiesce . . .

Available in April

An irresistible offer for you

Here at Reader Service we would love you to become a regular reader of Masquerade. And to welcome you, we'd like you to have two books, a cuddly teddy and a MYSTERY GIFT - ABSOLUTELY FREE and without obligation.

Then, every two months you could look forward to receiving 4 more brand-new Masquerade Romances for just £1.99 each, delivered to your door, postage and packing is free. Plus our free newsletter featuring competitions, author news, special offers offering some great prizes, and lots more!

This invitation comes with no strings attached. You can cancel or suspend your subscription at any time, and still keep your free books and gifts.

Its so easy. Send no money now. Simply fill in the coupon below at once and post it to - Reader Service, FREEPOST, PO Box 236, Croydon, Surrey CR9 9EL.

--- **NO STAMP REQUIRED** --->

Yes! Please rush me my 2 Free Masquerade Romances and 2 Free Gifts! Please also reserve me a Reader Service Subscription. If I decide to subscribe, I can look forward to receiving 4 brand new Masquerade Romances every two months for just £7.96, delivered direct to my door. Post and packing is free, and there's a free Newsletter. If I choose not to subscribe I shall write to you within 10 days - I can keep the books and gifts whatever I decide. I can cancel or suspend my subscription at any time. I am over 18.

Mrs/Miss/Ms/Mr _____   EP05M

Address _____

_____

_____ Postcode _____

Signature _____